Friends Forever

LYN ANDREWS

headline

First published in 2005
by HEADLINE BOOK PUBLISHING

1

Cataloguing in Publication Data is available from the British Library

ISBN 0 7553 0839 5

Typeset in Janson Text by Avon DataSet Ltd,
Bidford-on-Avon, Warwickshire

Printed and bound in Great Britain by
Mackays of Chatham plc, Chatham, Kent

Headline's policy is to use papers that are natural, renewable and
recyclable products and made from wood grown in sustainable forests.
The logging and manufacturing processes are expected to conform to the
environmental regulations of the country of origin.

HEADLINE BOOK PUBLISHING
A division of Hodder Headline
338 Euston Road
London NW1 3BH

www.headline.co.uk
www.hodderheadline.com

For my new grandson James Lewis Andrade: another little soul to cherish, especially after so very nearly losing him. And for Anita Stirling, a new friend from Northern Ireland whose beautiful oil paintings brighten up the walls of my study.

Lyn Andrews
Tullamore, 2004

Chapter One

———◈———

'WHAT DID SHE SAY? Will she let you come with me?' Bernie O'Sullivan's expression was full of suppressed excitement and suspense. In all her seventeen years nothing had been quite as important to her as the answer she now waited to hear from her best friend and soul mate, Molly Keegan.

Bernie fiddled impatiently with a strand of dark brown hair that had escaped from the loose knot on top of her head. The chignon was an unsuccessful attempt to make herself look more fashionable. She'd complained bitterly to her ma that it was impossible to be 'stylish' with long hair these days. Tess O'Sullivan had replied caustically that if she had the money to have it cut short then she could take herself into Tullamore town and be as 'stylish' as she liked; Tess herself was heart-scalded worrying where she was to find the money to put a decent meal on the table. But the issue that occupied Bernie's mind now had very little to do with a mere hairstyle.

'Well? Sure, don't be keeping me on tenterhooks!' she demanded.

Molly's grey-green eyes began to sparkle and she grinned at her friend. 'They agreed. I can go with you. Ma isn't very happy about it but Da said if the lads can make a good enough life for themselves in Boston then he can't see why I can't make a go of it in Liverpool. There's not a decent job to be had here for the likes of us and there's precious few jobs above in Dublin either.'

Bernie could have burst into tears of joy. She threw her arms around her friend. 'Oh, Moll, it will be *great*!'

1

Molly disentangled herself from Bernie's grip before it crushed the breath out of her. 'We'd better calm ourselves down and make some definite plans. Come on, we'll go to the far lock and sit by the bridge. It's quiet down there and there's plenty of shade.'

Grinning, Bernie linked her arm through Molly's and they began to walk down the narrow towpath, known as the canal line, which ran along the bank of the Grand Canal.

The weather for June in the Irish midlands was unseasonably hot and humid; the turf bog close by was always blamed for the dampness in the air winter or summer. Between green fields in which cattle grazed and the odd field of ripening barley, the scarred brown bog land was clearly visible. In the early summer months families from miles around all cut and turned the turf and carted it home to provide fuel for the rest of the year, as they had done for generations. It was backbreaking work but few complained. Coal was scarce and expensive.

There were a few houses, mainly single-storeyed cottages or cabins, between the thirtieth and the thirty-first locks. The former was known locally as 'Mitchell's Lock' after the family who had been lock-keepers for years. The latter was the Cornalaur Lock, referred to as the 'far lock'.

The trees and shrubs at the edge of the path threw patches of dappled shade across the calm waters of the canal, which reflected the cloudless, azure-blue sky and sparkled in the bright sunlight. Tall green rushes, yellow bog iris and water buttercup and clumps of creamy-white cow parsley grew in profusion on both banks and in the distance the graceful white shapes of a pair of swans could be discerned.

Bernie again fiddled with her thick, heavy hair. 'Ah, 'tis so hot! The first thing I'm after having done when we get to Liverpool is to get this mop cut!'

Molly grimaced and ran her fingers through her own long hair, which was thick, curly and auburn. 'At least it's not like this furze bush of mine! There's mornings when I can hardly get the hairbrush through it and Mam refuses to let me have it cut.'

'She won't be able to stop you now. We can do exactly as we please and there won't be anyone to be giving out to us.'

'Oh, there'll be plenty. You're forgetting that we're to go to your da's cousin and himself so respectable. Isn't that the only reason I'm allowed to go at all?'

Bernie laughed derisively. 'Respectable! When was any relative of Da's "respectable"? Sure, they have nothing, the same as the rest of us.'

Molly frowned. Both Mr and Mrs O'Sullivan had assured her parents that Matthew 'Matty' O'Sullivan and his wife Nellie had a grand house in Hopwood Street, Liverpool, and that he was a Checker on the docks. A very responsible job. They were a good-living Catholic family, one entirely suitable to keep a watchful eye on two seventeen-year-old girls fresh from the countryside and unused to big city life.

Bernie's da worked for her father as a casual labourer, helping out with the turf, the haymaking and the harvesting of the few fields of crops that Paddy Keegan grew on his not overly large farm. The Keegans' main income came from the dairy herd that her father was slowly building up. Her mother, Ita, kept chickens and ducks and geese and made butter. They were far better off than the O'Sullivans who lived in a small, run-down cabin beyond the Cappaloughlan Bridge. At one time there were fourteen of them crammed in it together until Bernie's four older brothers had taken the emigrant ship to New York. Her two eldest sisters had followed them, and then Katie O'Sullivan had gone to Australia with the Presentation Sisters and was now called Sister Assumpta, a source of great pride and joy to Tess O'Sullivan. It still left Bernie, Claire, Eileen, Tim and Ignatius – known as Iggy – at home.

Molly too had seen her brothers Denis and Mick go off to America. Every family in the county had had someone who'd left Ireland. There wasn't a living to be had for everyone. There was no alternative but the emigrant ship.

'But your da said they have a fine house and he has a good, responsible job,' Molly pressed. If her parents heard Bernie talking like this then it would definitely change things. She certainly didn't want that.

'I suppose to Da any kind of a regular job is just great. And how does he know what kind of a house they have? Sure, they never write to each other. I don't even know if Matty O'Sullivan *can* write. It's Ma and Nellie who write the letters and not very often either,' Bernie answered airily.

'He must be able to write if he's a Checker. Oh, for heaven's sake, Bernie, don't go saying things like that in front of Mam and Da or they'll change their minds and I'm not staying here for ever, I'm not!'

Bernie nodded emphatically. 'Neither am I. I'm not going to be buried alive here in the bogs with nothing to do but go to Mass, the occasional wedding and wake, get married and have gangs of kids. Never seeing anything or doing anything *exciting*! Never having any real money of me own. There's got to be more to life than all that. I certainly don't want to end up like Ma. Do you know how old she is?'

Molly shook her head. Much the same age as her own mam, she assumed.

'She's forty-six and she looks sixty-six!'

Molly frowned. Bernie had a point. 'Well, just don't say Matty O'Sullivan isn't respectable. Have you any money of your own?'

Bernie sighed. 'Not as much as I'd like. I've only been able to find odd bits of jobs lately. I'm fit for nothing. I've got my fare and a few shillings over and I've hardly a shoe to my foot.' She glanced despairingly at her old brown shoes. Despite her best efforts to polish them up the leather was scuffed and cracked and the heels were badly worn down. In fact her whole appearance depressed her. In addition to her much-hated hairstyle her print dress was faded and unfashionably long and it was tight around her waist. She was small and considered plump and the fashionable drop-waisted dresses with their shorter skirts would have made her appear thinner and taller. She envied Molly who was tall and slim and whose clothes were better and more modern than anything she owned. The green and white flowered cotton dress Molly wore today looked fresh, with its white pointed collar and wide belt that hugged her hips. Molly's flat shoes were of a light tan leather and her stockings were cream. Bernie had no stockings, cream, fawn or even black.

Molly was acutely aware that she was better dressed; in fact she always had been, since the day two girls had started in Junior Infants. Yet they had always been firm friends, despite the differences in their circumstances.

'I've got a few pounds saved up. I could give you enough for a new pair of shoes and some other things,' she offered, mentally vowing that once away from parental vigilance she would give Bernie some of her clothes. She would have to alter them, of course, but that wouldn't be a problem; Mam had taught her to sew from an early age, which meant she'd been able to find work doing alterations in Mrs Bracken's Drapery in Tullamore for three days a week. It didn't pay much but at least it was some kind of a job.

'I'll take a lend of it, Moll, just for shoes. I'll pay you back when we get work. We're bound to get jobs that pay a decent wage in a huge place like Liverpool.'

'I don't want you to take a lend of it, I said I'd *give* it to you! Didn't you save me from a desperate state altogether last week?'

Bernie laughed and her blue eyes danced with mischief. 'You mean when I told Tommy Coghlan you had scarlatina and couldn't meet him in Market Square at all?'

Molly shuddered. 'He's *desperate*!'

'Then why did you say you'd meet him in the first place?'

'Because he kept pestering me and Da likes him.'

'He only likes him because his da's got a shop and he's the only lad with all those sisters.'

'He's got so many spots on his face it looks like a bowl of lumpy porridge and he *picks* them!' Molly shuddered again. 'I don't care if his da had six shops. I wouldn't walk out with him.'

'You won't have to now. Liverpool must be just full of grand-looking lads and with money in their pockets to spend on two gorgeous girls like us!'

They'd reached the heavy shade of the trees overhanging the lock and with a little difficulty hoisted themselves up on to the wall that bounded the ruin of a small cabin and farmyard. On the opposite side of the lock the low single-storeyed lockhouse looked deserted in the morning sun; the only sounds to be heard were the water trickling through the lock gates, the birdsong in the hedge-rows and the distant lowing of cattle in the fields of the next village of Pollagh.

'When do you think we'll be ready to go?' Molly asked, idly kicking her heels against the warm stones of the wall and dislodging puffs of dry mortar.

Bernie looked thoughtful. 'In about two days? I've not much to pack.'

'Two days? That's a bit soon. I'd like to get a few things in town and I'll have to visit the aunts and uncles before I go.' Molly pulled a face, thinking of the advice and admonitions she'd have to endure from her many relations. Then she cheered up a little. She might get a few shillings as 'going-away' gifts. If she did, she'd give them to Bernie who certainly wouldn't get anything from any relations she might visit. Those who were left here in County Offaly were as poor as church mice.

'I wouldn't be bothered visiting any of mine! Sure, they won't care where I am. The only time any of them ever made a fuss was when our Katie went off to become a nun. Even me Auntie Norah from over in Galway turned up for that! It's Tuesday today, should we say we'll go on Saturday?'

Molly deliberated on this. Mam had only just agreed to her going at all. There would be all the washing and ironing, packing, visiting and arrangements to be made. 'Maybe we should leave it until next week. Say next Wednesday or Thursday, that will give us more time to get organised and I'll have to tell Herself she'll have to find someone else for the alterations.'

Bernie looked disappointed. It would take her no time at all to get 'organised' and she couldn't wait to get away from here. She'd had enough of living in the parish of Rahan to last a lifetime, but she realised that her friend had many more obligations than she did herself. She nodded slowly, idly plucking a piece of long grass and twisting it between her fingers.

'Come down to me tonight and we'll sort out the money and see if I've got anything that might do you to travel in,' Molly said.

'Won't your dresses swamp me?'

'I'll take up the hem and when we get to Liverpool I'm going to teach you to sew, Bernie O'Sullivan, if it's the last thing I do!'

'When we get to Liverpool I'll be able to afford things that fit me without having to alter them. But I'll come down when your da's after doing the milking,' Bernie replied, pleased and grateful that Molly had offered. Mrs Keegan might not be so amenable though, she thought.

Molly slid down off the wall. 'Do you think there's anyone in over there?' She nodded in the direction of the lockhouse.

'Why?'

'We might beg a cup of buttermilk before walking back, it's so hot!'

'A cup of water is what we *might* get from that auld skinflint – iffen he's at home at all!' Bernie sniffed, joining her friend on the grass verge.

Leaving the cool shade of the trees the two girls walked into the burning heat of the midday sun and across the narrow hump-backed stone bridge across the canal in search of refreshment.

Chapter Two

———•◦•———

'WHERE HAVE YOU BEEN? I seem to have got behind myself this morning. I'll have your da in for his dinner and the potatoes not even on to boil yet!' Ita Keegan looked crossly at her daughter while wiping red, work-roughened hands on her apron. Small beads of perspiration stood out on her forehead. The heat in the farmhouse kitchen was stifling for it was necessary to keep the range burning for cooking and heating the water.

She was a tall slim woman whose once fiery red hair was gradually turning grey in middle age. She worked hard keeping the house clean and tidy, cooking and baking for her family and tending the kitchen garden, her poultry and in addition spending hours in the dairy. On Thursdays she took her eggs and butter into Tullamore to sell.

'I'm sorry, Mam. I went to tell Bernie the good news; we walked down to the far lock.' Molly tied a clean apron over her dress and set about scrubbing the skins of the potatoes before transferring them into a pot of water that was boiling on the top of the range.

'Isn't it well for you that you have time to be chatting and strolling down the canal line?'

'I've said I'm sorry, Mam! Will I be setting the table?'

'You will so and have a look at that lump of bacon and see if it's nearly cooked. I've a loaf of bread already risen and ready for the oven.' Ita moved around like a small whirlwind between table, range, dresser and door – the latter to shoo out three hens that had taken the opportunity to forage inside the kitchen, thanks to Molly leaving the half-door open. 'And will you remember to shut the door after you come in next time and not have us invaded entirely by the poultry! I've swept this floor twice this morning already.'

Molly bit her lip and lifted the slab of bacon from its pan with the big metal fork and peered at it intently. It *looked* cooked.

Ita glanced over her shoulder and then deftly transferred the piece of meat to a large dish. 'Put it in the top oven to keep warm while those potatoes cook. So, I suppose she was delighted you're to go with her?'

'She is. I asked her to come down tonight so we can discuss . . . things.'

'Is she coming for her supper?' Ita was fully aware that food was always a scarce commodity in the O'Sullivan home and she was fond of Bernie.

'If you don't mind, Mam, and . . . and I was wondering if you'd mind if I gave her an old dress of mine?'

'You don't have any "old" dresses. What you grow out of does for Maria. It's not easy keeping four of you clothed and shod, especially the way those two eejits get through boots.'

'I know that, Mam, and I'm fed up telling our Tom and Aiden not to go kicking the toes out of them. You know they never listen. But maybe just this once I could give something to Bernie?'

'Has she nothing saved up for this new life in Liverpool?'

'Oh, Mam! How can she? She hasn't been able to get any kind of a job this past month.'

Ita sighed. Money was hard come by at all times but for the likes of Dessie and Tess O'Sullivan it was worse, although she would have thought with four sons and two daughters in America times shouldn't be so hard now.

'Well, just this once, seeing as it's her da's cousin who is going to take you both in.'

Molly smiled her thanks but wondered if Bernie's words about her da's cousins were correct.

'When we get the dinner over I want you to help me in the dairy; this weather isn't the best for butter.'

Molly nodded but was secretly dismayed. She hated churning. It was backbreaking work: hours of turning the heavy handle of the big butter churn, shoulders aching, arms aching and often at the end of the day, head aching as well. The only good thing that could be said was it was cool in the dairy. Still, hopefully she would go with Mam into Tullamore on Thursday to get the things she needed for her journey and give Mrs Bracken her notice.

The bacon, cabbage and potatoes were on the table when her father and Dessie came in from the fields.

'Wash your hands and then come to the table,' Ita instructed the two men.

'Ah, 'tis as hot as the hobs of hell out there. We're sure to suffer for this weather later on, 'tis unseasonal!' Dessie remarked, eyeing the big jug of home-brewed cider Ita had placed on the table. He was very thankful of these couple of days' work and the midday meal. Ita was a grand cook.

'Help yourself, Dessie,' Ita instructed.

'But not too much now or you'll be falling asleep on me this afternoon and there's three cartloads of turf to be brought down from the bog before the evening milking,' Paddy reminded him, sitting down and carving slices of bacon and helping himself to the big floury potatoes from the dish Molly put in front of him. He was a big man, well built with salt-and-pepper-coloured hair and grey eyes. His face was more weather-beaten than tanned.

'She's asked young Bernie down here this evening,' Ita informed her husband and Bernie's father.

'So, you're after letting her go then?' Dessie said, gulping down half a mug of cider.

'We are,' Ita replied.

'Seeing as Bernie's coming, don't you think it would be a good idea if Tess and Dessie come too? We could discuss the whole thing, make proper arrangements for travel. Dessie, you can stay on after you've helped me get my beasts back out into the pasture, can't you?'

Thinking there might well be a bit of supper in it for himself and Tess too, Dessie readily agreed.

'Then send our Tom up to see Tess after school, Ita,' Paddy advised.

'I will. Now, will you get on with your meal, I've plenty of work to do myself this afternoon.'

When Bernie returned home it was to find her mother sitting at the door of the run-down cabin looking with distaste at a bowl of small and rather shrivelled potatoes she held in her lap.

'Aren't they all eyes and poor looking?'

Bernie sighed. 'Where did you get them? Is that all there is for dinner?'

'Iggy dug them up from the patch beyond before he went off to school.' Tess waved a rather grimy hand in the direction of what passed for a 'pratie' garden.

'Ma, that lad's an eejit at the best of times! Even I know they're not ready to be dug up yet, they're hardly grown.'

'Well, there's nothing else in the house until your da gets his wages from Paddy Keegan and I can get into town. I can't ask herself at the shop and post office in Rahan for any more credit this month.'

Bernie shrugged. She took the bowl from her mother and went into the one room that served as kitchen and sitting room. There was no parlour, just one bedroom that led off the kitchen and another in the roof space, reached by a ladder. In the centre of the room was a large square table with two long wooden forms pushed under it. An old bentwood rocking chair was set on one side of the fireplace, a battered wicker armchair on the other. A few three-legged stools and a large press constituted the remaining furnishings. Not much to show for all Tess's years of marriage, she thought. Well, she wasn't going to end up like this. Even though it was stiflingly hot she threw a few more sods of turf on to the open fire, tipped the potatoes into the black iron pot that hung on a hook over the fire and poured the water from a chipped enamel jug over them. She was starving.

'Did ye use up all that water, Bernie?' Tess called.

'I did so. Why?'

'Then ye'll have to take the bucket up to the spring, that was the last of it.'

Bernie went back outside, yanking the bucket from its hook on the wall and wishing they had piped water as they did in Molly's house.

'Ma, what have you been doing all morning? Did you not know that was all the water there was?' It was a fair walk to the spring and she was hot, hungry and thirsty.

Tess rounded on her. 'Haven't I had enough to do with sweeping that filthy floor and using what water I had to wash the few bits *ye* left down for *me* to scrub while ye were off gallivanting with Molly Keegan!'

Bernie was instantly sorry. She had left her Mam to heat water and wash her few clothes which were now drying on the bushes and Mam was looking so tired. Tess O'Sullivan had been a fine big woman in her younger days but grinding poverty, constant hard work and worry and the carrying and giving birth to twelve children had more than left their mark. Now she was thin, bent and worn out.

'I won't be long and then I'll put on the kettle and we'll have a nice cup of tea. There *is* tea and milk and sugar?'

Mollified, Tess nodded. If there was nothing else there was always the makings for a pot of tea.

'Molly had great news, Ma! She's coming with me to Liverpool and I'm going down there this evening to sort everything out.' She eyed the washing. 'I'll get out the flat iron after dinner and do those few bits. This old dress will be filthy and sticky by then and I might even wash my hair, it will dry in the sun.'

Tess looked with affection at her daughter. She wasn't the worst and she'd miss her, but she was well used now to going to the station to see her children leave, knowing there was little chance of her ever seeing them again. She remembered them all in her prayers every night and thanked God whenever a letter or a parcel arrived, which these days wasn't very often. Ita Keegan had seen two of her sons go and now young Molly was leaving too, but she knew well that both Denis and Mick sent money home. No doubt Molly would too – well, maybe she would make sure Bernie didn't forget about her ma and da. Anyway, Liverpool wasn't *that* far away. If Bernie did well, maybe one day she'd come home to visit.

With an effort she got to her feet to get out the cups. There was a bit of soda bread left; they'd have that with the potatoes. Dessie would get a fine feed up at the Keegans' and that would have to do him. What she was going to give the kids when they got home she didn't know. Maybe later she'd walk up to Healion's at Goldsmith's Lot and see if Annie could spare a few eggs.

The afternoon passed quite quickly for Bernie. As she did her chores she daydreamed of all the things she was going to do when she got to Liverpool. Tess managed to scrounge four eggs from her ever-generous neighbour but was greatly relieved when young Tom Keegan had arrived and told her that she was expected with Bernie below at the house for a bit of supper and to discuss the girls' departure. She would have gone hungry herself otherwise.

'The four of youse behave while we're gone! I want no trick-acting out of ye or your da will have something to say to ye when we get back!' was the firm instruction to her four younger children as she and Bernie, now in a clean blouse and skirt and with her hair freshly washed and pinned up, took their leave at half past seven.

It wasn't far to walk and the fierce heat of the day had given way to the cool of evening. Small clouds of midges hovered over the waters of the canal which the rays of the slowly sinking sun had turned to molten gold.

Ita's door stood wide open as did all the windows in the two-storey house but Bernie knocked on the doorjamb just the same.

'Tess, come on inside and sit down, I've the tea whet and I'm just waiting for Paddy and Dessie to come back,' Ita instructed.

Tess dipped her fingers into the small holy water font on the wall and crossed herself and then sat down thankfully at the table, thinking for the hundredth time how fortunate Ita was in the fine house she had. And the furnishings! No one in the country districts had the electricity but Ita had oil lamps with fancy glass shades, not odds and ends of tallow candles.

'Molly, pour Mrs O'Sullivan a cup of tea while I finish carving up this ham, I'm sure she's in the want of it. Bernie, help yourself to either milk or buttermilk, it's cool enough. Molly brought it up from the dairy only a few minutes ago. Aiden, bring in that bucket of turf. Holy God, wouldn't it be grand, Tess, if we had the electricity and those new-fangled electric stoves and no need to be burning turf in this heat?'

Tess sipped her tea. 'I'd thank God if I had a decent range to cook on, so I would.' And I'd thank Him even more if I had decent food to cook on it every day, she added silently while hungrily eyeing the plates of ham, bread and butter, crumbly white cheese, potato cakes and barmbrack that Ita and Molly were placing on the table.

Aiden reappeared, lugging a large bucket of turf, followed by Paddy and Dessie, who eyed the veritable feast with appreciation. Two good meals in one day was more than he'd hoped for.

When everyone was seated, Paddy said grace and they all tucked in. The O'Sullivans tried not to appear to stuff themselves but it wasn't easy and Bernie wondered if she might ask Molly for a few slices of barmbrack to take home for her younger brothers and sisters.

When all the plates were empty, Molly and Bernie cleared the table and stacked the dishes in the sink. Young Tom, Aiden and twelve-year-old Maria were dispatched outside to play and the business of the night was finally embarked upon.

'Now, I've been talking this over with Ita and we think they should go next Thursday week, on the morning train from Tullamore. I'll take the trap and Dessie can take the cart. Between the two there should be enough room for everyone and their bits of luggage,' Paddy announced.

Tess nodded, casting a quick look at Bernie. She knew she was just itching to get off but her daughter showed no sign of disappointment or annoyance.

'Molly will have to say goodbye to her aunts and uncles and they'll both have to go to Confession on Saturday and Mass and Communion on Sunday. Father O'Brien wants to have a few words with them before they go.'

At this latter piece of information Molly shot her mother a sideways glance, wondering just when her mam had found time to see the parish priest. Bernie looked studiously down at the floor thinking of the lecture they were in for.

'Does Bernie have her fare?' Paddy asked.

'She does so, enough for the train and the boat,' Dessie informed him.

'And your cousin Matty can be relied on to give them a bed and look after them?'

Molly held her breath but Bernie remained silent.

'Ah, that he can! Haven't I already assured ye both he has a fine house and a steady, responsible job.' Dessie knew Liverpool was a big city but he wasn't sure exactly what kind of an area his cousin lived in. However, he was confident that with the good job Matty said he had the house was bound to be much better than the small, cramped cabin he himself called home. The girls would be safe with Nellie and Matty.

'And it's a decent Catholic family,' Tess added to her husband's assurances.

Paddy nodded. He was a caring man and had his children's welfare very much at heart. 'Then I'll give Molly a letter for him and a bit of money for his trouble. I know they'll find work as soon as they can and be able to pay for their keep, but it will help with the family finances until they do. I don't want them to be out of pocket on Molly's account.'

'That's very generous of you, Paddy. It will be appreciated.'

'Tess, do you have a proper address for them, so I can write to Molly?' Ita asked.

'It's number ten Hopwood Street, off Scotland Road, Liverpool, Lancashire. That should find them. I think the local church is St Anthony's. Isn't that what Nellie said in her letter, Dessie?'

Dessie nodded.

'Did she say anything about the house, how many bedrooms it has? Has it got a parlour? Is the area a decent one and are there any jobs in that part of the city or will they have to travel?' Ita pressed.

'Sure, she didn't say. To tell the truth, Ita, it wasn't much of a letter. There was a definite want of interesting information like that. Still, I suppose like the rest of us she's not a huge amount of time for writing letters. Hasn't she six kids of her own?'

'Mam, can Bernie and me go up to the bedroom now, to sort out some things? You remember I asked you earlier on?' Molly interrupted before Tess could elaborate further and her mother could start wondering if there would be room for another two at number ten Hopwood Street or would they be very overcrowded?

'Ah, go on up with the pair of you. I'll make a start on those pots.'

'I'll give you a help with them, Ita, you've given us a grand supper,' Tess offered, while Paddy passed Dessie a packet of Sweet Afton cigarettes and took down a small bottle of Power's from the dresser. It was a bit of an occasion after all.

Dessie thought it was a blessing that Bernie had set her heart on going to Liverpool and that his cousin Matty had providentially been willing to give both herself and Molly Keegan a roof over their heads. There had been no slap-up supper, cigarettes or drop of the 'good' stuff when the others had taken the emigrant ship. He relaxed into his chair, puffing gratefully on his cigarette.

Chapter Three

FOR MOLLY THE DAYS seemed to fly, for Bernie they dragged on
slowly. After that evening they saw very little of each other.
They had of course been summoned to the Parochial House in
Killina for the interview with the parish priest, something which
neither of them had anticipated with much pleasure but to which
they were resigned. They had sat for half an hour, listening
respectfully, and answered all his questions dutifully 'Yes, Father',
and 'No, Father'. They had paid far more attention when he told
them the story of the terrible plight of Maggie O'Dwyer who had
forgotten all the teachings of the Church and had committed the
dreadful sin of letting a lad take advantage of her. She had found
herself 'in trouble', to the utter shame and humiliation of her entire
family who had disowned her. She had been sent off to the nuns in
one of the Magdalene Laundries in a distant part of the country
where she still worked, her child given up for adoption. It was a
story they had heard many times, they'd known Maggie O'Dwyer,
but the priest's reiteration of it was sobering. Finally, fully aware of
what they must and must not do, they knelt for his blessing on their
new life.

Molly had gone with her mother into town on Thursday and
while Ita had attended to the business of selling her produce, Molly
had gone into the Drapery and given in her notice. The fact that
she bought three pairs of stockings, some cotton dress lengths and
a lightweight, longer-length cardigan mollified Mrs Bracken
somewhat. One pair of stockings she intended to give to Bernie,
whom she knew had purchased a new pair of shoes with some of the

money she herself had given her. She was determined they would both look decently turned out when they started on this huge adventure.

Then there had been the visits to her many aunts and uncles who had all made a fuss of her and wished her well. Some of them had even pressed a few shillings into her hand, despite her protests, for she knew it was money they could ill afford.

Bernie had packed and repacked her few bits and pieces half a dozen times at least, or so it seemed to Tess. 'She's that restless she's after giving me a headache just watching her! She can't wait to be off,' she'd complained to Dessie.

'Ah, leave her alone, Tess. She'll find out soon enough that life isn't a bed of roses over there either. She'll have to work damned hard for every penny, like the rest of us,' he'd answered.

Finally, to Bernie's enormous relief, the day of their departure dawned bright and sunny. They were all up early and there was soda bread, eggs and even rashers for breakfast, a rare treat that Tess had bought for the occasion out of Dessie's meagre wages. Bernie washed quickly and dressed in the pink and white sprigged cotton dress Molly had given her. It was a bit faded around the neckline and hem but she didn't mind: the fashionable drop waist with the short box-pleated skirt was all that mattered. In addition to the 'new' dress she had her black leather shoes with the small hourglass heel and the strap over the instep and the cream stockings. She wished they had a full-length mirror but they didn't. She also wished she had a hat but that had been beyond the limits of her resources too.

'Bernie, child, will ye stop admiring yourself and get out here! Your da will be along with the cart any minute now and we're to meet the Keegans at the grain store by the bend in the line,' Tess called.

Bernie glanced for the last time around the bedroom she'd shared with all her siblings and, smoothing down her skirt, picked up the small, dilapidated canvas bag which held all her belongings. She went out to join her mother and her younger brothers and sisters who had been given the morning off school to accompany her to the station.

Tess too had made an effort with her appearance. Her grey skirt was clean as was the dark blue blouse and despite the warmth of the day she had on a black knitted shawl. A small crocheted hat was crammed firmly over her greying hair.

'Will you childer sit still and not be driving me mad with your antics! I declare to God, you girls are like a bag of cats this morning!'

Bernie grinned. 'Ah, leave them, Ma, they're excited!'

'Well, I hope they'll be just as "excited" when it's time to go to school!'

'Here's me da now!' Iggy shouted, running along the track towards the farm cart which Dessie was driving. It was pulled by a sturdy-looking brown and white horse.

Tess shut the door of the cabin and shepherded her brood along the track towards her husband.

When everyone had climbed up and was settled he turned the horse around and they headed for the bend where the canal line joined the Cappaloughlan road, just behind the grain store. Molly, her parents and brothers and sister were already waiting in the trap. On her knee Molly clutched a brown leather suitcase, secured with a strap. A broad smile came over her face as Bernie waved to her.

'Paddy, let Tom and Aiden ride with Dessie, we're shocking cramped,' Ita instructed and the two boys gladly scrambled down and hoisted themselves on to the back of the cart to join the young O'Sullivans.

'Right, you go ahead and I'll follow,' Dessie said when the lads were safely installed.

'Wave goodbye to the canal, Moll, it'll be a long time before you see it again!' Bernie called.

Molly laughed. Sometimes Bernie said the daftest things but she could tell her friend was really excited. She felt excited too, but nervous at the same time and there was a tinge of sadness, but she pushed that to the back of her mind. At least it was a glorious summer morning. It wasn't pouring with rain or icy cold or blowing a gale as it could be in autumn or winter. They wouldn't be frozen or soaked by the time they got to the station and the crossing would be calm too. She'd only ever been up to Dublin once in her life, on an outing with her mam and da, but she was looking forward to seeing the city again, even if it would only be a fleeting visit.

They arrived at the station in plenty of time and the girls went to purchase their tickets to Kingsbridge Station while Tess and Ita tried to keep the younger children from disappearing or getting into mischief. There seemed to be quite a few people waiting for the Dublin train and soon the two women and both men were in conversation with a group of them.

'I meant to ask will there be anything to eat on the train? We'll be starving by the time we get to Dublin,' Bernie said, frowning.

'I shouldn't think so but Mam has packed me some sandwiches and buns. We can share those.'

Bernie smiled. 'Well, at least we had a great breakfast this morning. Did he say how far it is from the station to the ferry?'

'He said it's quite a way so we're to get a tram that will take us to the north wall. We should get into Dublin this afternoon and the ferry doesn't sail until ten o'clock.'

'Should we go for a bit of a stroll around the city then, seeing as we've got so much time?' Bernie had never been to the capital before.

'I suppose we could go and look at O'Connell Street and Grafton Street; there's some big expensive shops there. And then we could go and sit in St Stephen's Green for a while.'

'That'd be *great*! It would sort of get us used to being in a big city so we won't arrive in Liverpool looking like a pair of eejit culchies.'

'We don't look like a pair of "eejit culchies", we look very smart!' Molly laughed.

'By Tullamore standards!'

'Ah, will you give over with all that! Look, here's the train!' Molly said thankfully. She hated hanging around.

The two girls were hugged and kissed and admonished to behave themselves, go to church every Sunday, work hard and write home regularly. At last they boarded the train, put their luggage in the overhead racks and settled themselves in the third-class compartment, which was already half full.

As the engine emitted great clouds of steam, a piercing whistle and shuddered into movement Bernie grasped Molly's hand tightly. 'We're on our way, Moll! We're finally on our way!'

Molly smiled at her. 'I never thought a week or so ago that I'd ever be able to leave at all and now . . .'

Bernie nudged her and grinned. 'We'd better wave; Ma's acting like a windmill and I'll never hear the end of it if I ignore her now! It will be mentioned in every single letter for months to come!'

They'd enjoyed the journey, gazing intently out of the window as the train sped through the green fields and towns of Ireland towards the capital where they'd finally arrived just after lunchtime. They'd caught a tram to O'Connell Bridge and had spent the next couple of hours gazing into shop windows, looking longingly at the fashionable clothes displayed there and taking note of the many stylishly dressed women. There was plenty of poverty too, so Bernie noticed, but what really amazed her was how *big* everything was; and the streets were so busy and bustling compared to Tullamore. They'd had a pot of tea in a small café off Grafton Street and had then made their way to the peaceful, shady park that was St Stephen's Green. The shade was very welcome as the afternoon was very hot. Finally, after spending a few pence on some fruit and crubeens bought from the street traders in Henry Street, they headed for the dock area, joining an ever-increasing crowd of people, all carrying cases, bags and bundles. They made their way between the many carts laden with goods unloaded from the ships to the large covered shed from which they would embark. They joined the line of people waiting to purchase their tickets and when their turn finally came, Bernie asked how long they would have to wait before they would be allowed on board.

'About an hour I'd say,' the clerk replied, consulting a pocket watch. 'Aren't you culchies all the same, can't wait to get away. Find yourself a seat beyond.'

'See, we do look like a pair of eejit culchies!' Bernie hissed, glaring at the man who was no longer looking at them but was dealing with the next family of emigrants.

'Da says everyone in Dublin thinks anyone who doesn't live in the place is a culchie! Take no notice,' Molly replied as they pushed their way towards the opposite wall where there were a few rows of wooden benches, the only concession to any kind of comfort for the waiting passengers.

They sat down gratefully. They were both tired now.

'I'll be glad to get some sleep on the crossing.'

'We won't get much, Moll, not with all this lot on board and there's still more arriving. I didn't think it would be this busy. The country must be in a shocking state if so many people are having to leave it.'

'It is so, girl. We've given up on it entirely. We've sold everything we had in Mayo, not that it was much at all, and we're going to America,' a woman sitting next to her informed them.

'I've four brothers and two sisters in New York,' Bernie replied chattily. 'And my friend has two brothers in Boston and I've a sister a nun in Australia.'

'I've a cousin who has a daughter a nun in London. Have ye travelled far?'

'From Tullamore in Offaly.'

Molly closed her eyes and tried to doze. No doubt by the time they boarded the ferry Bernie would have told their neighbour her entire life story and would have learned a great deal about the woman, her children and all her relations in return.

She was roused from sleep by Bernie tugging at her arm.

'Will you move yourself, Moll! They're starting to queue up at the bottom of the gangway. If we want to get a decent seat we'd better get over there fast!'

They joined the line of people behind the family from Mayo and eventually made their way up the gangway and into the saloon. They got seats at the far end of the saloon, away from the already crowded bar and tried to find a comfortable position. It wasn't easy as the seat was little more than a slatted wooden bench but at least it was set against the bulkhead and they could lean their heads against that. Already the air was stuffy and warm and the smell of beer and spirits and tobacco smoke was making Molly's head ache and her eyes sting. People who couldn't find seats sat on the deck between the aisles and she was grateful that they didn't have to endure that at least.

'I hope it's not going to be as noisy as this all night or we'll get no sleep,' Bernie grumbled.

'Maybe they'll close the bar when we sail.'

'They probably won't close it until they've run out of ale! They must make a fortune out of it. There's always some who can find the money for drink. It's going to be a long eight hours.'

'Put your bag on the floor and rest your feet on it,' Molly advised. 'I'm going to roll my cardigan up and use it as a pillow even though it will be creased to death by morning and won't be fit to be worn.'

'I've a bit of knitwear in my bag, I'll get that out to use as a pillow.'

Bernie delved into the bag and brought out a faded blue short-sleeved jumper. She folded it up, jammed it behind her head and closed her eyes. Well, things could only get better from now on. If they could get some sleep the last part of the journey would soon be over and in the morning a whole new life would be waiting for them.

Chapter Four

———— ❧ ————

THEY WERE BOTH CRAMPED and stiff when they awoke early next morning.

'This place *stinks*!' Bernie said irritably, rubbing the back of her neck.

'It does so. I hate the smell of stale beer.' Molly wrinkled her nose at the profusion of fetid odours that hung over the room and then stretched. 'Will we go up on deck? At least the air is bound to be fresher.'

Bernie nodded, stuffed her makeshift pillow back into her bag and got to her feet. 'We look a pair of frights. My hair is coming down and our frocks are all creased.'

Molly grimaced but then grinned. 'I dread to think what I look like but never mind, everyone else looks destroyed too.'

Stepping around people still asleep on the cabin sole, they reached the door of the saloon and went up the companionway to the open deck. A stiff breeze instantly whipped at their hair, blowing the remains of sleep and the frowsy air of below decks away completely. There were a few people already on deck, peering intently at the distant skyline.

Clutching their belongings, they walked to the bow and leaned on the rail. Ahead of them lay the wide expanse of the Mersey estuary, the water sparkling like silver in the morning sunlight. On the starboard side they could see the lighthouse and the old stone fort at New Brighton and beyond it the houses, hotels, the ornate pier, the Ferris wheel and tower. The church of St Peter and St Paul with its huge verdigris dome had been built

27

on a rising incline of land and seemed to dominate the seaside resort.

'Do you think that's a cathedral?' Molly mused.

'I don't know, maybe it is; but sure, I bet you can have a grand time in a town like that,' Bernie said, her voice rising with excitement.

'And yer can spend a fortune an' all.'

They both turned to find a young deck hand leaning on the rail a few yards away. He grinned at them and pushed up the sleeves of his thick navy jersey, emblazoned across which were the words B. & I. Steamship Co. 'It's goin' ter be another scorcher all right. This yer first time ter the 'Pool?'

They nodded.

'What is that place over there?' Bernie asked.

'New Brighton. Parts of it are dead posh, big fancy houses an' hotels, but there's a fairground an' a ballroom an' all kinds of amusements, iffen yer've got the brass, like. If yer're hard up, there's the beach. Yer can gerra pot of tea fer tuppence an' fish an' chips fer fourpence.'

'We might go just to have a look around.' Bernie thought it sounded a great place: she'd never been to the seaside before.

Molly nodded. 'After we get settled and find jobs.'

He shrugged. He wasn't going to spoil their day by telling them that jobs were hard to find in Liverpool. He counted himself very fortunate to have steady work. 'Over on the port side yer can see the docks. There's eight miles of them. They start there at the Gladstone an' go all the way down to the Herculaneum in Dingle an' the overhead railway runs the full length of them. The "Dockers' Umbrella", we calls it.'

They followed his outstretched arm and took in the line of docks. It seemed to be full of ships, some of which looked enormous to their country-bred eyes.

'They go all over the world. "Gateway to the Empire", Liverpool is,' he informed them with pride, having decided to act as their official guide. 'Oh, me name's Jimmy McCauley, by the way.'

Bernie smiled at him. He was a good-looking lad of about

28

nineteen with brown curly hair and blue eyes. 'I'm Bernadette "Bernie" O'Sullivan and this is Mary "Molly" Keegan.'

'And are yer comin' here ter live?'

'We are. My da's cousin is giving us lodgings. He's a Checker on the docks.'

'Is he? Good job that, lorra responsibility.' He was clearly impressed.

Bernie glanced a little triumphantly at Molly.

'Can yer see them three tall chimneys? Well, that's the Clarence Dock Power Station – fer the electricity, like. Everyone calls them the "three ugly sisters".' He laughed. 'A bit further down yer can just make out the steeple of St Nicholas's church, it's Liverpool's oldest. It's really Our Lady and St Nicholas.'

'Don't you seem to know a huge amount about the place?' Bernie was full of admiration.

'Well, I should. I was born an' raised here. Me da comes from Belfast originally but it's shockin' there, what with all the fightin' over religion. Mind you, it's not that much better in Liverpool at times. Mainly on the seventeenth of March and the twelfth of July.' Seeing the look of consternation on the two girls' faces he launched once again into a spiel, drawing on his extensive fund of local knowledge and pointing out the buildings of the waterfront, which was drawing ever closer.

It *was* a big city, Molly thought. There were many fine buildings and the river seemed to be full of ships of all sizes. She could now make out the Landing Stage and the Pier Head, both of which seemed to be bustling even at this hour of the morning.

'Yer're in luck, the tide's in. Can yer see how level the covered gangways are?'

'You mean those sort of tunnels? Why is it lucky that they're level?' Bernie asked.

'Cos the Landing Stage is sort of floatin'. It rises an' falls with the tide an' iffen the tide's out, they're dead steep ter walk up. Yer'd be gaspin' fer breath by the time yer got ter the top.'

'Do you know how we get to Hopwood Street?' Molly asked. He seemed to know everything else.

'It's off Scottie Road. Get any tram that's goin' ter the Rotunda an' ask the conductor ter put yer off at the right stop. Is that where yer're stayin'?'

'It is. Do you know it at all?'

'Oh, aye!' he replied brightly.

This pleased Bernie. 'What manner of a place would it be?'

The smile remained firmly in place but he hadn't the heart to tell these two attractive young country lasses that they were heading for lodgings in a crumbling, fetid old house in one of the worst slum areas of the city. He knew just what conditions were like: his own home was in Blenheim Street, a few streets away. 'Oh, it's just an ordinary street. There's hundreds like it. Well, we'll be comin' alongside soon; I'd better shift meself. Good luck ter the both of yer an' take care of yerselves. Hang on ter yer purses too. There's plenty of thieves hangin' around the Pier Head. Remember, any tram goin' ter the Rotunda.'

The deck had become crowded and they watched him push his way through the press of people and disappear.

'What did he say his name was again?' Molly asked.

'Jimmy McCauley. Wasn't it good of him to tell us all those interesting things?'

'Sure, I thought he was a bit bold.'

'Oh, Moll! Don't be such an eejit, he was only being friendly.'

'Let's make our way back down; I think the gangway will be on the lower deck. I didn't like what he said about thieves.'

'I've got my bit of money in a little cloth bag that's hanging round my neck. I wasn't after taking any chances.'

'I'm making sure I've got a firm hold on my bag,' Molly said determinedly, tucking her small case tightly under her arm.

Half an hour later they found themselves with the crowd of people walking up the covered gangway to set foot finally on the cobbled roadway of the city that was to be their new home. When they were once more out in the bright sunlight, they stood and looked around. There were carts and lorries and even a few motor cars crowding the road. Above them on the raised track, a train rattled along while beneath the overhead railway another train puffed slowly down towards the block of soot-blackened warehouses known as the Goree Piazzas, a man with a red flag walking in front of the little engine. On the wall of the building that was the station for the overhead railway a sign proclaimed 'Permits to View the Liners Obtainable Here'. Across the expanse of cobbles, the three world-famous buildings of the waterfront stood in ornate grandeur, their once pale façades now covered, like every other building, in a coating of soot.

'Don't let's be standing here gaping, there's a line of trams over there,' Molly urged, ill at ease amidst the milling crowds and watchful for anyone who looked like a thief.

They made their way towards the tram terminus and peered intently at the name boards; they finally decided on a number nine, after being assured by the conductor that he'd put them off at the right stop. They paid their fares and then sat on the wooden seat and gazed out of the window. The vehicle rattled its way through the wide streets of the city centre, the trolley sparking overhead, and they were impressed by the fine civic buildings, shops, pubs and cinemas.

''Ere yer are, girls! Hopwood Street's just a bit further down on this side,' the conductor finally bawled out and they made their way to the platform.

'Sure, he's made a mistake! This can't be it!' Molly cried when they had alighted and stood on the narrow pavement looking around. There were plenty of shops and even more pubs, all of which were small, dark and decidedly shabby. Running off the main road were narrow, cobbled streets of the worst-looking houses she'd ever seen.

Bernie bit her lip but tapped the arm of a man in a greasy jacket and flat cap who was passing by. 'Can you tell me if this is Scotland Road? Is there a Hopwood Street near here or have we the wrong place entirely?'

'Aye, this is Scottie Road, luv, an' 'Opwood Street's on the next corner,' he replied affably.

'Oh, holy Mother of God!' Molly whispered, her heart sinking. The sun was getting warmer and the rubbish in the gutters was beginning to smell. Clouds of flies hovered over it and the piles of horse manure that lay in the road.

'They never said it was like *this*!' Bernie added. 'We can't stand here, Moll. We . . . we'd better go and find Matty's house; they're expecting us. It might be all right,' she added, not very convincingly.

They turned into the narrow street and looked at the tightly packed rows of houses. They were three storeys high, the brickwork crumbling and blackened, the steps leading up to the front doors worn and cracked. The doors themselves were peeling and half rotten, as were the window frames. The small panes of glass were dirty and fly-speckled. In some instances they were cracked or missing completely, the gap being filled with cardboard or rags. An iron gas lamp stood on the corner outside the pub but further down the gas streetlights were attached to the house walls by rusted brackets.

Molly gripped her case tightly. She couldn't see Matty O'Sullivan's house being any different to the rest.

Slowly they walked down the street, mentally ticking off the numbers until they drew abreast of a very low and narrow opening in the wall between two houses.

'What's down there?' Molly asked fearfully.

Bernie peered into the opening and then swallowed hard, unable to believe her eyes. Crammed into the tiny square of space were more houses, in an even worse state. A single gutter ran down the centre of the court, which was choked with rubbish. Two battered ashcans stood against one wall; in the far corner was what appeared to be a privy. Little or no light seemed to penetrate.

'Oh, God, Moll! 'Tis worse! There's more houses down there and they're *shocking*!'

Molly was panicking. 'What can we do? We can't go back, we've only just got here.'

'Let's . . . let's go and see what class of a place it is,' Bernie urged.

'Youse girls lookin' fer someone?' A woman had appeared on the steps of the nearest house. She was poorly dressed and looked careworn.

'My cousin, Matty O'Sullivan.'

'Oh, youse must be the young girls from Ireland. I'm Mrs Hardcastle; Nellie told me she was expectin' yer. 'Ave yer just got off the boat?'

They nodded glumly.

'Come on then, I'll walk down with youse. Always got the kettle on, 'as Nellie.'

They walked the short distance in silence and followed Mrs Hardcastle up the steps to number ten, which were just as worn as all the others. The house didn't look any better than its neighbours either.

Maggie Hardcastle pushed open the front door. 'Nellie, luv, yer lodgers 'ave arrived!'

The door at the end of the long, dim lobby was opened and a plump woman with dark hair scraped back in a bun, a long grey worsted skirt and faded green blouse, came out to greet them, wiping her hands on her coarse and stained calico apron.

'Bernie and Molly! Yer got here safe an' sound then. Come on inter the kitchen, yer must both be parched. I've the kettle on. Matty's gone ter work already and I'm tryin' ter get the kids ready fer school. They're actin' up somethin' shockin', they're that excited about meetin' yer.'

Both girls managed a smile as they were ushered into the small, overcrowded and already stuffy kitchen.

Maggie Hardcastle plumped herself down in a sagging armchair by the range while Nellie bustled about with mugs and the teapot and kettle. Six children of various ages and sexes stopped arguing and scrapping and stared at the two strangers.

'Clara an' Maisie, shift yerselves an' make some room fer Bernie an' Molly ter sit down. Franny, put yer boots on this minute an' go an' ask Mrs Kelly fer half a pound of broken biscuits, an' if yer behave yerselves, I'll give yer some ter take ter school with youse!'

'Biscuits, an' it's not even payday, now that's a real treat,' Maggie said.

The two girls smiled again and sat down at the end of the long bench Clara had pulled out from under the table, while the boy called Franny yanked on a pair of battered boots and went out.

Nellie put two mugs of steaming hot tea down in front of them. 'Youse must be worn out. Well, when we've had our tea, I'll get yer some breakfast. I should be shut of this lot in half an hour, then I'll show yer where yer can put yer things an' where yer'll sleep an' yer can have a bit of a rest, like. I've the place ter clean up and some shoppin' ter do, but I won't be disturbin' youse.'

Molly sipped her tea slowly, a cold feeling creeping over her.

Bernie gulped. 'Thanks, that'll be grand. Do we call you Cousin Nellie?'

'Just Nellie will do, luv. Now relax, this'll be a home from home, you see if it ain't. We all muck in tergether, we don't stand on no ceremony around here, do we, Maggie?'

'That we don't,' Maggie answered, eyeing the door hopefully, waiting for Franny to return with the promised biscuits.

Molly thought of the old saying: 'Out of the frying pan, into the fire', and felt tears of disappointment sting her eyes.

Chapter Five

WHEN AT LAST ALL the children had been sent off to school and Maggie Hardcastle had reluctantly departed after savouring the tea and biscuits, Nellie ushered the two girls into the lobby and up the rickety stairs, the banister rail of which was decidedly wobbly and unsafe.

'Yer'll have ter excuse the state of the place, it's always a mess at this time in the morning,' Nellie said breezily, closing the doors of the two small and very untidy bedrooms.

When they reached the top storey they realised they were to be given the room in the attic.

'Now, get yer things unpacked. There's a bit of a chest and Matty has put up a few pegs fer yer ter hang things up on. Come down when yer're ready an' we'll have a bit of breakfast.'

Nellie disappeared and Molly looked around in horror. The sloping ceiling made the room look tiny. There was one small window, which was half open but which did nothing to alleviate the stifling heat. The walls were covered in patches of damp, as was the ceiling. Bare boards constituted the floor on which was placed a straw-stuffed mattress. Over this was folded a single thin, coarse, grey blanket. A scarred and battered chest of drawers stood against one wall and a row of crude wooden pegs had been attached to the back of the door. There were no curtains and no sign of a gas lamp or even an oil lamp.

Bernie dumped her bag on the floor and sat down on the mattress. She was near to tears and smarting with humiliation at bringing her friend to a place like this. 'Holy Mother of God! What have we come to? Oh, Moll, I know we had nothing at home but everything here is so dirty and shabby-looking. It's . . . it's *filthy*! Why did they tell such lies? A grand house! Where do we have a wash? How do we wash our clothes? Where's the privy? There's no light even and the stink of the place! If he's got such a great job, why do they live like this?'

Molly sat down beside her and put her arm around her. She was feeling desperate herself but she had to cheer Bernie up.

'Maybe they can't afford to live anywhere else. Maybe . . . maybe he hasn't got such a great job at all. It's not your fault, Bernie. How were you to know?'

Bernie broke down and sobbed. All her bright dreams and high hopes lay in pieces. 'What are we going to do, Moll?'

Molly sighed heavily. She felt like breaking down in tears herself and sobbing alongside her friend but that wouldn't solve anything. Someone had to be practical. 'Sure, we can't go back yet. They'd all say we hadn't given it a chance and besides, we'd never get to leave again. We'll just have to make the best of it. Get jobs, save up some money and get a decent place of our own, somewhere better than this. It might take time but we'll do it. We *will*! Now, dry your eyes. Let's unpack our things and go down and ask her about finding a job. Never mind having a "bit of a lie down", we'll go out and see what we can find in the way of work.'

Bernie nodded and sniffed. Molly was right: they had at least to *try*. Molly was at least trying her best to look on the bright side of things, not that there was much of a bright side to anything as far as Bernie could see. Molly pulled her to her feet and she managed a watery smile.

It didn't take them long to unpack and Molly forced the window open a bit further, wrinkling her nose at the smell that was drifting up from the yard at the back. It was quite obvious that's where the privy was.

When they returned to the kitchen Nellie had rashers frying on the range but as soon as she saw their faces she pulled the pan off the fire and folded her arms.

'Sit down the pair of youse and tell me what's the matter. Yer chins are down ter yer boots,' she demanded.

Bernie looked apprehensive but decided to take the bull by the horns.

'It's not exactly what we expected. Everything is so . . . old and shabby. We never had anything at home but Molly's used to a grand house with nice clean things and . . .' Her voice trailed off as Nellie sat down heavily at the table, her shoulders slumped.

'Bernie, luv, we all try, believe me we *try*! None of us around here can afford ter live in a decent house in a decent area. There's no work, no money, sometimes there's hardly any flamin' food ter put on the table. I work me fingers ter the bone tryin' ter keep this place clean. I scrub the whole damned place from top to bottom twice a week with water I have ter drag in from the standpipe in the street an' heat up on the fire. I black-lead that range once a week, more often if I can afford the Zebo. I scrub me steps every day an' donkey stone them but yer've seen the filth of the streets. We're all fightin' a losing battle against the muck an' the fault lies in the flamin' houses themselves. They should all be pulled down. There's animals better housed than we are around here. Have yer seen the state of the courts that are crammed in behind these houses? They're a livin' disgrace! We've no gas; no water; and only two privies fer four houses. How can I afford decent furniture an' beddin' with all the kids ter feed an' clothe?'

'But doesn't Matty have a grand job? Isn't he a Checker on the docks?' Bernie interrupted.

'He was, years ago, but he couldn't lay off the drink or the horses, the stupid sod, an' there's too many others ready ter fill yer shoes when yer get the push – an' he did! Like everyone else, he gets what work he can. He goes down ter the stands twice a day. Sometimes he gets work, sometimes he doesn't. Oh, I was so mad at him for ages. Then when yer mam wrote an' asked could yer come here I was that mortified with him that I couldn't tell her he was now just one of thousands of casual dock labourers. I had me pride, God help me!'

The two girls looked at her with pity. Poverty and unemployment in the countryside was bad enough but it seemed to be far, far worse in the towns and cities. At least in the country there was fresh air, clean water and no overcrowded slums rife with disease. No matter how poor you were there was always a patch of land to grow a few vegetables on and neighbours who would help out.

'We didn't know. We didn't understand how things ... are,' Bernie said contritely.

'We'll manage and we'll help as much as we can with the chores,' Molly offered.

Nellie gave a wry smile. 'The chores would kill yer, luv!'

'We're not afraid of hard work,' Bernie added.

'I hope yer're not afraid of the flamin' vermin an' bugs either? There's the usual mice an' rats, then there's the bed bugs an' cockroaches an' the bloody fleas an' lice. The whole place is a breeding ground fer them. At night the bugs come out of the walls in their hundreds! Matty burns them off the bedsprings an' the kids kill them with the candles an' believe me, they stink!' Nellie covered her face with her hands. Whatever kind of homes these two girls had come from, they had to be better than *this*. She hadn't felt so utterly defeated and humiliated in years.

Fighting down the waves of disgust that were engulfing her at the visions Nellie's words conjured up, Molly got to her feet and put her arm around the older woman's shoulder. 'I said we'll manage and we *will*! Now, will we be after having those rashers? Bernie will make the tea.'

Nellie pulled herself together. 'Yer're a good girl, Moll, understandin', like. Sometimes ... sometimes I just feel like givin' up, but there's always the kids ter see ter...'

Molly nodded and smiled. Nellie must have been like them once. Full of hopes and dreams for the future.

Bernie made the tea and Molly did her best to set the table with what few dishes there were and they sat down to the best breakfast that Nellie could provide.

'That was grand, it really was,' Bernie said when they'd finished. 'Sure, it's a great treat to have rashers in our house. Ma's always in debt to herself at the shop and post office.'

'Dessie works fer yer da, Molly, doesn't he?' Nellie stated.

'When there's any extra work to be done. And talking of work, Nellie, do you think it will be hard for us to get decent jobs?'

'It won't be easy, luv. There's factory work. Rope works, soap works, animal feeds, tanneries and the like. The work is hard and dirty, the hours are long and the pay's rubbish and some of the girls who work there are real hard cases. Are yer trained fer anythin', like?'

'I can sew. I did alterations,' Molly replied.

Nellie looked impressed. 'Yer might get somethin' in the big shops in town. Did yer serve yer time?'

Molly shook her head. Neither did she have any references.

'Oh, well, yer can at least try. There's Lewis's, Blackler's an' Frisby Dyke's. I expect the really posh ones like Hendersons an' George Henry Lee an' that Bon Marché would expect yer ter be time-served. What about you, Bernie, luv?'

'Sure, I'm fit for nothing but factory work by the sound of it. All I can do is clean and cook a bit.'

'We've got a bit of money and Da sent you a letter and a few pounds for our keep until we get work. That should help,' Molly informed the older woman.

'Ah, God luv him!' Nellie cried gratefully. 'I'll go up ter St John's Market an' do some proper shopping. The markets are open from early mornin' ter very late at night, always have been fer as long as I can remember. Yer can get great bargains there at the end of the day because yer can't sell what's left as "fresh" next day. It's much cheaper than buying stuff in the shops, although sometimes it's not as convenient. And I'll call in at Paddy's Market on the way back; get a few more bits of crockery an' beddin' too. Yer can both come with me if yer like?'

'We thought we'd go and have a look around, familiarise ourselves with the area and see if there are any jobs,' Molly informed her.

'But if you're going to the markets later on we could come too,' Bernie added.

Nellie got to her feet. 'That's settled then. Youse go an' sort yerselves out and I'll get stuck into cleaning up this pigsty as best I can, like I do every day of me flamin' life.'

Bernie and Molly tidied themselves up, having a quick wash in a bowl in the tiny scullery, put on some clean clothes and went out. They walked along Scotland Road towards the city centre, looking into shop windows and occasionally calling in to enquire if there was any work available. Each enquiry met with the same response: there was nothing. When they reached the end of Byrom Street they walked on towards St John's Gardens at the back of St George's Hall: a haven of peace and quiet amidst the bustle and grime of the city with formal flower beds and clipped shrubs, statues and benches for people to rest on. Thankfully, they sat down on one.

'I've got two pounds and four shillings; how much have you got left?' Molly asked.

Bernie fished out the little cloth bag that hung around her neck on a piece of twine and emptied it. 'Five and sixpence. It's not much, Moll, is it?'

'I know Da put three pounds in the envelope for poor Nellie, so we should be all right for food for a bit. Do you think we should buy ourselves a jug and basin set for that bedroom so we will be after having a bit of privacy to wash?'

Bernie nodded. She was well used to washing in front of her family but Molly wasn't and she was being so good about everything – like not having a decent bed or pillows or sheets or even a proper towel. 'Maybe we can get a few bits for ourselves at this market too. A towel, a couple of sheets for the bed – things like that.'

Molly shook her head. 'Let's not be after buying things like that just yet. Let's get work and wages first.'

'Will you try for a job in those shops she mentioned?'

'I will so but if I can't get anything I'll have to try the factories.'

Bernie shuddered. 'They sound desperate.'

'Beggars can't be choosers, Bernie, but I was thinking about what you said about only being able to clean and cook. Would you try for a job in service, do you think?'

'In service? You mean work for someone in a big house?'

Molly nodded.

'We don't know anyone with a big house. We don't know if there *are* any big houses in this desperate kip of a city.'

'There must be. It can't all be like Hopwood Street – just look at all these grand buildings. There's got to be money here.'

'Sure, I don't know. Wouldn't they expect me to live in? What would you do?'

Molly shrugged. 'Stay with Nellie or get a room of my own.'

'I can't let you do that. I begged you to come with me, I won't be after abandoning you.'

'Let's see what we can get first. It was just a thought. Now, will we spend a couple of pennies on a pot of tea and something to eat, if we can find somewhere cheap? We don't want to go back just yet. I think she's had enough of us for one morning.'

Bernie managed a smile and they got to their feet and made their way out of the gardens and into the Old Haymarket. Crossing the wide road they spotted a shop bearing the name J. Lyon & Co. Ltd that also advertised a Tea Room on the upper floor. That would do.

Chapter Six

———◆·■·◆———

I T WAS LATE AFTERNOON when they finally returned to Hopwood
Street after looking around the city centre. They had stood in
envious wonder before the windows of big department stores like
Blackler's, Lewis's, Owen Owen, Bunney's and the exclusive and
expensive Bon Marché, Hendersons and George Henry Lee.

'There's money in this city all right!' Molly had exclaimed
as they'd noted the many well-dressed men and women and
the gleaming motor cars in Bold Street, which was Liverpool's
equivalent of London's Bond Street.

To save money and because it was a lovely afternoon, they'd
walked back. They were tired but determined to spend their
precious money on things more important than tram fares.

The house didn't look much better for Nellie's efforts, although
they noticed that the steps had been scrubbed and whitened as had
a small area of pavement outside, although how long it would stay
like that after the kids came home from school was a debatable
matter.

'I went up ter the Home an' Colonial Stores an' got a few bits fer
the tea. We'll have ours first cos when the kids get home they'll eat
me out of house an' home an' Matty hasn't been back, so that's a
good sign. He must have got a whole day's work and he doesn't get
that very often, I can tell yer,' Nellie informed them.

She looked much cleaner and tidier than she had that morning,
Molly noticed. Her calico apron was clean, as was the blue and
green paisley print dress, although the colours were faded.

'We had no luck with work so we had a wander around the

shops. Wouldn't you need a fortune to buy some of the things they have? And the style!' Bernie grimaced. 'We really felt like a couple of culchies.'

'Ah, you young ones are always thinking of fashion. Have yer had anythin' ter eat at all?'

'A cup of tea and a bun in Lyon's Tea Shop.'

'Well, sit down. There's a bit of ham and bread and marg.'

They chatted on about the price and variety of the goods in the shops until one by one Nellie's offspring arrived home and greedily ate what their mother put down before them, pushing and shoving each other and trying to steal bits from each other, amidst much slapping and admonitions to 'behave yerselves an' don't be makin' a holy show of me' from Nellie.

After the meal they were all chased out into the street to play while the women washed the few dishes.

At six o'clock Matty appeared, looking hot, tired, dirty but pleased with himself. Bernie, who had never seen him before, was struck by his resemblance to her da.

'So ye arrived safely then? Aren't ye two fine-looking girls? A credit to your mas and das.'

'They are indeed and Molly's da is a very generous man. Sent money with her, he did, for their keep until they get work. We're off to the markets later.'

'Sure, money slips through her fingers like sand on the seashore,' Matty laughed.

Nellie glared at him. 'Chance would be a fine thing! Did yer get a full day then?'

'I did so.'

'Then yer'll have a few bob in wages – or have yer already been inter the pub?' Nellie looked at him suspiciously.

'Ah, now, Nellie, give over with that! I had one pint, that's all, and aren't I entitled to it slaving away in a stinking hold all day. Isn't the shirt stuck to me back with the sweat?'

Nellie raised her eyes to the ceiling. 'Get inter the scullery with yer an' get a wash. Yer're not sittin' down ter eat in that state.'

Matty handed her some coins and then, winking at the two girls, went into the scullery where they heard him singing 'The Fields of Athenry' rather tunelessly. Bernie and Molly exchanged glances. He was clearly a bit of a rogue, but as welcoming as Nellie had been.

It was after eight when they all left the house and headed up the street toward Scotland Road. Nellie insisted they get the tram to Lime Street. They would walk from there to St John's Market; it was just a 'step away'. Both girls were looking forward to the visit, having never been to a big indoor market before.

Nellie quickly made for a stall selling meat and began a lively bargaining process, determined to get as much as she could for her money.

'Will we leave her to it and have a look around?' Bernie suggested, having little interest in tripe, brisket or hearts.

They wandered slowly between the many stalls, which offered most commodities a housewife would need. Molly purchased two towels and a nice white earthenware jug and bowl set, patterned with pink flowers, and Bernie bought a tablet of Sunlight soap.

'Now we'll have the height of cleanliness and the luxury of washing in private,' she laughed as they went to rejoin Nellie.

'That feller must think I was born yesterday! Wanted ter charge me sixpence over an' above what we agreed! I gave him a piece of my mind, I can tell yer, an' I took me custom elsewhere. I got a good deal from the feller further down.' Nellie indicated the hemp bag over her arm, now half full. 'I just want ter get some vegetables and we'll be able ter have a great feed over the weekend and there'll be enough left for a good pan of scouse on Monday too. What did yer buy?'

'Some soap, towels and a jug and bowl for the bedroom, so we won't be after adding to the confusion in the scullery first thing of a morning,' Molly informed her.

If she thought getting washed in the bedroom was an odd thing to do when everyone else washed in the scullery, Nellie said nothing. They left the market and headed back to the tram stop.

Paddy's Market – officially St Martin's Market – was on Great Homer Street and was frequented by many people but especially the sailors from the foreign ships in the docks. There were all kinds of stalls but people mostly went for the clothes, which were piled in heaps on the floor. It wasn't uncommon to see sailors of all nationalities walking back to their ships wearing two or three overcoats and as many as five hats, one on top of the other. They were quickly resold when they arrived back in their home ports. All this information was imparted by Nellie as the tram rattled along Byrom Street.

Molly and Bernie were fascinated by the antics of both customers and vendors and watched bemused at the scenes enacted in front of them. Nellie bargained hard for towels and quilts and even some sheets, all of which had seen better days but were better than no linen at all. When they finally left, clutching their parcels, it was nearly dark and a clock suspended outside a pawnbroker's shop informed them it was a quarter to eleven.

'I'm wore out but it's been a great day all right, better than I've had in a long time, I can tell yer,' Nellie announced.

'I think we'll sleep well tonight,' Bernie added, yawning.

'Yer can use them sheets an' yer can pass that blanket I put out fer yer back ter Matty an' me. Take the quilt too.'

'It's too hot for blankets and quilts, just the sheets will do,' Molly replied, marvelling that even though she had nothing Nellie had willingly given them the blanket off her own bed.

'We'll stop off at the chippy and get somethin' fer supper. I'm starving an' youse two must be too.'

They were hungry and the smell coming from the chip shop was very appetising. To Molly's amusement Nellie asked her to pass over the new bowl, which she then asked to be filled with a fish supper for all of them.

'Perfect end to the day!' she exclaimed, beaming as, clutching the bowl to her chest, her fully laden bag on her arm, they turned into Hopwood Street.

* * *

Despite the stuffy room and the uncomfortable mattress both Molly and Bernie slept soundly, exhausted by the events of the last twenty-four hours.

Molly awoke first and stared around in confusion until she remembered where she was. She sat up and ran her fingers through her tangled curls. Then she noticed the red lumps on her arms and remembered with horror Nellie's words about the bed bugs. She jumped to her feet and tore off the thin cotton nightdress. She had been bitten all over.

'What's the matter? Why are you leaping around at this hour and in just your knickers?' Bernie asked, irritably.

'I'm eaten alive and so are you! Oh, God! Bernie, I don't think I can stand this! I can get used to anything but not bugs!' she cried.

Bernie jumped up quickly. 'We never, never had bugs at home! Ma would die if she could see the state of us! Oh, Moll, we've *got* to get out of here as quickly as we can. We *have* to find work!'

Molly was pouring water from the jug into the bowl which she had carefully washed before going to bed. She splashed it all over her and began to soap herself. She'd never felt so unclean in all her life.

'We'll go out today, Bernie, and not come back until we've got ourselves some class of a job. And we'll call into a pharmacy and see if there's anything at all that we can buy to get rid of these horrible things!'

'Don't you think that if there is something Nellie would have got it?'

'Sure, she wouldn't waste money on things like that. I think they've just sort of got used to it, accepted it.'

Bernie grimaced. There must be houses in this city that were free from bugs and vermin, surely, although certainly not around here.

Over breakfast they tried to make light of their bites and the revulsion and despair, but informed Nellie that they would probably be out of the house the entire day.

'I've got ter hand it ter yer both; there's not many young girls who take lookin' fer a job so serious, like. There's a few in this street I could name who'd sooner lie in bed all day than look fer work!'

Molly thought they must be totally mad.

When they got to Scotland Road they decided to start their quest by going into St Anthony's Church, lighting a candle and saying some prayers to the Blessed Virgin to help them in their task. It was cool inside and they both felt better for their short visit.

'Well, where do we start?' Bernie asked as they emerged into the sunlight.

'Shall we call at the Parochial House and ask for advice?' Molly suggested.

'Sure, it can't do any harm.'

They were ushered into a small room that obviously served as some kind of an office and told by the housekeeper that Father Ryan would be with them in a few minutes.

They stood feeling a little apprehensive until at last the parish priest appeared.

'Two new faces, I see!'

'Yes, Father. We've come to Liverpool to find work. We're staying with Matty and Nellie O'Sullivan in Hopwood Street. Matty's my da's cousin. I'm Bernadette O'Sullivan and this is Mary Keegan.'

'God bless you both and you're very welcome here. I know Matty and Nellie well. A good Catholic mother is Nellie. Life isn't easy for her.'

Molly nodded, noticing that the priest didn't have much to say about Matty. He obviously knew all about the drinking and gambling that had cost him a good job and condemned his family to dire poverty.

'We'll be at Confession tonight and Mass and Communion tomorrow,' Bernie put in quickly.

'We're desperate to find work, Father, and we don't know where to start, so we thought we'd ask your advice,' Molly informed him.

'Sit down. Now, do you have any skills?' It would be easier for them if they had but he doubted they did. By their accents they were from the rural midlands.

'I can sew quite well, Father, but I didn't serve an apprenticeship and I have no references.'

He nodded.

'And all I can do is clean with a bit of plain cooking but we *have* to get work quickly!'

It didn't look promising but he felt he had to try to help. Two naïve young girls with no jobs and no money could find themselves in all kinds of moral danger in a city like this, full of unscrupulous, heathen seamen. 'I know you will be good Catholic girls, from good homes.'

'Oh, we are indeed, Father! We were taught by the Presentation Sisters in Killina,' Bernie interrupted.

'My da's a farmer and he does what he can to give work to Bernie's da and others.'

The priest nodded. 'I can give you both character references and Mary, if I were you I'd ask – politely – for an interview with the head of the ladies' wear departments in Blackler's, Bunney's, Lewis's and Frisby Dyke's. If there's nothing there, try some of the smaller shops. Bernadette, I think I can actually help you. I have a friend, a very devout man but not of this parish, whose wife has become sick lately and who just might be willing to take on someone to help in the house. I'll give you the address and a note. I can't promise anything but, please God, he might consider taking you.'

'Thank you, Father,' Bernie replied, although she really didn't want to be parted from Molly.

'It's very good of you, Father. We just didn't know where to turn and well, we didn't really want to have to try the factories. They sound desperate places.' Molly thought he was less stern and far more generous and accommodating than Father O'Brien back home. She was truly very grateful to him.

He could understand their reluctance. They were country girls and they'd find it very hard indeed to work in the factories. They were confined and stinking places, and some of the girls and women who were employed there were coarse and ungodly. Not all of them, many were quiet and hard-working, but it was best not to expose these new arrivals to such women if it could be avoided. They were his parishioners; they were his responsibility.

'Wait there now while I put pen to paper and, God willing, by the end of the day you'll both be gainfully employed.'

After he'd left the room Bernie looked apprehensively at her friend. 'What if I have to live in?'

'Then you'll have to. You can't turn it down, not after he's recommending you. And it's got to be better than factory work.'

Bernie nodded glumly.

'I'll be just fine. I'll stay with Nellie and save every penny until I can get somewhere else. Don't you be after worrying about me, I can look after myself.' But Molly spoke with far more confidence that she felt.

Chapter Seven

Tʜᴇʏ ʟᴇғᴛ ᴄʟᴜᴛᴄʜɪɴɢ ᴇɴᴠᴇʟᴏᴘᴇs and Bernie also had a piece of paper bearing the name William Ernest Montrose, Esq., of number sixteen Winslow Street, off County Road, Walton. She had been instructed to get a tram as it was a long way to walk and ask to be put off at Spellow Lane. Molly was to go in the opposite direction, into the city centre.

'How will we know if we've been successful?' Bernie asked.

Molly looked thoughtful. 'You'll at least know at once if they'll take you on. It will take me longer – much longer.'

'Shall I meet you somewhere? I'll have to get the tram back anyway.'

'I'll meet you outside that posh shop in Bold Street, Cripps, as near to half past twelve as I can.'

'I'll wait a bit further down, the feller in the uniform they have outside that place won't be taking kindly to the likes of me hanging around the door.'

Molly nodded her agreement and Bernie made to cross the busy road to her tram stop on the opposite side. Molly caught her arm. 'Good luck, Bernie.'

'And good luck to you too, Moll.'

Bernie didn't have long to wait for a tram and after paying her fare and asking to be put off at Spellow Lane, she sat down and looked out of the window. She knew she really was fortunate but she was nervous without Molly's support and she hated the idea of leaving Molly on her own, despite her friend's insistence that she would be fine.

There were shops and houses either side of Walton Road but she noticed that the area was better than Scotland Road, far more prosperous and much cleaner, and she was surprised when the conductor shouted out that this was her stop. She'd expected it to take much longer to reach her destination.

Winslow Street was the second road on the right after the busy junction. She'd stopped for a few minutes to gaze into the windows of the large Co-op shop and check her appearance. She looked tidy if nothing else but she wished she had a hat.

The houses were of the Victorian terrace type, not exactly big but substantial, and they were all well kept. Paintwork was clean and fresh, windows sparkled and brass doorknockers were gleaming. The stone steps were not worn and cracked like those in Hopwood Street. The windows of every house sported pristine white lace curtains.

She stopped outside number sixteen and took a deep breath, knowing that her progress had been noted from behind many of those lace-curtained windows. She'd never been inside a house like this in her life before and it was daunting.

Her knock was answered at length by a rather frail-looking middle-aged woman with light brown hair and pale blue eyes. Despite the warmth of the day she wore a fine-gauge wool dress in sage green trimmed with cream braid, which was, Bernie noted, quite stylish.

'Good morning, ma'am. I have this letter for Mr Montrose. Father Ryan from St Anthony's sent me.'

Ellen Montrose took the envelope. 'You'd better step into the hall, child. My husband isn't at home, he's at his work until lunchtime but I'll see what Father Ryan has to say.'

Bernie stepped inside and looked around. The walls were papered halfway up in heavy anaglypta, which had been painted cream. Above them the wallpaper was brown with a pattern of cream roses. All the woodwork was varnished brown. On the floor was a brown and cream patterned rug and the stairs were carpeted. A couple of small, gold-framed pictures of rural scenes hung on one wall and on the other was that requisite of every Catholic home, an image of the Sacred Heart at the base of which burned a little red lamp.

Ellen Montrose scanned the neat lines of copperplate and felt very relieved. She had been trying so hard to keep the house in first-class order since she had come out of hospital, but it was so hard, she tired so very quickly. By the end of the day she found it a huge effort even to cook William's evening meal. She had protested that she was fine, quite able to manage, when William had said he was worried about her health but privately she had confided in Father Ryan. James Ryan was an old friend of William's; they'd been brought up in the same street, attended the same school until James had gone off to the seminary, but they'd kept in touch and it had been Father Ryan who had married them and baptised and then buried their child who had only lived a few days. Her health had never been good after that and there had been no more children.

'You have only just arrived in Liverpool, Bernadette?'

'I have so, ma'am, and . . . and it's not what I expected.'

The appalling slums of Scotland Road must have been a dreadful shock to the poor girl, coming as she did from the Irish countryside, Ellen thought. She was an attractive little thing, not dressed in the height of fashion but clean and tidy.

'Come into the kitchen and let's have a chat,' Ellen said kindly.

Bernie had never seen such a clean and tidy kitchen. It was painted in a pale green and the shelves that ran along one wall were lined with green and white checked oilcloth. All the pans and utensils were stacked neatly and were highly polished. Under the window was a sink with brass taps, beside it a scrubbed wooden draining board and her eyes widened as she saw a modern stove for the first time.

'Oh, ma'am, haven't you every possible comfort! Everything is so . . . bright and modern!'

Ellen smiled. 'I have indeed. Mr Montrose is very considerate and generous. Sit down.'

Bernie sat at the table, which was covered in the same oilcloth as the shelves.

'Father Ryan is right; I haven't been at all well since my operation. I get tired very quickly. I really do need some help.'

'I can clean and wash and iron and cook plain meals, ma'am.' Bernie was eager. It would be a positive joy to clean this house and cook in this kitchen. There was electricity, gas, running water. There would be nothing heavy to do at all.

'I'm sure you can and Father Ryan says you are a good Catholic girl, diligent and honest.' He'd also said that if it would be at all possible to take Bernadette, they would be doing him a great favour, for he feared she might otherwise slip into a life of degradation, poverty and worse. Ellen had taken an instant liking to the girl with her lilting accent and unaffected, simple manner. She would teach her to cook more adventurous meals and how to use the more complicated appliances.

'I am indeed, ma'am,' Bernie answered seriously.

'Then I'll discuss it with Mr Montrose this evening and get word to Father Ryan. I'm sure you will suit me fine, however, Mr Montrose will decide how much he is to pay you but if you could come at, say, half past eight in the morning until five in the afternoon, Monday to Friday, and until twelve lunchtime on Saturday, that would give you Sunday and Saturday afternoon off. Would that be agreeable, Bernadette?'

'Oh, it would indeed and thank you, ma'am! You see I have no trade, no training and I don't think I could bear to work in one of those factories.'

'Indeed not. I hear they are really dreadful places. I don't of course expect you to wear any kind of uniform, just something practical and neat. Mr Montrose won't be able to afford to pay you a very big wage. We're not wealthy people. I'm just warning you, I don't want you to be disappointed, Bernadette.'

'Ma'am, I'll be very grateful for *anything*. Won't it be a real pleasure to work in a place like this?'

'Then this evening go up to see Father Ryan and I'll expect you at half past eight on Monday morning. Now, shall we have a cup of tea?'

Bernie scrambled to her feet. 'Let me make it, ma'am! You just sit there and take your ease.'

Half an hour later she made her way back towards the tram stop. She felt she was walking on air. Mrs Montrose had showed her how to fill and boil the electric kettle, and where the tea and sugar and milk where kept (in the small, cool and very tidy larder). She'd handled the nice white cups and saucers, decorated with broad bands of green, as though they were the finest bone china. There was even a teapot to match them. She'd only ever been used to the old brown teapot at home and Nellie's was an even poorer affair. Then she'd been taken on a tour of the house; never had she seen such luxuries. Smart linoleum, rugs, polished furniture, brass bedsteads, good quality bedding, lampshades. Switches on the wall that you just flicked and on came the light. Gas fires in the bedrooms – an unheard-of luxury. And on top of everything else a bathroom with a big white enamel bath standing on claw feet, a washbasin and a toilet that flushed. No need to go outside in all weathers to a ramshackle earth privy. And she didn't even have to live in, although she would have considered it heaven to live in a house like that.

Her mind was still reeling with everything she had seen when she got off the tram outside Central Station and walked the short distance to the bottom of Bold Street. She couldn't wait to tell Molly all about number sixteen Winslow Street and the fact that she would get Saturday afternoon and all day Sunday off, and of course she would be home by half past five each evening and would have the whole night to herself. Could anyone ask for anything more? She just hoped her friend had been as lucky.

She didn't have long to wait until she spotted Molly's auburn curls but some of her euphoria dimmed when she saw the dejected expression on her face.

'No luck then, Moll?'

'None. I've been to Lewis's and Blackler's but they had no vacancies. Blackler's said they'd put my name on the waiting list though.'

'That's better than nothing at all, Moll.'

'What about you? How did you get on?'

'Great! I'm to start on Monday morning.' She was finding it

hard to suppress the torrent of excitement that was bubbling up in her but she didn't want to depress Molly further.

'How much will you get? Will you have to live in?'

'I won't, I'm to work eight-thirty until five each day and until twelve noon on Saturdays with Sunday off. But I don't know how much they'll pay me. It's up to Himself to decide and he was at his work. I've to go to see Father Ryan tonight but I don't care, Moll! You could almost work there for nothing, it's a little *palace* and she's so nice.'

Molly smiled. 'I'm really glad for you, Bernie, I am.' She was relieved that one of them had work and also for the fact that she wouldn't have to face life in Hopwood Street without her friend.

'Where are you going to try next? I'll come with you, wait for you.'

'Bunney's on the corner of Lord Street and then Frisby Dyke's further up. After that I don't know.'

'You'll get something, Moll, I know you will!' Bernie said emphatically. 'Things are going to get better, I just feel it.'

Molly had no luck at Bunney's and it was with a feeling of increasing disappointment that the two girls walked up Lord Street to Frisby Dyke's.

Bernie said she'd wait for her just outside the front doors and Molly went in and asked for the ladies' wear department.

As she climbed the stairs to the first floor she rehearsed what she would say.

'May I help you?' The young assistant looked friendly, despite the austere black dress with its plain white Peter Pan collar.

'Could you tell me where I might find who is in charge here? I'm looking for work. I can do alterations of all kinds and I don't mind doing other things too.'

'It's Miss Freemantle you should see but I don't think there're any vacancies. We have two girls who do the alterations and there's myself, Miss Greenwood and Miss Hepworth to see to the customers and the stock.'

Molly bit her lip. It looked a nice place to work.

'But I do know there's a vacancy in the soft furnishings depart-ment. My friend who worked there left to get married. Would you be interested in that?'

'What are soft furnishings?' Molly asked, feeling very embar-rassed.

'Curtains, cushions, braid, antimacassars, tablecloths and napkins, lampshades, things like that.'

'Oh, yes, that would be grand. I'd like that but . . .'

'But what?'

'I've no experience.'

'Don't tell them that! You're Irish, aren't you?'

Molly nodded.

'Tell them you worked in a big shop in Dublin then, somewhere like Cleary's. I've an auntie in Dublin and I went to visit her once.'

'But I didn't. I don't even come from Dublin but they'll know that by my accent. I'm from the midlands.'

'Believe me, they won't know the difference, I don't. You're just *Irish*. You'll soon pick it up, it's not hard.'

'But what if they find out?'

'Do you want the job or not?'

'I do so!'

'Then go and ask for it. Have you any kind of a reference?'

'I've got a character reference from my parish priest.'

'Go on then, it's on the third floor. Ask for Mrs Stanley, she's the manageress and she's not a bad old stick. Dora, my friend, got on well with her. Good luck.'

Molly grinned at her. 'Thanks, I'll need it.'

Chapter Eight

———◦·❊·◦———

I T HAD TAKEN ALL Molly's resolve and confidence to inform Mrs Stanley that she had worked in the soft furnishings department of Cleary's for two years after she had moved up to Dublin from Tullamore. She had no references from them because she had had to give notice rather suddenly to come to Liverpool when the chance had arisen, but she handed over her reference from Father Ryan and hoped he would forgive her for all the barefaced lies she was telling. She also prayed that he had put nothing in the letter about her never having lived or worked in Dublin.

'And have you any experience of helping customers with curtains? It's rather specialised,' the manageress asked at length, folding the letter and handing it back to Molly.

'I'm afraid not, ma'am, but I can sew quite well. I can do all kinds of alterations and I have made some of my own clothes. I'm sure I could learn quickly.'

'I'm sure you will be able to. You do seem a very capable girl and with your experience and the fact that we haven't found anyone at all suitable up to now, can you start on Monday?'

Molly could have kissed her. 'Oh, I can so, ma'am!'

Mrs Stanley gave a tight little smile. 'You will call me Mrs Stanley, if you please. We will provide your shop dress, which must be kept neat and clean at all times. Two white collars are provided; they are detachable. Black stockings and shoes, if you please, and, Miss Keegan, it would improve your appearance if you had your hair cut. It would look much tidier.'

'Yes, yes, I will, ma'— Mrs Stanley. It's such a furze bush!'

'Quite. The wages are twelve and sixpence a week, rising to fifteen shillings when you are twenty-one. The hours are eight o'clock to six on Monday, Tuesday and Wednesday and eight until eight o'clock on Thursday, Friday and Saturday. We don't open until nine in the morning but your first hour will be spent cleaning and tidying and restocking.'

Molly nodded. The hours were long but she wasn't complaining and twelve and sixpence, rising to fifteen in four years' time, wasn't to be sneezed at.

Mrs Stanley smiled. She had been impressed by the priest's letter and the girl's manner and experience. 'Then I'll introduce you to the other members of staff, show you where the cloakroom is and the locker where you will keep all your belongings. Then I'll introduce you to Miss Venmore, the timekeeper. It goes without saying that I expect you to be punctual, diligent, polite and obliging. If you are in any doubt about anything, do please *ask*. Don't try to muddle through, that just causes expensive mistakes and disapproval and disappointment for the customers.'

'I will so,' Molly agreed firmly. It would all be new to her but she liked the idea of that. She had a feeling that she would enjoy working at Frisby Dyke's; there were so many lovely things. Her mam would love to come and see the stuff they had here; there was nothing like it in Tullamore.

Bernie had decided to go in and was debating whether she could afford to buy some of the pretty hair slides they had on a counter on the ground floor when she caught sight of Molly, who was beaming.

'You got a job? You did?'

Molly nodded and took her arm and they went out into the street.

'What? How much are the wages? When do you start?'

'Let's go over the road to the Kardomah Tea Room and I'll tell you everything. We can afford a treat now.'

They settled themselves at a small table in the window and ordered a pot of tea and two toasted teacakes. 'Whatever they are!' Molly whispered.

'I don't care, I'm starving!' Bernie hissed back.

'I didn't get a job sewing. I'm to be an assistant in the department selling curtains, cushions, lampshades and things like that for the home. Soft furnishings, they call them, and they've got some gorgeous things! Mam would only be delighted to have a look around the place. I heard about it from an assistant in the ladies' wear department. I did have to tell a few lies though.'

'Lies? What kind of lies?'

'She said I was to tell them I had experience, so I said I'd worked in Cleary's in Dublin.'

'Oh, Holy Mother! You never did?'

'I *had* to! I wanted the job so badly, Bernie.'

'I know, Moll, but I just hope Father Ryan will understand that. You'll have to tell him in Confession.'

Molly bit her lip. 'I know.'

'God will understand though and it's not really a *desperate* lie. You did need the work; we have to get out of Hopwood Street.'

'The only thing that worries me is in case I forget that I'm supposed to have been living in Dublin for two years and I don't know the place at all. What if someone asks me where exactly I lived?'

'Just give as little information as you can. Say it was near Mountjoy.' It was the only part of Dublin Bernie had ever heard of and that was only because of the jail there.

'I don't want to have to go on telling lies.'

'Then don't. Say you weren't very happy there and you don't want to talk about it.'

That was good advice, Molly thought.

'How much will you get?'

'Twelve and sixpence, rising to fifteen shillings when I'm twenty-one.'

'That's a *fortune*!'

'I know but things are more expensive here, so she said when she took me to meet the timekeeper.'

Bernie grimaced. 'I bet she doesn't live around Hopwood Street.'

'The hours are long though. Eight 'til six Monday to Wednesday and eight 'til eight on Thursday, Friday and Saturday. I only get Sunday off.'

The tea and cakes arrived. The 'teacakes' were large flat currant buns, toasted and swimming with melted butter.

'Um, they're grand!' Bernie announced delightedly, her mouth full.

'They provide me with the black dress and two white collars but I've to have black stockings and shoes and get my hair cut.'

Bernie grinned. 'I'll have mine cut too. Sure, we'll go when we've finished this. Your one who brought the tea has nice hair, I'll ask her if she can recommend somewhere we can go.' She caught the eye of the waitress who came over to them.

'Is there anything wrong, miss?' the girl asked, frowning.

'Not at all, but we were wondering, well, you have such lovely hair, so fashionable, and we'd both like to have ours cut but we don't know where to go.'

The girl smiled and patted her short, shiny dark bob. 'I have mine cut at Marcel's. It's just a small shop in Harrington Street which runs at the back of Lord Street here. They don't cost the earth and they can usually fit you in if you can wait. I don't have time to wait, with working, so I book an appointment. They stay open late two nights a week.'

'I've just got a job over at Frisby Dyke's and I have to have black stockings . . . and I could do with some other things too,' Molly said hesitantly.

'Marks and Spencer is the best value. It's on Church Street. I get my stockings and "unmentionables" there. Woolworth's is great too, there's nothing over sixpence.'

They thanked her profusely and finished their tea.

They waited with mounting excitement in the small hairdressing salon in Harrington Street. The two girls and an older foreign-looking man who they deduced must be 'Marcel' appeared to have great expertise in their chosen profession and snipped confidently at all lengths of hair.

It was Molly's turn first and she rather shyly pointed to the picture of a young woman with a short bob that was displayed on the wall.

'You've lovely hair! Customers pay a fortune to have their hair permanently waved to look like this,' the assistant informed her.

'There's just too much of it!'

'I'll thin it out for you. And I'd suggest a side part rather than a fringe. A fringe won't sit right. Your hair is too wavy.'

Molly looked a little disappointed but the woman smiled. 'It will look great, I promise!'

It did, Molly was relieved to see when finally her long auburn hair lay in thick strands on the floor at her feet. Her head felt so much lighter and the short wavy style suited her.

'Don't you look different altogether? It's grand, Moll, it really suits you,' Bernie exclaimed.

'It feels so airy and light!'

'Your turn next, is it?' the woman asked.

Bernie couldn't wait to sit down in the chair.

When they emerged they felt exhilarated. Bernie was delighted with the short bob that came just below her ears and the full fringe suited the shape of her face.

'Don't we both look the height of fashion now?' she laughed.

'We both look so different that they'd not recognise us at home. Oh, I wish Mam had let me have it cut years ago. It will hardly take any time at all to wash and dry.'

'Will we go to those shops she told us about?'

Molly nodded her agreement and they both walked down towards Church Street.

'Would yer look at the pair of youse! Yer look years older!' Nellie exclaimed when they finally arrived back in Hopwood Street, clutching brown paper parcels.

'I had to have it cut for the new job,' Molly informed her.

'So I thought I'd have mine done as well,' Bernie added.

Nellie beamed at them. 'That's great news about the job. Sit down an' we'll have a cup of tea an' yer can tell me everythin'.

63

Alice, you take them parcels upstairs for Molly and Bernie an' don't go nosin' at what's inside!'

Young Alice did as she was instructed while the two girls informed Nellie of the events of the day. She exclaimed over their good fortune, their forthcoming steady wages and marvelled at Bernie's description of the house in Winslow Street.

Later that evening they both went up to St Anthony's Church for Confession, something Molly was not looking forward to as she would have to tell Father Ryan, who had been so kind, that she had committed a sin in telling barefaced lies to get the job. That would hurt and disappoint him and add to her shame. She was greatly relieved to see that Father Ryan wasn't taking Confession, it was another priest. Of course she would have to tell him but that didn't seem so bad. She was told to say four decades of the Rosary as a penance and she promised never to sink to such deception ever again. Afterwards they both went to the Parochial House: Bernie to find out how much Mr Montrose was willing to pay her and Molly to thank the parish priest for his help.

They were ushered into the same room as before and waited.

'Ah, I was expecting you, Bernadette. I've had word from William Montrose. He's most relieved that Mrs Montrose has admitted she needs help. I understand she thinks you'll be very suitable and that you're to start on Monday morning?'

'I am so, Father, and it's a grand house. It will be a pleasure to work there for Mrs Montrose.'

'They are good people and I'm sure you'll learn a great deal from Ellen. Now, you're to be paid seven and six a week. I know it's not a great deal but it will be regular and you have to admit the work won't be hard or taxing and the hours certainly aren't long.'

'I'm delighted with that, Father. Really I am,' Bernie assured him. It was more than she'd expected or hoped for.

'And how did you get on, Mary?'

Molly still felt a little guilty thinking about the lies she'd told. 'I got work too, Father. I'm to start on Monday too, in the soft furnishings department at Frisby Dyke's. I was very lucky, someone had left to get married, and your reference really did help.'

He nodded, much relieved. 'So, I hope that you will both be diligent, honest and punctual in your work and not waste your wages.'

Bernie decided to take the bull by the horns. 'Father, we're very grateful to Nellie and Matty for taking us in but . . . well . . . it's a bit crowded and not very . . . clean . . .' she faltered.

'Nellie does her best, child, they all do. The conditions people are forced to live in are disgraceful.'

'We know that, Father, we . . . we're not criticising her, really we're not!' Molly added. 'It's just that we're not used to things like . . . bed bugs and lice and no water.'

'When we've got enough money we'd like to find somewhere else, somewhere better,' Bernie interrupted. 'I'm sure she won't mind, the kids are all having to sleep in the same room so we can have the one in the attic.'

The priest understood. 'That's very commendable of you. When you feel you have enough saved up, come and see me and we'll see if we can find you a couple of rooms in a house in a decent area.' He at least could tell them *which* area, for there were districts in this city where two Irish Catholic girls would definitely not be welcome. Religious bigotry was rife and not only in the enclaves of the predominantly Catholic Scotland Road area or fiercely Protestant Netherfield Road area. He knew of cases where Catholic families who had moved into streets in the more genteel areas of the city had been ostracised, particularly if they were Irish and, frankly, he was also a little worried in case Bernadette unintentionally carried bugs or lice into Ellen Montrose's house. He'd have to warn Ellen to be vigilant.

They thanked him again and left, promising to be at Mass in the morning.

'We'll work out how much we'll need for expenses and how much we're going to give Nellie, then we'll know what we can save and how long it will be before we can get out of this kip!' Molly said with relief.

'Don't forget I still owe you for the things we got today.'

'You had to have a couple of working dresses, Bernie.'

Bernie nodded. They'd bought stockings and some underwear in Marks & Spencer, and two plain cotton dresses and a couple of aprons as well. They'd been a bit extravagant and had splashed out on some scented soap and fancy hair slides in Woolworth's and had also bought a hat each, the fashionable cloche type, for, as Molly had said, every respectable girl and woman had a hat.

'It won't take us long, Moll. We won't buy anything else. What we've got will do us for the rest of the summer.'

'I've still got those dress lengths. I could make us a decent frock each for Sundays.'

'And where would you do the cutting out and sewing? Sure, the stuff would be filthy in no time in Nellie's kitchen and with all those kids pawing at it.'

Molly looked thoughtful. 'I have a lunch hour, as Herself called it. Maybe I could do it then.'

'Take it to work?'

Molly nodded. 'I'd ask first, of course. They do alterations so they might even have a sewing machine I could use.'

Bernie looked doubtful. 'I wouldn't count on them letting you use it, Moll.'

'I can ask. There's no harm in that. I can't wait to get out of here! For the first time since we arrived I really feel as if life is going to be just great. I was beginning to think we'd made a desperate mistake.'

Bernie linked her arm through Molly's and grinned at her. 'Things can only get better from now on, Moll.'

Chapter Nine

———◦·✦·◦———

MOLLY AND BERNIE WERE both feeling a little nervous on Monday morning as they set off in opposite directions. They had been up very early and scrubbed themselves all over with the new scented soap, so they felt clean and fresh, despite the red bite marks which they had liberally dabbed with calamine lotion they'd bought from a pharmacy.

They had been advised by the chemist to keep all their clothes packed in camphor paper in as airtight a drawer as they could find to discourage the bugs, even though they bemoaned the fact that this would cause heavy creasing. Molly had bought a fine-toothed comb, which Nellie called a 'nit comb', and they meticulously went through each other's hair with it at night and prayed they wouldn't find that anything nasty had taken up residence there.

'At least now it's short it will be easier to go through,' Bernie had said grimly, determined not a single bug or louse should find its way into Mrs Montrose's spotless home.

Nellie had advised Molly to take a bit of 'bread and scrape' for her dinner as she doubted anything would be provided and it would cost her a pretty penny to be buying a meal each day. She assumed Bernie would be given something to eat at midday. She had agreed to accept seven shillings a week for their lodgings; it would be a very welcome addition to her precarious and often meagre budget and she could feed them quite cheaply if she shopped at the markets. After they'd taken out their weekly tram fares, they were left with ten shillings and eight pence between them. They'd decided to keep the eight pence for things like soap and shampoo and other minor necessities and to save the ten shillings.

'In four weeks we'll have two pounds. I wonder how much it will cost to rent two decent furnished rooms?' Molly had mused.

'I'll ask Mrs Montrose. She might have some idea. Nellie won't.'

'We'll have to feed ourselves and pay for gas and electric as well as travelling expenses.'

'We'll only really need one good feed a day. We'll manage, Moll, and surely the rent won't cost much more than eight or nine shillings.'

'Even if it costs ten we'll still have ten shillings left between us and that's not bad really.'

Bernie had grimaced. 'If we can stick this kip for four more weeks!'

They'd parted company on Scotland Road, wishing each other luck, Bernie dashing to catch a tram that was already standing at the stop.

Ellen Montrose was waiting for her and to Bernie's surprise so was her husband, who hadn't left for work. He was a tall, thin man with sparse grey hair and heavy spectacles, dressed in a dark, immaculate three-piece suit. A heavy gold watch and chain adorned the front of his waistcoat, his black boots shone and his white shirt glistened with starch.

Ellen introduced her. 'This is Bernadette, dear.'

'Good morning, Bernadette. I'm glad to see you are punctual.'

'Good morning, sir,' Bernie answered politely, thinking he looked far stiffer and formal than his wife.

'I see you've had your hair cut. It suits you,' Ellen said pleasantly.

'Thank you, ma'am. I thought it would be tidier.'

'I trust you will work hard and not be in any way insolent,' Mr Montrose interjected. He was looking pointedly at the pink dabs of calamine on the bits of her arms not covered by the sleeves of her dress.

Bernie was beginning to feel slightly uncomfortable and hoped he wasn't going to stay at home all day. 'Oh, no, sir! I mean, sure I'll work hard and do as I'm bid.'

'Then I'll be off to the office,' he informed them, much to Bernie's relief.

She'd had a good day, Bernie thought as she walked along County Road for the tram that evening. She'd washed up the breakfast dishes, made the bed and cleaned the bathroom. Mrs Montrose had showed her how to use the Ewbank carpet sweeper on the carpet in the parlour and she'd dusted and polished all the furniture. She'd washed the kitchen floor and then she'd made tea and sandwiches for Mrs Montrose's lunch and had been quite surprised when she'd been told to lay two places at the kitchen table.

'I really didn't expect . . . anything, ma'am.'

'But you can't work all day without anything to eat, child.'

'I often did, ma'am,' she'd replied, thinking of the days when she'd had little more than soda bread and potatoes to eat.

After that she'd cleaned all the windows and her employer had supervised the making of a steak and kidney pie and scones, things Bernie had never made before. She'd been quite astonished when the lad from the butcher's had called with what he called 'Mrs M.'s usual order' and handed her a parcel of neatly wrapped meats. She'd been a bit confused about paying him but he'd said Mr Montrose paid the account by the month.

'An' dead on time too! Never lets it be owin' fer even a day,' he'd informed her with some admiration.

She'd learned that a weekly order from the Co-op was delivered too. The bread and milk were delivered each day and paid for on Saturday mornings and the coalman came once a fortnight. It was all so *different*, she'd thought, but then the poor woman had been sick and probably hadn't been able to go to the shops or carry heavy groceries home.

Monday was usually washday but as it was her first morning it had been postponed until tomorrow. She wasn't at all concerned, however. It couldn't be hard in a house like that.

Nellie's house looked even more drab and dirty when she got back. Poor Nellie, but sure, if she had all the things Mrs Montrose had, the place would still be a kip, she thought. Nellie was right, the whole street should be demolished and new houses built. She didn't know how Nellie and her neighbours found the heart to go on scrubbing and cleaning when everything and everyone around them defeated their efforts.

Molly arrived home at a quarter to seven. 'You wouldn't believe the wait I had before I could get on a tram and even then there was such a crush!' she informed them.

'It's always the same, luv. Everyone's comin' home from work at the same time,' Nellie sympathised.

'How did you get on?' Bernie asked. Molly looked tired and the severe black work dress made her appear pale.

'Not too bad. You have a fair bit of cleaning and tidying to do before the shop opens and I seem to have been on my feet for hours and hours. There's such a lot to learn too. All the different fabrics and types of braid and which can be washed and which have to be "dry cleaned" . . .'

'How do you "dry" clean something?' Bernie asked, mystified.

'It's done in special places, apparently, but I don't exactly know how.'

'An' costs an arm an' a leg too, I'll bet,' Nellie added.

'There's so many different styles of lampshade and they all have special names. And I'll be expected to help with curtain measurements.'

'Sounds dead complicated ter me,' Nellie muttered, never having had a decent pair of curtains in all her married life. Even her mam had had to borrow a pair for the front room the day she'd got married to Matty.

Molly brightened a little. 'Still, I got a cup of tea and a sandwich. They have what they call a "canteen" where you can get a bite to eat and it doesn't cost much so I won't need to take anything tomorrow.'

'There's a good dish of scouse and plenty of bread to dip in. You must be starving,' Nellie announced, ladling the stew out.

'I am,' Molly agreed.

After their supper the two girls decided to go out for a breath of air as the evening was sultry and the small house stifling. They walked down toward the Leeds to Liverpool canal, which bore little resemblance to the Grand Canal back home. There were no reeds or water flowers on these banks, no trees or shrubs, no birdsong.

'Did you ask about the price of renting rooms?' Molly asked.

Bernie shook her head. 'I just didn't get round to it.'

'Well, I did. Joan, one of the girls in my department, said you can rent a whole house for ten shillings a week out in the furthest suburbs. Places like Norris Green and Fazakerley. The council are building whole estates of brand-new modern houses there but they're for families and they're quite a long way out. But if we try Walton or Anfield we should get a couple of decent rooms for about seven shillings a week.'

'That's what we're giving Nellie.'

'Yes, but we'll have gas or coal and electric on top of it and our food and expenses. Oh, and they always want a month's rent in advance.'

Bernie looked crestfallen. 'That will take up our two pounds.'

'We'll just have to wait for a week longer. We can't move out with no money for light or food or fares. Never mind, it's only an extra week.'

Bernie nodded and they walked on in silence until they were interrupted by the shouts and yells from a group of lads who were milling around the edge of the canal. Some were splashing around in the dirty water; others were jumping up and down on the bank.

'What are they up to? Sure, that's a terrible racket they're making.' Bernie shuddered. 'I wouldn't swim in there if someone paid me – even if I *could* swim!'

Suddenly a lad of about ten detached himself from the group, ran over to them and grabbed Molly's arm. 'Miss! Miss, will yer 'elp us! It's me brother! Oh, come quick!'

'What's the matter with him?' Molly asked.

''E jumped in, miss! 'E's a dead good swimmer is our Alfie but 'e 'asn't come up!'

'Holy Mother of God!' Bernie cried in alarm and they all ran over to where the group was huddled together. All were white-faced and quiet; some were shaking.

'Where did he go in? How long ago?' Molly demanded.

'Just . . . just down there, miss! 'E's been gone ages!' a scruffy lad with a shock of black hair replied. His lips were blue and he was shivering.

Molly kicked off her shoes but Bernie grabbed her arm.

'Moll, for God's sake, you can't go in after him! God knows what you'll catch and you could get into difficulties too!'

'I *have* to! You can't swim!'

'Oh, save 'im, miss! Please, please? Me da'll kill me! We're not supposed ter be swimmin' in the cut at all!' Alfie's brother sobbed, clinging to Molly's skirt.

Molly peered into the turgid, stagnant water and began to strip off her stockings. God alone knew what was down there but a lad's life was at risk and she had to stifle her fear and revulsion.

The sound of footsteps pounding over the hard-baked ground made them look around. A young man was hurtling towards them at full pelt, his arms working like pistons and his face flushed. He was followed by two more.

Obviously someone else had gone for help, Molly thought with relief.

'Quick! Quick, there's a lad drowning!' Bernie yelled. 'She's after going in too but she's not that strong a swimmer and I can't swim!'

'He went in down there.' Molly pointed to the spot.

In an instant two of them had dived into the water fully clothed.

'The bloody little fools! There's that much rubbish chucked in there it's a bloody deathtrap!' the third panted.

Molly gathered the shivering and sobbing lad to her as they watched the two older lads' heads finally appear.

'Jimmy, will I go for the scuffers? Is there any sign of him?' the young man still standing beside Bernie shouted.

His mate dragged himself out of the water, shaking his head. 'It's like a bloody scrapyard down there. I can't see sight nor sign of him, not that yer can see much at all. The poor stupid little sod!'

'It's *you*! It's Jimmy McCauley!' Bernie cried, recognising the young deck hand from the ferry. She dragged off her cardigan and put it around him; he was dripping wet and shivering himself.

He looked at her blankly for a few seconds before recognition dawned. 'Bernie O'Sullivan from the Dublin ferry boat!'

'Jimmy, someone's goin' ter have ter tell the kid's parents and the scuffers'll have ter be informed. Someone's goin' ter have ter get his . . . him out – eventually,' his friend hissed, glancing at both Molly and the boy she was holding.

'Well, he can't be going, the state he's in, nor the other one either!' Bernie said, jerking her head in the direction of the second young man who had now dragged himself out of the canal.

'I'll go and get the scuffers then,' Jimmy's friend said reluctantly.

'And I'll take this one here home,' Molly volunteered. 'Where do you live?' she asked Alfie's brother.

'He lives in Blenheim Street, a bit further down ter our house,' Jimmy replied.

'In the same street as yourself?' Bernie said. 'Then you know him?'

He nodded. 'His mam's goin' ter be in a right state!'

Molly looked anxiously at Bernie, dreading having to go and tell the poor woman about this appalling tragedy.

'Won't it be better if we all go back to Nellie's first? You lads can get dried off and she'll give you a cup of tea and then we can decide what to do about . . . things,' Bernie suggested.

'That might be a good idea,' he agreed. 'Yer'd better bring the whole lot of them, they're all in shock.'

Nellie too was shocked and appalled when Molly explained why the group had invaded her kitchen.

'Sweet Jesus have mercy on him! And have mercy on his poor mam! Have youse lot no thoughts fer yer poor mams? They struggle an' slave ter bring yer inter the world and ter bring yer up an' yer go doin' stupid bloody things like this! How many times have yer been told not ter go swimmin' in the bloody cut!' she cried.

Matty took charge. He sent Tom Birkin, the only one of the three young men who was not dripping wet, to Athol Street Police Station and his own eldest son to inform Father Ryan.

'You lads sit down there and Nellie will give you all a cup of sweet tea. You girls get towels so these lads can be after drying themselves and I'll go up to the pub and get a drop of brandy. We're all in the want of it.' He turned to the group of ashen-faced boys. 'The police will want to talk to all of you and they'll send down a diver. When they've been and His Reverence has been to break the terrible news to the family, you can all get off home.'

Young Alfie's brother clung to Molly. 'I don't never want ter go 'ome! They'll blame me! Me da will belt me black an' blue!'

'Ah, don't be daft! I'll have a word with him,' Matty tried to console him.

'I was supposed ter be mindin' our Alfie! 'E's younger than me!' the boy sobbed.

'Was,' Jimmy said bitterly, wringing the water out of his shirt.

To Bernie and Molly the next hour seemed to stretch into an eternity. They passed cups of tea and 'drops' of brandy around the small kitchen while Nellie dabbed at her eyes and chased her own offspring upstairs 'out of harm's way'. Finally a constable and a sergeant arrived.

Everyone was asked for their account of the tragedy, after which the young boys were told to go to their homes.

'Will yer send down a diver?' Jimmy asked.

The sergeant nodded, snapping shut his notebook. 'You say the parish priest has gone to inform the parents?'

'He has,' Nellie replied. 'And the Council should do something about the rubbish in that cut!' she finished angrily.

'The kids shouldn't swim in it! There're enough notices up and if you lot didn't go throwing your rubbish into it in the first place it wouldn't be the deathtrap it is!' the constable retorted.

'Sure, the Guards in this country aren't very sympathetic!' Bernie muttered to Molly. Nellie just glared at the pair as they turned and left.

Jimmy and his mates got to their feet. 'We'll be pushin' off ourselves now. Thanks, Mrs O'Sullivan, for the tea and brandy.'

'Yer're welcome, lad,' Nellie replied heavily.

Bernie followed them down the lobby. 'It was a brave thing to do. If there's that much stuff down there you could have been drowned yourself.'

'Yer don't think about yerself at the time. She was all fer goin' in after him an' yer said she wasn't much of a swimmer.' Jimmy jerked his head in the direction of the kitchen where Molly was helping Nellie to clear up.

'You are all right in yourself, though?' Bernie pressed.

'Wet an' I'll probably get a dose of sick stomach from the filth in the water, but I'll be all right.' Suddenly he smiled. 'Yer look different. Yer've had yer hair cut.'

Bernie nodded.

'And how are yer gettin' on? I didn't have the heart ter tell yer on the ship that this is a flamin' slum.'

'Oh, we're doing grand! We have jobs and we're going to be moving out to a place of our own before long.'

'Really? Will yer let me know where yer're going?'

'I will so.'

He hesitated. Before joining his mates, who were already down the front steps, he asked, 'Would yer like ter go out one evening? Take yer mind off what happened tonight?'

Bernie was taken aback. This was something she'd never expected. He seemed a nice enough lad and he was undoubtedly brave . . . He was quite good-looking too, but she'd only met him once before. Still, as he said, it might take her mind off the tragedy *and* he was the first lad who had asked her to go on a proper outing. She might enjoy his company.

'I would so.'

'I'm off termorrow night then it's back ter workin' on the "cattle boats". I'll call fer yer about eight. Will that be too early?'

'No! That will be just grand.'

He turned and left and she stood watching the little group as they made their way up the street in the gathering dusk. What a very strange day it had been. She felt utterly exhausted. One part of her was still stunned and shocked; another part, however, was looking forward to seeing Jimmy McCauley again.

Chapter Ten

———⋄❈⋄———

THE WHOLE NEIGHBOURHOOD WAS stunned and saddened by the death of young Alfie Bradley. Pennies were collected from the houses in all the surrounding streets to help the bereaved family with the cost of the funeral. Dire warnings were given to all the children about the danger of going anywhere near the canal no matter how hot the weather got.

Molly wrote home to her mother, giving her all the news. She didn't make any mention of the conditions she and Bernie were living in, saying that very soon they hoped to be moving, as Nellie was really very overcrowded. She promised that as soon as she could she would send Ita some of the nice pieces of material that were left over in her department. Called 'remnants', they could be bought by both staff and customers alike, although as staff she would get them a bit cheaper. They would make gorgeous cushion covers. She knew the news would be passed on to Tess, as Bernie hadn't yet written to her ma; she also knew that Tess expected Bernie to send money home. She hoped Tess would understand when they finally moved from Hopwood Street and could tell both families about the dreadful conditions they had escaped from. Bernie did intend to send money home, when they got settled and worked out their finances. It was just a matter of time.

She was also pleased but a little apprehensive about Bernie's proposed outing with Jimmy McCauley.

'It was very brave of him to go diving in like that after poor Alfie but you don't really *know* him. We only met him for a few minutes on the boat,' she said doubtfully.

'And I'll never get to know anything about him if I don't go. He seems very nice and it *was* a brave thing to do.'

'Where are you going?'

'I don't know. He didn't say.'

'Don't let him take you to a pub.'

'Wouldn't he be an eejit to try! I'm only seventeen and you have to be twenty-one. We'd be shown the door and I'd be mortified altogether.'

'I suppose he's got a decent enough job.'

'Nellie says he's damned lucky, there're so many lads his age who can't get work.'

Molly sighed. There were large numbers of men and boys hanging around the street corners or tramping the city streets looking for work. It made her very thankful that they had been so fortunate.

Bernie had been given a very nice red rayon two-piece which Mrs Montrose didn't want any more. The skirt was box pleated and the top, which hugged her hips, had navy ric-rac braid around the collar and the cuffs of the short sleeves. Mrs Montrose had said it had been a 'bad buy'. The colour made her look deathly pale and the skirt was far too short for a woman of her age. William hated it on her, she'd confided. He'd said it made her look 'cheap' and had instructed her to give it to some 'deserving case'. Bernie had been delighted with it. The colour suited her and the skirt was just the right length.

'Oh, ma'am, it's only *gorgeous*!' she'd exclaimed.

'Then take it home, it might do you for Sunday best,' Ellen Montrose had urged.

Bernie hadn't said she would wear it for an outing with a young man. She didn't think her employer would really approve.

'Yer look too smart fer around here, Bernie! Get him ter take yer somewhere decent,' Nellie said when she came down, all dressed up in the two-piece, her cream stockings and black shoes. Her cream felt hat with the green ribbon bow didn't exactly match but the outfit was far better than anything she'd ever had in her life before.

'He might take you ter the cinema,' Nellie mused.

'I wouldn't want to suggest that, Nellie. It's a bit expensive.'

'It's not *that* dear an' he must earn good money. Oh, it's years since I was in one of them places!'

'Well, I'll see what he suggests. I don't want to appear bold.'

Molly smiled at her. 'You're not in the least bit bold and you look gorgeous. He'll be delighted with you.'

'That he will,' Nellie agreed. 'He's a decent enough lad. I know his ma. He comes from a good home. Hard up like the rest of us but clean livin'.'

Clara poked her head around the kitchen door. 'Ma, that feller what was here the other night when that Alfie Bradley was drownded? He's standin' on the doorstep.'

'Well, fer God's sake don't leave him standin' there! Where's yer manners? Bring him in!' Nellie bawled at her.

Bernie made for the door. 'I'll go on out to him! He might be a bit embarrassed.'

'It'll be the first time a lad from around here will be embarrassed about comin' courtin'!' Nellie laughed. 'An' make sure yer're back here by half past ten at the latest. No decent girl stops out half the night,' she added.

'She's a bit of a dragon, isn't she?' Jimmy laughed as Bernie closed the kitchen door. Nellie's words had been clearly audible.

Bernie grinned at him. 'Ah, she's not the worst. She's very good to us in her own way.'

'Yer look really great. That's a nice outfit.'

Bernie smiled a little shyly. She wasn't used to compliments from lads. 'The woman I work for gave it to me,' she informed him and then could have bitten her tongue. There really wasn't any reason for him to know it was second-hand.

'I bet it didn't look half as good on her! Would yer like ter go ter the pictures or would yer like ter go dancin'? There's the Charleton, it's at the junction of Scottie Road an' Byrom Street. It's usually a good night – a bit quiet, like, this early in the week. Yer can't move at the weekends, though.'

'I've never been to a dance hall. I've never been to the cinema either,' Bernie admitted. They were both tempting.

'Then I'll have ter take yer ter both. Will we start with the pictures? Looks like a good film on at the Derby, an' it's not far to walk.'

Bernie nodded. They had almost reached the top of the street.

Jimmy took her hand. 'We'll call in to Ainsworth's and get some sweets.'

Bernie blushed. 'Ah, you're spoiling me!'

'Well, I asked yer out, didn't I? Yer can't expect a girl ter get all dressed up an' just take her fer a walk or a tram ride.' Another idea occurred to him. 'One weekend when I'm off I could take yer on the ferry ter New Brighton. That place yer were askin' about on the boat when we came up the river.'

'Oh, I'd be only delighted to go there!'

'Great. That's two more outin's fer the future.'

Bernie smiled at him. He was talking about their 'future', and that pleased her. She did want to spend more time with him. No lad had treated her like this before. He was considerate; she felt it really mattered to him how she felt, what she thought, where she would like to go. She liked him; she liked him a great deal.

She'd been fascinated by the moving pictures and she'd shed a few tears when the beautiful young heroine had tragically died of consumption just before her wedding day. It had been a very sad ending. 'Dead soppy,' Jimmy had called it but she hadn't cared. He'd bought her a quarter of Everton Mints in the little newsagents and a drink of fizzy sarsaparilla at the cinema and he'd had her back in Hopwood Street at a quarter past ten. She'd felt a little light-headed when he'd kissed her on the cheek, saying he'd be off again a week on Saturday and they'd go dancing and would Molly like to come too as his mate Richie 'fancied' her?

'Did yer have a good time then?' Nellie asked. She was struggling to darn a pair of socks that appeared to be held together almost entirely with darning wool. Molly was neatly patching a pair of trousers belonging to young Franny.

'I did so. We went to the Derby Cinema.'

'That flea pit!' Nellie said derisively.

'It wasn't *that* bad and the film was lovely but so sad.'

'Well, at least he brung yer home on time.'

Bernie took off her hat and Molly folded the trousers. 'Will we have a cup of tea before we go up?'

Nellie flung down the sock in disgust. 'I can't do nothin' with this! Aye, put the kettle on, luv.'

'He's going to take me dancing a week on Saturday and he asked if you'd like to come too, Moll.'

Nellie looked at her askance. 'Do yer want her ter look a right wallflower?'

'No, he said his mate Richie would like to take Molly. He was the other lad who dived into the canal.'

Molly looked a little startled. She hadn't taken much notice of Jimmy's two friends; she'd been too upset at the time.

'Yer might as well, Molly. Yer haven't had much fun since yer got here. Go on, luv, live a bit!' Nellie urged. In her experience, as a woman you got very little pleasure out of life so you had to grab whatever was going while you were young, before you lost your looks.

'We can't dance. Well, I can do a bit of step dancing but not these modern dances,' Molly replied.

'I bet those two can't either! Yer'll soon pick it up and anyway the place will be packed so there'll probably only be room ter shuffle around the floor. No one will notice if yer've got two left feet.'

'Will you be too tired after working all day, Moll?' Bernie asked. She didn't want to force the outing on Molly.

'Ah, she'll forget all about being tired. Yer're only young once, is what I say!' Nellie urged.

Molly smiled. 'Sure, it will be an evening out.'

'That's the right attitude, luv. Let some feller put his hand in his pocket an' give yer a good time. Bernie, there's no fresh milk, it's gone off with the heat. Yer'll have ter use the "conny onny", the condensed stuff,' Nellie informed them with resignation.

* * *

Molly decided that for this, their first big outing, they should pull out all the stops. They had ten evenings in which to conjure up new outfits.

'I've got those dress lengths. The yellow and white flowery one will suit you and the blue and cream one will do for me.'

Bernie was incredulous. 'You'll never get two dresses done in *that* time!'

'*I* won't but *we* will. It's about time you learned how to do simple seams and hems. We won't do anything complicated, like pleats. Just plain boat necklines, no sleeves and we'll gather the skirts into the bodices.'

'I'll look like a sack of potatoes in a gathered skirt. I'm too small. Ah, Moll, you just see to your own. I'll wear the red outfit again.'

'No, you won't, Bernie O'Sullivan! If I can use the sewing machine at work we'll do pleats for yours,' Molly replied determinedly.

Bernie did tell Mrs Montrose that she was going dancing, in a foursome with Molly and the two young men who had so bravely tried to save young Alfie Bradley. She had told her employer the whole story in detail and Ellen had promised to have a Mass said for the boy at St Francis de Salles, the parish church.

'At which ballroom, Bernadette?' Ellen enquired.

'I don't think it's a *ballroom*, ma'am. More a dance hall. The Charleton; I think it's in Byrom Street.'

'I see. I can't say I've heard of it. The Grafton Ballroom is very nice as is the Rialto, and there is one here on County Road, above the Co-op. Blair Hall, it's called. I've never been but I believe it's very select. Mr Montrose isn't a great dancer these days. What will you wear?'

Bernie pulled a face. 'Molly is insisting that I learn to sew. She's good at it and she's got a couple of dress lengths which I have to admit are nice and fresh looking. I'm to have a yellow and white flowery one.'

'That should suit you, with your lovely dark hair. I think Molly is right. It's a very useful thing to be able to make your own clothes;

they are getting more and more expensive. I had to pay fifty-nine shillings and sixpence for my winter coat last year. Mr Montrose nearly had a fit. It is very nice though. Java brown bouclé wool with a lovely musquash collar and cuffs and it will last for years.'

'I suppose it will, ma'am,' Bernie agreed, thinking that she would never spend nearly three whole pounds on a coat even if it did have a fur collar and cuffs.

Ellen Montrose looked thoughtful. She was growing increasingly fond of the girl. It was so pleasant to have someone to chat to during the day and under her supervision the child was fast becoming quite a good cook. Indeed William had remarked only yesterday how good Bernie's first shepherd's pie had been. 'I have some white beads, not very expensive ones, that would set it off perfectly and perhaps you could buy some yellow ribbon and make a headband? I believe all the young girls are wearing them. Three-quarters of a yard should be enough to go around, tie in a small bow and leave the ends loose. It won't cost much. The Co-op should have a good selection in their haberdashery department.'

Bernie smiled. 'I'll call in on my way home this evening, ma'am, and I'd be delighted with a lend of the beads.'

'With a "loan" of the beads, but you can keep them. Wear them whenever you wear the dress. And you must tell me how you enjoy your evening.'

'Oh, I will indeed, ma'am,' Bernie promised.

She bought three-quarters of a yard of inch-wide yellow satin ribbon on her way home and spent an hour tying and retying it, much to Nellie's amusement and the avid curiosity of the younger girls.

'She's dead good ter yer, that one, isn't she?' Nellie said with a tinge of envy in her tone.

'She is so. Sometimes I feel sorry for her. She doesn't seem to have any friends or relations, just Himself – and he's an auld misery from what little I've seen of him.'

Nellie looked thoughtful. 'Sometimes I'd think meself very fortunate not ter have any relations or kids but then I suppose the old sayin's true. "None to make yer laugh and none ter make yer cry." I'd miss havin' a good old jangle with the neighbours though.'

'They don't go in much for standing chatting on the front steps in Winslow Street,' Bernie informed her.

'Right then, we'd best get the tea over if youse two are goin' ter start with all this dressmakin'. I promised Molly I'd have this table cleared an' scrubbed clean by seven o'clock. She's dead clever, isn't she?' Nellie had picked up the Butterick paper pattern Molly had bought in Ireland which showed a picture of two versions of a simple, drop-waisted sleeveless dress.

'She will be if she can get me to make something that halfway matches that picture,' Bernie said grimly, hoping Molly had gained permission to use the sewing machine in her lunch hour. If she hadn't she was sure they wouldn't get finished in time – unless they stayed up all night, every night.

Chapter Eleven

━━━◆◆◆━━━

MOLLY WAS BUSY NEXT morning as there was a new delivery of furnishing fabric.

'Miss Keegan, I'd like you to check these rolls of fabric with me. I'll check them off on the invoice as you read out the name, colour and number from the roll ticket. Then we'll inspect them for possible flaws in the weave and pattern. You can't be too careful. Anything not up to scratch will have to go back,' Mrs Stanley instructed her.

It took them over an hour as they were both interrupted by customers. Molly was as polite and obliging as she could be, knowing she had a favour to ask when the opportunity arose.

'Thank goodness this is the last roll, there will be no time for a break this morning I'm afraid. It's only three-quarters of an hour to lunchtime.'

'I don't mind that at all, Mrs Stanley. Isn't this the most gorgeous material? Look at the way the light catches the gold weave of the brocade. Wouldn't it look grand trimmed with some of that heavy ivory fringe?' Molly mused, fingering the rich fabric with something akin to reverence.

The manageress nodded. 'It would, Miss Keegan. It would lift it, give it the appearance of true elegance. You have a good eye.'

Molly smiled and blushed slightly at the praise. 'Sure, it was just a thought. Shall I put this roll out on display?'

'Yes, near the front, and you might as well drape a couple of yards of that ivory fringe over it, just to give customers an idea of the effect.'

Molly thought it was now or never. 'Mrs Stanley, may I ask a big favour?'

'What kind of favour?'

'During my lunch hours may I have permission to use the sewing machine, please? My friend and I have been invited out and I've promised to make us both new dresses. To sew them by hand will take so long that I don't think they would be ready in time. I'll be very, very careful with it.'

Mrs Stanley looked a little surprised but considered the matter carefully. At last she nodded.

'As long as you confine it to your own time and provide your own thread and pins. If the machine is damaged in any way you will of course have to pay for it to be repaired.'

Molly was delighted. 'I will so but as I said I'll be very careful with it.'

'I didn't realise you were competent enough to make your own clothes, Miss Keegan.'

'Oh, I couldn't make something like a coat or a jacket, but skirts and blouses and simple dresses.'

'Very commendable and useful too. I must bear that in mind.'

'Thank you, Mrs Stanley,' Molly replied, thinking that Bernie would be as relieved as she was that the machine could be used.

The frantic evening dressmaking sessions were the cause of much amusement, interest and sometimes complaint to the entire family and quite a few of the neighbours, who crowded into the kitchen to see how things were progressing. Maggie Hardcastle spoke for them all when she said, 'It's not often yer get someone around 'ere what can run up a couple of posh frocks in such a short time.'

On Thursday, Friday and Saturday evenings Molly was tired when she got home and didn't feel a bit like sewing, but each evening Nellie was as good as her word. She had the table cleared and scrubbed and was eagerly looking forward to a couple of hours of what she called 'relaxing entertainment'. Molly had to do her bit.

By the appointed Saturday both dresses were finished and Bernie had promised to give them a final pressing when she got home from work at lunchtime. She was thrilled with the long double string of small white beads Mrs Montrose had given her and she'd bought a cheap white bangle for her wrist from a man who was selling bits and pieces from a suitcase on the corner of Scotland Road and Kew Street when she'd got off the tram one night.

She was dressed and waiting when Molly finally arrived home.

'Oh, Bernie, you look gorgeous, so cool and fresh! I'm so hot and sticky and my feet are killing me!'

'I've asked Nellie to heat up some water while you have your supper. The towel's nice and clean and there's some of that lavender water Mrs M. gave me yesterday. There was more than a quarter of the bottle left and she was after throwing it out! You'll feel much better when you've eaten and are washed and dressed and you've splashed some of that scent on.'

Molly smiled and began to strip off her black shop dress while Bernie went down to bring up her evening meal. She had been thinking all day about Richie and she had to admit that she wasn't all that keen on going out with him. Of course she hardly knew him; she hadn't taken all that much notice of him on the terrible night young Alfie had drowned and he might turn out to be very nice indeed – once she got to know him better, but did she *want* to get to know him better? She sighed. She didn't want to disappoint Bernie and, as she'd said to Nellie, at least it was a night out.

Nellie was vociferous in her praise when they both finally came down into the kitchen to wait for Jimmy and Richie to collect them.

'Ah, God, would yer look at the pair of them! Like a pair of princesses yer are! Give us a twirl!'

Both girls obliged, grinning in self-conscious amusement but secretly delighted.

'Clara, go and get Maggie and Ethel and Aggie! Tell them ter drop what they're doing and come and see the finished outfits,' Nellie instructed.

'Nellie, don't be making an exhibition of us!' Bernie protested.

'What if the lads come and find us being paraded like a pair of spancelled goats to the entire neighbourhood?'

Nellie was not to be deterred. 'It's not the *entire* neighbourhood and they won't be here just yet.'

Molly felt her cheeks beginning to redden as the three women plus four of their daughters trooped into the kitchen, although she knew they both did look well. She was pleased with their handiwork; there had even been time to trim both dresses with a few rows of braid around the necklines and hips. Bernie had insisted that she spend a little money on some blue glass beads and a length of cream satin ribbon for a headband and Nancy, Maggie's eldest daughter (who sometimes wore rouge and lipstick and was considered 'fast' by Nellie), had even sent in a small box of Phulnana face powder that had cost twopence. Not that either of them had dared use it for, as Bernie had said, if they did it was sure to be reported back in Nellie's next letter which might even result in an anxious request to Father Ryan to oversee their moral welfare far more intensely.

Everyone heaped praise upon them until young Clara announced that the two lads were coming down the street and the neighbours slipped out of the back door.

Molly felt rather embarrassed as she walked up the street with Richie, a few steps behind Bernie and Jimmy. Quite a lot of the neighbours were standing on their doorsteps chatting and they all waved.

'What's the big deal? Yer'd think we were a flamin' May procession,' Richie said somewhat cuttingly. He was a tall, thin lad with reddish-blond hair and freckles.

'It's the frocks. Molly and me have been making them and they've caused a bit of a stir,' Bernie informed Jimmy.

'Yer both look really great. Yer'll be the best dressed girls there.' Jimmy meant it; he thought they both looked lovely – particularly Bernie.

'Are we going to the Charleton? Mrs M. says the Grafton and the Rialto are really nice and so is a place on County Road, Blair Hall.'

'They're a bit too classy fer the likes of Richie and me.'

Bernie looked doubtful. 'You mean we'd have to have nicer outfits than these?'

'I dunno but I've heard they charge two shillin's each admission an' that's a bit steep.'

'That's shocking! The Charleton will be just grand,' Bernie said cheerfully. It wasn't fair to be asking him to spend a fortune on her.

The dance hall was above some shops and was reached by a fairly narrow staircase. Neither Bernie nor Molly had been very impressed by Richie's suggestion that they call into one of the many pubs for 'a swift half' before they went dancing.

'We're only seventeen and we're not going to be mortified by being asked to leave!' Bernie had snapped at him. Molly had raised her eyes to the sky and Jimmy had just shrugged.

The place was already crowded as the band was the popular and well-known Ernest Zeffer's Premier Dance Band who were playing a spirited version of 'Paddling Madeline Home'.

'Sure, Nellie was right. It won't matter much that we can't do more than a few steps, no one will notice,' Molly said *sotto voce* to Bernie.

'I don't know, Moll, there's quite a few looking at us already.' Bernie was quite flattered with the attention they were attracting.

'It's dead hot in here already,' Richie muttered to Jimmy. 'We'll be parched in half an hour. We should have gone for a bevvy.'

'Stop yer moaning! I told yer they weren't old enough ter go inter pubs and neither are we. And they're decent girls.'

'Well, are we going to dance at all, Jimmy, or are we going to stand here chatting all night?' Bernie asked.

'All right, come on, let's "trip the light fantastic", as they say.' Jimmy grinned and, taking Bernie's hand, elbowed his way on to the dance floor, followed by Richie and Molly.

The evening was going very well, Bernie thought. She was enjoying herself and they appeared to be the 'belles of the ball' as Jimmy had laughingly said. It was obvious that most of the people who frequented the Charleton Dance Hall were acquainted with each other; as both she and Molly were strangers they were proving a bit of a novelty to the men and a source of interest and speculation to the girls and women. Every detail of their appearance was noted and discussed, with admiration and envy. Nor had they danced solely with their partners. They had been asked to dance by half a dozen different lads.

Once her initial shyness had worn off Molly too found she was enjoying herself. She wasn't very keen on Richie, though. He didn't seem to be able to string more than a few words together and his only interests seemed to be his work as an apprentice on the railway and Everton football club, neither of which she knew anything about nor had any wish to. A couple of the other lads who had asked her to dance were older, in their early twenties, and more interesting and attentive. She'd liked one in particular: Billy Marshall he'd said his name was. He was better dressed and spoke with less of a heavy accent than the others. He was quite handsome too, with very dark brown hair and eyes. He said he came from Everton Valley, which was in a better area than Scotland Road and Vauxhall Road.

'You're by far the prettiest girl here and the best dressed,' he'd told her

Molly had blushed. 'You've a fine line in flattery. You could turn a girl's head, if she were to take any notice of you,' she'd answered but not sharply.

'It's not a line! It's the truth,' he'd protested.

She'd just smiled and let him lead her into what she hoped was a fairly passable quickstep as Ernest Zeffer launched into 'My Blue Heaven'.

By the time the dance was over he'd ascertained where she lived, where she worked and the fact that she hoped to be moving very soon.

'So, if you move where will you go dancing?' he enquired.

'Oh, I don't know. It depends on where we move to. Bernie, my friend, works in Walton. She says it's quite nice there.'

'It's not bad and not short on dance halls either. There's Swainson's and Blair Hall and then there's the Aintree Institute and the Orrell Park Ballroom but they're a bit further out. They're the decent ones, anyway.'

'I've heard of Blair Hall.'

'It would suit you better than here.'

'An' what's wrong with here?' Richie demanded, glaring at both Molly and Billy.

'Nothing much, except it gets a bit crowded and some of the fellers are bevvied,' Billy Marshall answered offhandedly.

'And some fellers go in fer pinchin' other fellers' girls!' Richie snapped. He was still aggrieved that he hadn't been allowed to go for a bevvy and the fact that Molly didn't seem a bit interested in him had annoyed him even more.

'I didn't know she was your girl.'

Molly felt her temper rising. How dare he! 'I'm not his girl! This is the first time I've ever been out with him. I hardly know him.'

Richie was getting really angry now. He'd spent good money on her and she'd hardly danced with him at all – in fact she'd barely spoken to him. 'Well, I asked her out an' I paid fer her!'

Molly's cheeks burned and her eyes glittered dangerously. 'I'm not some class of an animal! Just because you paid my admission doesn't mean you own me! I'll give you the money. I won't be spoken about like that!'

'You apologise to Molly, you thicko! Your trouble is you don't know how to treat a decent girl,' Billy Marshall snapped.

Molly screamed as Richie let fly with his fist, sending Billy Marshall sprawling backwards. Then all hell seemed to break loose. Fists were flying in all directions; girls were screaming; men shouting.

Jimmy grabbed both Bernie and Molly and dragged them towards the door, just as the four burly doormen came charging up the stairs to sort out the miscreants before the police were called.

'Let's get out of here quick! That bloody fool Richie will end up in the flaming bridewell before the night's over.' Jimmy bundled them both down the stairs.

'He deserves to be thrown into jail! He started it.' Molly was still shaking with anger and humiliation.

'I could see he was getting dead narked because you were dancing with that feller but I never thought he'd start a flaming fight.'

They'd reached the street and Molly's temper was diminishing but Bernie was still highly indignant.

'A nice place you were after taking us, Jimmy McCauley. Half of the lads in there were drunk! And isn't he a beast carrying on like that? We're not used to such goings on.'

Jimmy was contrite. 'I'm sorry, Bernie, I really am. I know some of the fellers go ter the pub before they go there but I never expected Richie ter behave like that.'

'I didn't really like him much at all, even before he started fighting,' Molly said.

Jimmy was trying to think of something to placate them both and salvage something from the evening. He was really angry with Richie.

'Look, why don't we go to Fusco's? They're Italian an' the ice cream is the best yer'll ever taste. Yer can even sit down in the back an' eat it. It's too early ter go home yet.'

Bernie calmed down a little and glanced enquiringly at Molly who looked undecided. She didn't want to ruin Bernie's night out by refusing Jimmy's suggestion outright, nor did she want to be what Nellie termed a 'wallflower', but she was exhausted.

She smiled. 'Thanks, Jimmy, it sounds great but why don't you take Bernie? I'll get a tram home; I'm really tired. It's been a long day and I've got a bit of a headache. I wouldn't be much in the way of company.'

Jimmy was quite relieved. 'If yer're sure, Molly.'

Reluctantly Bernie decided that after all that had happened she couldn't let Molly go home and face Nellie on her own. 'I'll come with you. We can go to Fusco's another night, Jimmy. I'm a bit tired myself.'

Jimmy was disappointed but just nodded. The evening had turned into a disaster and all because of Richie's temper. 'I'll see you both home then.'

Molly went straight indoors but Bernie stood on the step.

'I really am sorry, Bernie. I will see yer again, won't I?'

She smiled at him. 'Of course you will. I don't think those two were suited anyway and it's not your fault. You only wanted us to have a great night.'

He grinned with relief. 'I've got next Sunday off. If the weather's good will I take yer across to New Brighton?'

'That would be really grand, Jimmy. I'd love that.'

He bent and kissed her. Bernie's arms slid around his neck and her lips parted beneath his. Jimmy held her more tightly but as his kisses became more and more passionate Bernie pulled away, a little breathless.

'I . . . I think I'd best be going in, Jimmy. It . . . it's not that I don't want to stay here with you, but . . .'

'I'm sorry, Bernie, I was rushing you a bit. I'll see you next week?'

'You will so. Goodnight and thanks.' She turned and went indoors. The evening hadn't been a complete and utter disaster, not as far as she was concerned.

Nellie took an entirely different view of the matter. 'A nice carry on, I must say! Askin' yer out dancin' and then startin' a fight! A nice pair them two is!'

'It wasn't Jimmy's fault, Nellie, and he did ask us both to Fusco's and he saw us home.'

'An' I should think so too after all yer hard work at gettin' them frocks made and dollin' yerselves up ter the nines. I hope the scuffers keep that feller locked up all night an' I hope the Magistrates give him a hard time in the mornin'! They don't take kindly ter disorderly conduct an' neither do I. Now, I'd get ter bed the pair of youse. Molly looks destroyed altogether, as Matty always puts it.'

'Where is he?' Bernie asked.

Nellie looked decidedly annoyed. 'Gone ter the flamin' pub with Bert Hardcastle. The pair of them won a few bob at pitch and toss and before Maggie and me could get a penny of it offen them they were off like a shot! Old habits die hard with Matty O'Sullivan,' she finished bitterly.

Bernie looked at her with sympathy then gently shoved Molly towards the door. Nellie had a lot to put up with, she thought sadly.

They hung the dresses up behind the door.

'We *did* look great, Moll, but I'm sorry it turned out the way it did after all that hard work.'

Molly managed a tired smile. 'We were the centre of attention, weren't we, and I think that was some of the trouble. But I'm determined on one thing and that is we're really going to make an effort to save now and get out of this place. No more dance halls for me, not for a while yet.'

Chapter Twelve

FOR THE NEXT FOUR weeks both girls worked hard and saved every penny they could. Molly found her work increasingly interesting and less confusing. She also found that Mrs Stanley's bark was worse than her bite and that if she asked for help it was always willingly and patiently given. She began to learn how to match colours and fabrics. How to pick out cushion covers, lampshades and curtain material so that they coordinated; in fact Mrs Stanley remarked that she seemed to have a certain talent for it. A good eye for colour, was how she'd put it. Molly had been pleased with the praise. She began to look forward to having what she thought of as 'a home of her own', even if it would only consist of a couple of rooms in someone else's house, and to think of what kind of materials she could use for her own 'soft furnishings' – when she could afford them.

Bernie hadn't told Ellen Montrose how that Saturday evening had turned out. She had just said they enjoyed themselves, although it had been very crowded and hot, and they'd got home early, a condition stipulated by Nellie – something her employer thoroughly approved of.

'So, will you be going again, Bernadette?' Ellen Montrose enquired.

'I don't think so, ma'am. Not to that place anyway. I think you were right when you said there are some nicer places.'

'And what about the young man?'

Bernie had blushed a little. 'He's asked to take me to New Brighton on the next Sunday he's off, ma'am.'

'I see. Well, if this weather holds it should be a lovely day out for you. There's plenty to see and do and there are some nice hotels and of course cafés,' she added, remembering that the girl didn't earn very much and probably neither did the young man concerned. She hoped that the girl wasn't going to get seriously involved; she was still so very young and had little experience of life.

Bernie had thoroughly enjoyed her day trip. Jimmy had spared no expense. They'd gone on all kinds of amusements, had ice cream and lemonade, paddled in the sea, gone up the tower – which was higher than the one at Blackpool – seen a minstrel show on the Pier and had a slap-up fish supper.

The light had been fading as they walked along the water's edge, Jimmy's arm around Bernie's shoulder.

She smiled up at him. 'It's been a great day, hasn't it?'

'It's always a great day when I'm with you, Bernie.' Suddenly he was serious. 'Yer're all I ever think about these days an' I can never wait until I see yer again. I count the days, honestly I do.'

Bernie felt a warm, intensely happy feeling wash over her. 'I count the days too, Jimmy. I feel ... well, that I'm only really happy when I'm with you. Sure, I'm not very good at putting what I feel into words. Oh, I can blather on about things that don't really matter much but when it comes to things that do matter I get a bit lost.' She wanted to tell him that she felt sure she loved him but she felt shy and tongue-tied.

Jimmy bent and kissed her gently on the mouth. 'Do I *really* matter to you, Bernie?' What he wanted to say was did she love him but he was afraid to ask straight out.

There were tears in her eyes as she reached up and stroked his cheek. 'You do. You're the person I care most about, I mean that.'

'Bernie, I've never felt like this about anyone before an' I mean that.'

She slid her arms around his neck and he held her tightly. She knew he was telling the truth, she couldn't not believe the deep sincerity in his voice. He didn't have to say it; she *knew* he loved her.

When they got the ferry home to Liverpool, they were tired but very happy.

Molly and Bernie had had a serious talk with Nellie about their plans and while she understood how they felt, Nellie wasn't entirely sure that it was the wisest thing for two seventeen-year-olds to set up home on their own.

'But we won't be on our own. We'll be living with someone,' Bernie protested.

'I know that but will they keep their eye on the pair of youse the way I do? Or will they only be interested in gettin' their rent every week? After all, yer're family, Bernie, and iffen anythin' happened ter yer I'd never forgive meself. How could I face yer mam?'

'Sure, what can happen to me?'

Nellie had shaken her head. 'Yer never know in a city like this.'

Bernie had thought that if she were in any danger it would surely be in an area like this rather than in some quieter, more respectable suburb, but she didn't voice her thoughts aloud.

'We won't be having much money to be going out all the time. We'll have things to buy and we'll have to keep ourselves,' Molly added.

Nellie had sighed heavily. 'I know yer've been brought up proper, like, but young girls have been known ter go off the rails, especially if there's a lad involved.'

Suddenly becoming aware of what Nellie was really worrying about, Bernie had shaken her head. 'Ah, Nellie, surely you don't think we'd be after doing anything like *that*?'

'I don't think yer would but yer just never know. Look at Ethel's girl. The quietest of the lot was their Violet and she fell in with some feller an' he was married only we didn't know it at the time. The next thing yer knew she was havin' ter be sent off to the nuns in Wales. Poor Ethel could hardly hold up her head fer the shame of it. She was *ruined* entirely, was Violet. No decent feller would want ter marry her now.'

'Well, Moll and me aren't like that.' Bernie was emphatic.

'And Father Ryan said we were to go to him when we were ready and he'd help us,' Molly put in.

Nellie had raised her eyes to the ceiling. 'God Almighty, I sometimes wonder what that man is thinkin' of! Sometimes I really wonder does he not see what goes on around him? Well, all I can say is he must have great faith in the pair of youse, so don't yer go givin' him cause to regret his trust or his kindness. Or makin' a disgrace of us all either,' she'd added firmly and the subject was closed.

The second week of July was stiflingly hot. The tar on the city streets melted, sticking to shoes and boots and wheels. Hordes of ragged urchins played in the waters of the Steble Fountain and, despite all the warnings, the local lads were once more swimming in the Leeds to Liverpool canal. Of an evening people flocked down to the riverfront, taking the ferries to Seacombe, Birkenhead, Wallasey and New Brighton just to try to cool down in the slight breeze.

In Hopwood Street and its adjacent courts it was almost unbearable. The old houses trapped and held the heat, which was added to by the fires kept burning in the ranges. The gutters and privies stank and the flies were a torment. Women sat on their doorsteps, unable to endure the stifling heat of their kitchens. Men and boys hung around on the street corners until late at night and even the children, who usually played games in the street until it got dark, had little or no energy for their usual pursuits. The pubs did a roaring trade to the detriment of household budgets; great hardship ensued for many families.

Bernie found it a blessing to go to work. The light, airy rooms of the house in Winslow Street where every window was open were a welcome relief from Nellie's house. Mrs Montrose found the heat tiring and in the afternoons went for a rest in her bedroom, instructing Bernie not to do too much in the way of heavy work but to spray the yard and especially the grids and around the dustbin with DDT to deter the flies. A large quantity of brown sticky flypapers had been purchased from the chandlers and had been hung in every room. Bernie changed them regularly and thought that Nellie should invest in a few. They certainly helped.

Molly was very tired after being on her feet all day in the heavy atmosphere of the shop. They were not busy, except for the sale of muslin and lightweight cotton bedding, and the time dragged. It was almost unbearable on the crowded trams and when she finally arrived home on Wednesday night after having to stand crushed between two sweating clerks for most of the way, the sights and sounds and smells of Hopwood Street almost brought tears of despair to her eyes.

She found Bernie standing on a chair, struggling to attach a flypaper to the ceiling.

'I don't think it's going to be much use. It won't stay up,' Bernie cried in exasperation as the flypaper, the drawing pin and a chunk of plaster all fell to the floor.

'I don't think it'll help much either, luv. We'd need ter have the whole flamin' ceiling covered with brown sticky paper. The damned things are like a bloody plague and sometimes I think them flypapers cause more disease than they prevent,' Nellie said wearily.

'Only if they're left hanging there when they're full. They have to be changed regularly,' Bernie informed her.

'And who has the money fer that? It's all the muck and rubbish that attracts them.'

Bernie gave up in disgust. 'I'm going to try and hang it over the window in the bedroom, otherwise it will be a complete waste of money.'

Molly followed her up to the attic room. 'Sure, I don't think I can stand much more of this, Bernie. Will we go up and see Father Ryan tonight? We've two pounds seven shillings saved up.'

Bernie nodded. The heat in the room and the smell wafting up from the yard was making her feel sick.

Neither of them felt hungry, so after having a wash and changing their clothes they went up to see the parish priest.

'Oh, it's you two again. His Reverence is worn out with this heat and being up half the night on sick calls,' the housekeeper informed them irritably.

'We're sorry to hear that but hopefully we won't be disturbing him again after this evening,' Molly said placatingly.

The woman nodded curtly and disappeared.

Father Ryan did look very tired, Bernie thought, when he at last appeared.

'We're very sorry to be bothering you, Father, but we've got enough money saved up to be able to move,' Molly informed him.

He nodded, sitting down heavily in the black leather armchair. Conditions in the Parish were dreadful and the risk of an epidemic of disease was increasing by the day.

'It's just a couple of rooms we need, we don't mind if they're not completely furnished. A bed, table, chairs, something to cook on, that's all we'll want to start with,' Bernie added. 'It's really awful at Nellie's.'

'I know, child. Well, let me look in the newspapers. Sometimes there's advertisements. I think Walton will be best. It's quiet and there are plenty of shops and churches. It will be near work for you, Bernadette, and the trams into town are frequent for you, Mary.'

'Will we wait, Father, or shall we come back?' Bernie asked.

The priest got to his feet with an effort. 'Wait here, there's no sense in you going back to Hopwood Street and then having to drag back here again,' he advised. Of course, they could have looked at the advertisements themselves but they had little idea of the geography of the suburbs or which were or were not decent areas to live and he had encouraged them to rely on him for this kind of information.

'At least it's fairly cool in here,' Bernie said quietly.

'More than that, it's clean,' Molly added.

He returned in ten minutes with a folded page of a newspaper. 'There are two I think you should enquire about. I've marked them. They are both in the parish of St Francis de Salles. Father Stephens is the parish priest, I know him well. If you get lodgings I'll let him know.'

Bernie took the paper and looked at the addresses. 'I know where both are, Father. We'll go straight there.'

He nodded and then fixed them both with a serious gaze. 'You *can* be trusted to behave yourselves? I know you've been well brought up, so don't betray your parents' trust or mine. If you need help you must come to me or to Father Stephens.'

'We will, Father, and we won't be getting ourselves into any kind of trouble. We just want a decent place to live.'

'Let me know how you get on and if I'm not here leave word with Mrs Mulrooney. Have you informed Nellie?'

'We have so.'

'Then get off with you now and good luck.'

The heat hit them as they left the building and walked through the churchyard. There seemed to be a great deal of noise coming from the Throstle's Nest pub on the corner, the door of which was wide open.

Molly ignored it. 'Where are they?'

'One is in Arnot Street and the other is in Ismay Street. They're further down County Road. I don't think the houses are as big as they are in Winslow Street but that doesn't matter.'

'Does it say how much they want?'

'No. Just "furnished rooms to let".'

'Let's get the tram and hope they haven't already been taken,' Molly urged.

They called at number five Ismay Street first, only to be told that the rooms had already been let out. They had the impression that even if they hadn't the landlady wouldn't have welcomed them.

'I didn't like the look of Herself at all,' Bernie confided as they walked in the direction of Arnot Street where there was a large school on one corner.

'She didn't like the look of us either,' Molly replied, grimacing.

Number three Arnot Street was a neat-looking little house with a green-painted front door and cream cotton net curtains at the window.

Molly knocked.

The woman who opened it was elderly and a little stooped.

'Mrs Hayes? We've come about the furnished rooms. Are they still available?'

'They are. Won't you come in?'

They followed her into the lobby and Bernie looked around. It wasn't as fresh or as modern as Mrs Montrose's; it smelled a little musty. They were ushered into a parlour, which contained an old-fashioned sofa, a heavy sideboard, a small table, two ladder-backed chairs, a tub chair and an overstuffed pouffe.

'There's this room and a bedroom and we share the kitchen.'

'It's . . . very nice,' Molly ventured.

'May we see the bedroom?' Bernie asked, thinking it was very cramped and dark looking.

'You do have the money? You do have steady jobs? You're very young. Why don't you live at home?' The questions were fired at them in a brisk, almost quarrelsome voice.

'We have a month's rent in advance, we both have good steady work and we came to Liverpool for a better future. We're Irish, ma'am. We have been living with relations but they are very overcrowded. I'm Molly Keegan and this is Bernie O'Sullivan.'

'I see. Then you're both Catholic? I know Father Stephens very well, do you know him?'

'No, ma'am. Father Ryan at St Anthony's is our parish priest. He's been very good to us.'

'How old are you?'

'Seventeen, ma'am,' Bernie replied.

'Very young. Very young indeed to be leaving your home and travelling to another country.'

'We know but there's no work there, ma'am.'

'Will you not be calling me "ma'am", you're not servants!' the old lady snapped.

'I suppose I am. I work for a Mrs Montrose in Winslow Street, sort of "in service",' Bernie informed her.

'And I work at Frisby Dyke's.'

The old lady nodded. 'Well, there's just me here now. My family have all grown up, got married and left. The rent is six shillings a week; you put your own money in the gas and electric meters. Buy your own coal and food. You keep the place clean and tidy and I don't allow gentlemen callers, not that girls of your age should be entertaining gentlemen. Well, do you want the rooms or not?'

They were both taken aback. They hadn't even seen the bedroom or where they were to cook or discussed what the toilet facilities were like.

'Yes! Yes, it will be just grand,' Molly answered quickly before Bernie could prevaricate. Anywhere was better than Hopwood Street.

Chapter Thirteen

'WHAT DID YOU SAY that for?' Bernie asked after Mrs Hayes had gone out to get what she called a 'rent book'.

'Bernie, I can't face living at Nellie's for much longer! This isn't bad. It's clean, at least.'

'But we haven't seen the rest of it yet and she's a bit odd. What am I to do about Jimmy? She said no gentlemen callers.'

'We'll sort something out. Hush, she's coming back.'

Molly was handed the small card-backed book and duly handed over twenty-four shillings in advance rent. They were then shown the kitchen, which was very similar to Nellie's except that it was cleaner, and much better furnished and equipped. There was a small scullery off it, which contained a sink, and they were thankful to see there was at least cold running water. The coal was kept in the small yard in two small bunkers and the privy was also in the yard but was also very much cleaner than the one Nellie shared with the house next door.

The bedroom was on the first floor, above the parlour, and contained a brass bedstead, a washstand, a single wardrobe and a chest of drawers. Everything was very dark and heavy and old-fashioned, Molly thought, but it looked comfortable and she was certain there were no bugs in this house.

'When would you like to move in?' their new landlady enquired.

'Would tomorrow night be suitable?' Molly asked. 'We don't have much. Just our clothes and some bits and pieces. It would be after nine o'clock though as I work until eight.'

'I usually go to bed at ten at the very latest but I suppose I could make an exception this once,' Mrs Hayes replied with rather a bad grace.

Surreptitiously Bernie nudged Molly. She wasn't sure about this at all.

Molly ignored her. 'Thank you. We'll get here as quickly as we can.'

'Then I'll see you tomorrow evening. I'll give you your keys then.'

Once out in the street Bernie looked back at the house with some trepidation. 'She's not very friendly, is she?'

'Well, do we really want the landlady to be in on top of us by the minutes?'

'I don't think she really approves of us.'

'Oh, she'll be fine when she gets to know us.'

'What am I going to do about Jimmy?'

Molly sighed. 'You'll just have to meet him at the top of the street and say your goodnights there too. Sure, you never know, when she's used to us she might let him come calling. She's had a family of her own after all and they're married so she must have allowed "gentlemen callers" at some time. Let's get back and break the news to Nellie.'

'Don't forget we have to call at the priest's house first,' Bernie reminded her.

Father Ryan was pleased to see them both.

'So, how did it go?'

'Very well, Father. We've got rooms at the house in Arnot Street with a Mrs Hayes. She's rather strict, she has quite a lot of rules and regulations, but it's nice and clean,' Molly answered.

He was relieved. 'Well, that's no bad thing. It means she will be keeping her eye on you and that she's a decent, respectable woman.'

Bernie said nothing. In her opinion it meant Mrs Hayes was far too strict but she couldn't say that to a priest.

Nellie hadn't expected them to find somewhere quite so quickly. 'Yer've been dead lucky. Decent places are snapped up quick. Are yer sure there isn't somethin' wrong with it?'

'It looked fine. A bit old-fashioned and dismal but . . . grand,' Molly informed her.

'It could be Herself, she's a bit odd,' Bernie said.

'How do yer mean "odd"? Cracked? Mad?'

'No! She's just an old lady, probably a bit lonely. Her family are all married and I suppose she's set in her ways.' Molly shot a warning look at Bernie. If Nellie thought the woman was not in her right mind she would put her foot down and insist they remain here.

'There's a lot of owld ones like that but perhaps I'd better come an' see fer meself. Yer told her yer'd be there tomorrow night?'

They both nodded and Molly bit her lip. This was just what she hadn't wanted.

On the following evening they packed their few belongings, leaving the jug and bowl and the sheets, as there had been a real china bowl set on the washstand in Arnot Street and the bed had been made up.

Most of the neighbours called in to say goodbye and admonish them 'not ter forget where we are' and 'come an' visit us'. Bernie had given Nellie a note for Jimmy which Nellie promised to deliver by hand to his home in Blenheim Street; there was no other way in which Bernie could let him know where she was going and she wasn't due to see him again until the following weekend when he was off again.

Despite all their protests Nellie insisted on accompanying them and it was nearly a quarter to ten when the three women got off the tram on the corner of Arnot Street, all carrying parcels.

'It's a better area, I'll give yer that, an' these houses are much better than them falling-down old dumps we has ter put up with. I wonder how much rent she pays?'

'Maybe she owns it.'

Nellie looked at Molly in astonishment. 'No one *owns* their house, except them that are really rich.'

'Da does and he's not rich at all.'

'It's different in the country, luv. Well, I have ter say she keeps her brasses well.' Nellie looked with approval at the gleaming brass knocker and letter-box. 'She doesn't donkey stone her steps though,' she added, peering at the neat step that was devoid of the whitening she spent so much time rubbing on her own.

'Ah, she's an old lady. You can't be expecting her to be down on her knees,' Molly said by way of an excuse. She had lived in Hopwood Street long enough to know that it was a heinous crime not to scrub your steps daily.

'Me poor owld Mam did hers until the week before she died,' Nellie muttered.

'You've finally arrived then? I had almost given you up and locked the door. Who's this?' Mrs Hayes asked, peering suspiciously at Nellie.

'I'm Mrs O'Sullivan, her cousin, an' I've come ter see that this is a fittin' place fer the pair of them to be livin',' Nellie announced firmly.

'Indeed? Well, I can assure you that it's more than "fitting", as you put it, for two young girls who, if they were mine, I wouldn't let out at this time of night on their own,' was the cutting reply.

Bernie cringed. This didn't bode well for Jimmy being able to visit. And it wasn't all *that* late: Nellie at least gave her until half past ten to be in. She'd expected to gain more freedom in a place of their own, not less.

'Can we come in?' Molly asked, not wishing to start off on the wrong foot with an argument between Nellie and the old lady.

'Put your stuff in the front room and then come into the kitchen,' Mrs Hayes instructed, holding open the door.

'She's got some good stuff. Old-fashioned but good,' Nellie said, glancing around quickly. 'And it's nice and clean. A bit musty-smelling, like. Bit of fresh air wouldn't go amiss. Them windows probably haven't been open in years.'

Molly thought that it smelled a great deal better than Nellie's house, musty or not.

Mrs Hayes sat down beside the kitchen range and indicated that they all do the same.

'Seeing as you're here, you can listen to what I have to say to these two. I've been thinking about them all day and while I understand that it's been necessary for them to come to find work here, they're still very young and need to have an eye kept on them.'

'Isn't that what I've been doing?' Nellie interrupted.

'I've had a talk with Father Stephens and informed him of their circumstances and he's promised to take care of their spiritual welfare.'

'Didn't Father Ryan do exactly the same?' Nellie was getting a little irritated with this high-handed attitude.

Mrs Hayes ignored her. 'And I intend to see to their moral welfare. While they are living under my roof they are my responsibility and I feel sure that that is something their parents will approve of. I've had five children of my own and I brought them all up decently, even though I was a widow for many years. None of them ever brought any trouble to my door. So, you'll both be in by a quarter to ten at night. I won't have drink brought into the house and I don't approve of smoking. You may entertain the occasional female friend but, as I've already said, no gentlemen callers.'

'Now hang on a minute, don't yer think that's bein' a bit harsh? They're seventeen an' if yer can't have a bit of enjoyment out of life when yer're young it's a sad state of affairs. God knows yer don't get much enjoyment as yer get older.' Nellie had seen the looks of dawning disappointment on both their faces.

The old lady rounded on her. 'I suppose you approve of such carryings on?'

Nellie was outraged. 'No, I do not! I'm a decent woman an' I've brung my family up decent too! We haven't got much but we're not . . .' She struggled to find the right word. '. . . deranged,' she finished emphatically.

The old lady's lips twitched in a smile. ' "Depraved" I think you mean and I wasn't implying that you were. Well, we'll see how

109

things go. I might relax some of the rules but not those on smoking or drink. I've only got their welfare at heart. If you like I will personally write to their parents and assure them that their daughters are being well minded.'

'I don't think that's necessary. I'll write ter Tess and tell her meself,' Nellie replied coldly. She thought the old woman was taking far too much on herself and was being unreasonable. They were paying her for their lodgings, after all, and deserved some privacy.

'Suit yourself. I really *have* only got their welfare at heart.'

Nellie nodded stiffly and Bernie looked down at her feet miserably. This was what she had been afraid of.

Molly tried to lighten the atmosphere. 'Mrs Hayes, would you mind very much if later on I made some new soft furnishings for the rooms to sort of brighten them up?'

'You can sew?'

Molly nodded.

'She's a fine dressmaker. Made two lovely frocks, she did,' Nellie put in, determined to impress upon the old lady that both girls had many good points not to say talents in their favour. 'And I have ter say this place needs a bit of cheerin' up.'

'I can purchase remnants from work and sometimes damaged stock, usually lampshades, and I can measure for curtains and probably make them too,' Molly added quickly.

Mrs Hayes nodded. The girl looked quite capable. 'Right then, here are your keys and now you'd better get unpacked.'

Nellie got to her feet. 'I'll get off home then. Now, remember the pair of youse, if yer need me yer know where I am.'

They both saw her out while Mrs Hayes remained in the kitchen.

'Don't take no notice of that owld tartar! Yer're paying her rent, yer deserve some privacy. Don't let her be runnin' in and out ter yer by the minutes, make that clear. Be polite but firm. Start as yer mean ter go on!' Nellie hissed.

'I think she does mean well,' Molly whispered.

'She's old-fashioned, that's what she is. Livin' in the past. Yer was right, she's set in her ways all right but don't take no nonsense out of her an' if she starts acting up then come fer me.'

'We will,' Molly promised.

Bernie said nothing. She was regretting ever setting eyes on either number three Arnot Street or their landlady.

Chapter Fourteen

A S MOLLY GATHERED UP her things Bernie sat down on the sofa.
'I don't like it here, Moll. I don't like it at all. It's all very
well Nellie saying don't stand any nonsense out of her . . . It's worse
than living at home!' She was near to tears.

Molly sat down and put her arm around her. 'Bernie, it's going to
be grand, it *is*! I don't think she's as bad as she's making out to be.
She'll get used to us and when she sees we're hard-working and
aren't going to cause her any trouble she'll relax a bit. She didn't
object to us trying to brighten the place up, did she? We don't
smoke and we don't drink and I know having to be in at a quarter to
ten is early but we don't go out very often.'

'*You* don't.' Bernie was not convinced.

'But you're not out every night of the week. You only see Jimmy
when he's off and that's not really very often. I'm sure that she
won't mind making it half past ten, just for you, on special
occasions.'

'But she said no "gentlemen".'

'Gentlemen *callers*. I think she means you won't be able to bring
him in and spend the evening here and you don't do that anyway.'

'I know but I might *want* to, especially in the winter, and I
thought that when we got a place of our own that's what I'd be able
to do.'

'By that time she will have got used to us and she might even
allow that. He's a decent lad with a steady job; I'm sure she'll like
him.'

Bernie sniffed. She wasn't so sure.

'Let's look on the bright side. Tonight we'll be sleeping in a proper bed with clean sheets and no bugs. We've got a wardrobe and a chest for our things and there's a nice washstand too. The kitchen is clean and tomorrow we can do some food shopping; we don't need coal just yet so that will be a saving and once we get those meters sorted out we'll have electric light and gas for that little ring so we can boil a kettle. It's a *start*, Bernie! It's almost our *own* place.'

Bernie managed a wry smile. 'But with *her* rules and regulations!'

'Sure, they're no worse than those at home and at least now we've got our own money to spend.'

'I'm glad I told Jimmy I'd meet him at the top of the street when I see him next,' Bernie said.

For the first time in weeks they slept in a comfortable and clean bed and in the morning, after putting a few pennies in the gas meter, they boiled the kettle, got washed and made some tea. Of their landlady there was no sign but the tea caddy and sugar bowl were on the kitchen table and the milk bottle was standing in an earthenware pot filled with cold water to keep it cool.

Bernie agreed to do the food shopping on County Road at lunchtime and Molly said she would buy some new towels in hers.

Mrs Montrose, who had been informed by Bernie of their move, had been a little concerned by Bernie's lack of enthusiasm.

'Are you not happy about the rooms in Arnot Street, Bernadette?'

'They're much better than where we were before, ma'am,' she'd replied but then had decided to confide in her employer.

'I'm sure she does mean well. I agree with Molly: she will unbend in time. Don't forget, she doesn't really know you yet.'

'I'm sure you're right, ma'am,' Bernie had answered, still not convinced.

They had settled in very well, Molly thought, by the middle of the following week. They had established a routine for the cooking and cleaning and shopping and it was a real pleasure to come home after a long and tiring day to a peaceful house where there was plain but well-cooked food on the table and where you could have a wash, get changed and then sit and read or sew or just chat about what had happened that day. It was all so very different from Nellie's crowded, noisy and decrepit house.

She had already started to keep her eye out for remnants that she thought would look good as cushion covers and she had seen some nice lace antimacassars for the sofa and chair. It would be some time before they could afford new curtains or an eiderdown and bedspread set like the lovely quilted satin ones that had just arrived, but by Christmas she hoped to have saved enough to buy some.

Bernie was looking forward to seeing Jimmy but was apprehensive and a little jumpy when at last she left the house on Saturday evening. It was still very warm and she had decided to wear the yellow and white dress again, but without the beads or the bangle, and Molly had unpicked the green ribbon bow from her hat and replaced it with the yellow satin she'd used as a hair band.

'That looks just as nice and it matches. We can always put the green one back if needs be. Now go on and enjoy yourself,' she'd urged. She was going to have a quiet evening cutting out and tacking some rose-pink damask she'd got for half of nothing which would just make three cushion covers.

'Where can we go? I've to be back so early.'

'He'll think of somewhere – and don't be looking around you in that furtive way, you'll only make people think you're doing something wrong,' Molly advised.

As she walked up the street Bernie tried not to appear 'furtive'. At least she knew Mrs Hayes wasn't watching her as the old lady's rooms were at the back of the house.

Jimmy was waiting for her, leaning against the railings of the school.

'Yer look nice. This is a bit better than Hopwood Street, isn't it?'

She smiled but then shrugged.

'What's up?'

'Oh, it is nice and clean and so quiet but, well, the landlady's a real dragon. You won't be able to call for me or see me in and I have to be back for a quarter to ten.'

'Yer've got a key, haven't yer? Yer can come an' go as yer please! An' what's she got against me?' Jimmy was indignant.

'It's not *you* particularly. I can't have "gentlemen callers": she thinks I'm too young. She thinks we're both too young to be allowed out at all! She's old and a bit odd you see. She says we're her responsibility.'

'That's daft! Yer pay yer own way, don't yer?'

Bernie nodded. 'Six shillings a week and we keep ourselves. But it is much nicer than Nellie's.'

Jimmy took her hand. 'I was goin' ter take yer dancin' too, to that place above the Co-op.'

Bernie was disappointed. 'I'm really sorry, Jimmy.'

'Never mind, Bernie, let's make the most of what time we've got. We'll buy some sweets an' drinks an' get the tram ter Walton-on-the-Hill an' then walk ter the park. It's nice there an' they don't shut the gates in the summer until late. I'll have yer back in time, don't worry.'

It wasn't the same as going to a nice dance hall, Bernie thought, but it was better than not being out with him at all.

Walton-on-the-Hill was a nice little place, she thought, quite rural really with its old stone church surrounded by trees that overhung the graveyard. There was a very old schoolhouse there too and a pub called the Black Horse. There were also public swimming baths and some rather grand-looking houses lining Queens Drive, the wide thoroughfare that, according to Jimmy, led down to the park.

The park itself appeared to be huge, with acres of rolling green lawns, brightly coloured flower beds and shrubberies. They walked along until they found a quiet bench under a canopy of beech trees where they sat down. He put his arm around her.

'Yer're very quiet, Bernie. Don't yer like livin' there? Do yer miss Nellie an' her gang?'

'I do a bit. Oh, I don't miss all the muck and the bugs and the flies but there was always someone in and out, plenty of chat, the antics of the kids . . . It's so quiet now and . . .'

'Yer've got Molly.'

'I know but, well, Molly has all the girls she works with to talk to all day, I only have Mrs M. And Molly is used to having more space and their house was always quieter than ours.'

Jimmy was very concerned. 'I don't like ter see yer upset, Bernie.'

'I'm not, not really. I suppose I'll get used to it, but it's not really the way I . . . planned things!'

Jimmy didn't say anything but he was thinking. He had a bit of money saved up, he had a steady job, and he knew that he loved her even though he'd never told her so. He'd never felt like this about any other girl. She was only young but he knew lots of girls who were married at her age. His own mam had been.

'What if yer had a place of yer own? I mean really yer own, would yer feel lonely?'

Bernie was surprised. 'All mine? Without Molly?'

'I mean, with me. Get married, like?' He felt himself blushing. He hadn't meant it to come out like that but he hadn't wanted her to think he was asking her to live 'over the brush' with him.

Bernie's eyes widened and she felt her heart leap to her throat. 'You mean . . . you and me . . .?'

Jimmy nodded. 'We could get engaged, like. Surely that owld one couldn't object ter me then? I love yer, I really do. I think I knew that when I first saw yer on the ferry, I just didn't realise it at the time.'

Bernie laid her cheek against his. He *loved* her! He wanted to *marry* her! She'd never felt so happy in her life before. 'Oh, Jimmy!'

'Well, will we get engaged then? We can save up an' get a house of our own in no time an' yer won't have ter put up with that owld one.'

'You're not just asking me because you feel sorry for me or you think I'm really unhappy there?'

'No! I've just told yer I love yer!'

Despite being overjoyed Bernie realised that she would be leaving Molly to pay the full rent on her own and that maybe her friend would feel as though she was being deserted.

'What about Molly?'

'She'll be all right now. She's got a job an' a place ter live an' someone ter keep an eye on her. She's got the girls she works with fer company an' yer will still be able ter see her; she can visit as often as she likes.'

Bernie felt happier, Jimmy was right; she was sure Molly wouldn't be upset. Molly wasn't like that. She was the best friend anyone could ever have. Her eyes shone with love and joy. 'I'd love to get engaged and I love you too, Jimmy. I really do!'

They walked home with their arms around each other, making plans. The next time Jimmy had a day off they would go into Liverpool to buy the ring. Bernie had said she didn't really need one, that she'd wait for the wedding ring which was all her mam had ever had, but he had insisted and what's more he'd said they were going to T. Brown in London Road, one of Liverpool's better class jewellers.

'They'll be after charging a small fortune, surely. Won't we need the money for more useful things?' she'd asked, uncertainly.

'We'll get "useful" things as wedding presents, an' besides, if we're ever hard up, yer can always pawn it,' he'd laughed.

'I haven't got much money and I won't be able to save an awful lot either. I've still got to pay my share and I don't earn as much as Molly.'

'I'm not sayin' we'll dash out an' set a wedding date, Bernie. We'll get married in, say, nine months' time, plenty of time ter get the necessities.'

She nodded. She would have to save up enough for a dress because her mam certainly couldn't afford to pay for one. Then she realised that she would have to get her da's permission. She was under age and they didn't even know she was walking out with anyone.

'What's wrong now?' Jimmy asked, seeing her expression change.

'I'm going to have to write and tell Da about you. I'll need his permission.'

'Surely he won't refuse?'

'Oh, I don't know. He's never met you and not likely to either.'

'Well, we'll ask Nellie ter help out there. She knows me an' she knows my mam. Get her ter write a glowin' letter about me.'

Bernie brightened up. She would do just that and she'd ask Nellie to make sure she put in all the details about how brave he'd been in trying to save young Alfie Bradley – there had in fact been some talk about him getting a medal from the Liverpool Shipwreck and Humane Society. She'd put all that in her own letter to her da but if Nellie did too it would give it more credibility. Surely Da couldn't refuse?

It was very nearly a quarter to ten when they got back to the top of Arnot Street. Jimmy pulled her into the doorway of the school and took her in his arms. He kissed her for a long time.

She was flushed and shaking a little when she finally pulled away. 'I'd better go now.'

'Don't ferget, I'm comin' ter call fer yer next week when we go fer the ring.'

Bernie nodded. She was going to have to inform Mrs Hayes now but she wasn't dreading it at all. 'I'll be ready.'

'And if that one kicks up, just get the tram up ter me mam's house. She'll soon put her straight.'

'I haven't even met your mam yet.' Bernie was apprehensive.

'I know, an' she's goin' ter be a bit surprised at our news, but she knows all about yer an' she said yer sound like a decent girl an' one with a bit of sense ter get yerself out of that flamin' slum so quickly. It's something she never managed. I think yer'll both get on like a house on fire. She's great, my mam.'

Bernie smiled at him. 'I'm so glad.' At least if the worst happened and she was thrown out she had somewhere to go.

Chapter Fifteen

———◆———

MOLLY WAS SO ASTONISHED that she just gaped at her friend speechlessly.

'Well, aren't you going to congratulate me, Moll?'

Molly pulled herself together. 'Oh, Bernie! Of course!' She flung her arms around her friend and hugged her tightly.

'I'm so happy, Moll. I was so surprised when he asked me!'

They both sank down on the sofa, Molly completely ignoring the three half-finished cushion covers she'd spent hours making.

'I'll write to Da tonight and we're going to ask Nellie to write to him too. I'll pray he won't refuse his permission. Then we're going to save very hard before we get married. He's insisting I have a proper ring too – and probably quite an expensive one!'

'It is what you really want, isn't it? You do really love him?'

'Of course I do! I know it's a serious step to take – "until death us do part" – but I *know* I want to spend the rest of my life with him.'

'It's very sudden.'

'I know but . . . you do like him?'

Molly smiled. 'Of course I do. I'm just asking you the questions everyone else will ask. You know what older people are like; they think we're too young for *anything*. Oh, but when will you tell Herself in there?' Molly was beginning to feel a bit apprehensive now.

'Should I tell her now? I'm going to have to face her before next week. Jimmy's going to call here for me.'

Molly looked doubtful but then she squared her shoulders. 'Let's go and get it over with. I'll come with you. The worst she can do is tell us to leave and give us back some of our advance rent.'

Bernie nodded, grateful that she had Molly's support.

'I see you got home on time then,' Mrs Hayes said as they both entered the kitchen. The old lady had been reading the *Liverpool Echo*; the page was open at the 'Births, Marriages & Deaths' section.

'I did so and I have some good news to tell you.'

'Indeed?'

Bernie took a deep breath. 'I'm getting engaged.'

There was silence in the kitchen; the only sound the ticking of the clock on the wall.

'I said I'm—'

'I heard you the first time! You never mentioned that you were walking out with anyone. Does that cousin of yours know? Does Father Ryan know? Does your employer know?'

'No. I mean, Nellie knows I was walking out with Jimmy, she knows him and his family but the others don't know about us.'

'How long have you known him? You've hardly been in Liverpool for more than a month. Has he taken advantage of you?'

Bernie was wilting before the barrage of questions.

'She met him on the ferry boat, Mrs Hayes, and then we witnessed him very bravely trying to save a young local lad from drowning. They've been courting ever since. He really is a very decent lad,' Molly interrupted.

'But that's hardly enough time to get to know him, let alone agree to marry him. He could be a blackguard of the first order!'

'He's not!' Bernie cried. She could see the old lady was getting angry.

'You're little more than a child!' the old lady said dismissively.

'I'm old enough to know my own mind and I love him!' Bernie retorted.

Mrs Hayes fixed her with a quelling glance. 'I very much doubt it but seeing as I'm not your mother or even your legal guardian there is very little I can do to stop you. You do realise you will have to have your father's permission, though, and if he has any sense he won't give it.'

'I do so and I intend to write to him tonight.'

'And Nellie will write too and I'm sure he won't refuse,' Molly added. She was certain Dessie wouldn't object. To have Bernie married and off his hands would be one less worry for him.

The old lady picked up the newspaper. 'You had better inform your cousin of these developments and hope that indeed she approves. I certainly do not!'

'I will,' Bernie answered. She hadn't expected her news to be greeted with cries of joy but she hadn't expected such outright disapproval.

Molly pushed her towards the door and when they were back in their own room they both sank down gratefully on the sofa.

'Well, at least she didn't show us the door. She might come round, in time,' she said thankfully.

'I don't think she will but I don't really care, Moll! At least we've both still got a decent roof over our heads.'

Molly grinned at her. 'Shall we have a cup of tea to celebrate? We haven't got anything stronger.'

Bernie giggled. 'She'd really throw us out if we had but I'm not risking going into that kitchen again tonight. I'd better get that letter done to Da.'

'I'll make it. We'd better go and see Nellie tomorrow, after Mass.'

'I didn't expect ter see youse two again so soon! What's up now? Have yer changed yer mind? Is she layin' down the law?'

'No, we're settling in grand and she's not been too bad. Bernie's got some news for you.'

Nellie looked a little suspicious. 'What?'

'Jimmy asked me to marry him last night and I said I would and we're going for the ring next week,' Bernie blurted out.

'Jesus, Mary an' holy St Joseph! Matty, did yer hear that?' Nellie cried.

Matty looked up from his newspaper; he hadn't really been listening.

Not knowing how Nellie was going to react, Bernie plunged on. 'I know we haven't known each other long but I do love him and he is a decent lad and he's got a steady job and he doesn't really take a drink or gamble and he's insisting that I have a proper engagement ring from somewhere called T. Brown's in London Road and we're going to save up and get married in about nine months' time. Oh, Nellie, you do approve, don't you? I told Father Ryan after Mass and he didn't have ten fits. He asked me if I was absolutely sure, if I really understood the commitment and when I said I did he said I was getting a good steady lad and that we should both go and see him for a longer chat and he congratulated me.'

'Will yer just slow down, Bernie! Just let it all sink in.'

'She's written to her da but she'd like you to write to him too and tell him what kind of a lad Jimmy is,' Molly urged.

Nellie shook her head. 'It's all a bit fast but I can't say a word against him. Yer could do far worse, I suppose. The two of youse have got it all planned out, haven't yer?'

Bernie nodded emphatically.

'A proper ring, yer said? Well, he must have a few bob put away. There's nothin' cheap in that place, I can tell yer. The likes of us can usually only afford ter look in the window. He must think an awful lot of yer, Bernie. I never got no engagement ring.' Nellie shot an indignant look at her husband.

'Ah now, Nellie, be fair, did any of the women around here? We had no money for such things,' Matty reminded her.

'It's all very nice, Bernie, luv, but wouldn't yer be better off keepin' that money an' buyin' furniture?' Nellie suggested, being more practically minded.

Bernie didn't look convinced. 'Aren't we going to save up for things like that?'

Nellie shook her head. Bernie was young and the thought of being able to flash around an expensive ring was obviously very appealing. She'd find out soon enough that married life was no bed of roses, especially when the kids came along. And even though Jimmy McCauley had a steady job now there was no guarantee he'd have it for ever. She sighed. Well, if the worst happened Bernie could always sell or pawn the ring.

'So, you approve then?' Bernie pressed. At least there had been no mention of her being too young – and anyway, she'd be eighteen by the time she got married.

'I suppose so. Just as long as yer're absolutely sure that it's what yer want. Marriage is fer ever and it really is fer better or worse, fer richer fer poorer.'

Bernie nodded. 'I know and I am absolutely sure. So, will you write to Da and tell him all about Jimmy?'

'I will, luv. I suppose he's told his mam and da?'

'He will have done by now.'

'Flo McCauley's a nice woman. Good-hearted an' hard-workin'. Yer'll get on well with her.'

Greatly relieved, Bernie smiled. 'Will I put on the kettle?'

She was ready and waiting when Jimmy called for her the following Saturday afternoon. Of their landlady there was no sign; in fact they had seen little of the old lady during the week either. She had been very relieved when the letter from her parents had arrived on Friday morning. Usually the replies to her letters were quite slow in coming but obviously her news had shaken things up. Her da had written briefly, giving his consent; her mam's contribution was much longer, but all that mattered was that the letter had arrived.

They got off the tram at the bottom of London Road. The jeweller's was almost at the very end of the street and they paused in front of the window. Bernie was stunned at the prices. Some of these rings cost more than a man would earn in six whole months.

'Is there anythin' there that takes yer fancy?' Jimmy finally asked. 'I've got five guineas.'

Bernie stared at him. 'You're never going to spend all that on a ring, I won't let you! You can furnish half a house for that!'

'I don't mind, honestly. Yer're worth it, Bernie.'

Bernie shook her head. 'No, I couldn't let you do that. You worked too hard for that money. There's one there, at the back, that's very pretty and it's only three guineas.' She shook her head

again. She never thought she'd see the day when she'd say something as fatuous as 'only three guineas'.

'All right then, if you insist. Let's go in.'

The bell above the shop door tinkled musically as they entered
and a tall, slim and very elegant woman approached them.

'May I help you?' she asked in a pleasant, well-modulated voice.
She was smiling but Bernie was a little overawed by her and hung
back. Jimmy had no such qualms.

'We'd like to buy an engagement ring, please. She . . . my young
lady has seen one she likes in the window.'

Despite her nervousness Bernie felt pleased and excited. She'd
never been called a 'young lady' before and Jimmy's voice had been
full of pride.

'Of course. If you would just point it out to me I'll bring it to
you. Please do take a seat, both of you.' The assistant indicated a
quiet corner of the shop where a small table and two rather delicate-
looking chairs had been placed, obviously for just such customers
as themselves.

She brought the ring, resting on a little black velvet cushion and
placed it on the table. 'Have a good look at it and try it on. It's a
very important and special purchase and we want you to be
absolutely satisfied that you've made the right choice. Take your
time and if there is anything else you'd like to see don't hesitate to
ask.'

Jimmy took the ring, which was in the shape of a small heart set
with tiny diamond chippings, and slipped it on to Bernie's finger.

Bernie looked at it and her eyes filled with tears. It was beautiful.
She'd never had anything so beautiful in her entire life.

'Do yer like it?' Jimmy asked.

She could only nod; there was a huge lump in her throat.

Seeing the not uncommon sight of a young bride in tears of joy,
the jeweller smiled and discreetly passed her a clean white lawn
handkerchief embroidered in one corner with a small yellow
horseshoe. 'You may keep that. Now, you're quite sure? It's no
trouble at all to bring you a few others to try on.'

Bernie found her voice. 'No, this is the one! It's just gorgeous!'

'It doesn't need altering at all?'

Bernie moved it around on her finger. 'No, it's a perfect fit. It might have been made especially for me.'

'Then we'll take it. Can she keep it on?' Jimmy asked, seeing Bernie was reluctant to take it off.

'Of course. I'll give you the box though and as a gesture of thanks and good luck for your future together, we always give a box of half a dozen silver-plated teaspoons with every engagement or wedding ring that is purchased. It's company policy.'

'Oh, that's really lovely!' Bernie was quite overcome.

'That's dead good of yer!' Jimmy added. He'd been told it always paid off to go to really classy shops if you could afford it: this proved it.

Jimmy handed over the money while Bernie sat and admired her ring, wriggling her fingers up and down so that the stones caught the light.

The woman returned with a hand-written receipt for Jimmy and a square leather-covered box, which she handed to Bernie. 'There's also a sprig of lucky white heather in the box. I wish you both every joy in the years to come.'

They thanked her profusely and when they were once more out in the street Bernie looked up at her fiancé, her eyes still swimming with tears.

'What are yer crying fer?'

'I'm just so happy! It's gorgeous and we've even got our first wedding present – and she gave me this lovely handkerchief too. What more could I ask for?'

Jimmy grinned and then bent and kissed her. 'Let's go an' show me mam. She's dyin' ter meet yer.'

Chapter Sixteen

———◆◈◆———

Bernie felt a little shy and apprehensive as she walked with Jimmy down Blenheim Street. It looked just like Hopwood Street, she thought, and made a mental note not to let any semblance of pity or distaste show if the home of her future mother-in-law resembled that of Nellie.

'Don't look so frightened, she won't eat yer! I told yer she's dyin' ter meet yer,' Jimmy assured her.

She managed a smile and squeezed his hand as he led her down the dark, narrow lobby. The kitchen did look like Nellie's in so much as it was the same size and had a big iron range, but there the resemblance ended. It had been recently lime-washed; the lino on the floor was clean as was the cotton lace curtain at the window. The big table had been scrubbed white and the chairs, although plain and serviceable, had bright patchwork cushions. There were cups and saucers set out on the table with a sugar bowl and milk jug, rather than the assortment of chipped mugs Nellie used with the sugar still in its blue paper bag and the milk in its bottle.

'So, yer're Bernie. He's never stopped talking about yer, luv, an' he was right. Yer're a pretty lass an' if yer make him happy then yer'll make me happy. Yer're very welcome.'

Bernie relaxed and smiled. Mrs McCauley was a small, plump, jovial woman with greying hair and bright blue eyes. Her dark dress was clean and the apron she wore over it was spotless. 'I'll do the best I can, I promise,' she assured her.

'Sit yerself down an' we'll have a cup of tea but first let me see the ring.'

Bernie proudly held out her hand.

'God in heaven! Isn't that a gorgeous piece of jewellery! There's not a woman around here who has anythin' like it!'

'I wouldn't let him spend what he was willing to pay.'

Jimmy's mother shook her head. 'That lad is a fool where money is concerned.'

'Now, Mam, I saved it up.' Jimmy was indignant.

'Aren't you the fortunate one ter be able ter have money ter save,' his mother retorted, indicating that they both sit down while she lifted the kettle from the range.

'We intend to save every halfpenny we can from now on,' Bernie informed her.

The older woman nodded. 'It won't be easy fer yer, luv, not if yer've the rent an' gas an' electric an' food, but any girl as young as you who has managed ter get out of this flamin' slum in such a short time will find a way. I'll do what I can ter help yer. Come here a couple of nights fer yer meal, that should save a few shillin's, an' we can get ter know each other better. We'll have a good chat when meladdo here is away workin' on the ferry. His da works the night shift so we'll have the place ter ourselves, more or less.'

'Thanks, I'd like that and it would help,' Bernie replied before remembering that she and Molly shared the cost of everything and she really couldn't ask her friend if she could pay a little less.

'So, have the pair of youse thought about a date yet?'

Bernie shook her head. 'We want to be able to afford a place of our own and some decent furniture. We thought we'd wait about nine months.'

'Can yer stick that owld one fer that long? I hear she's a bit of a tartar.'

'Sure, I'm after hoping that now I've got the ring she'll see we're serious and let Jimmy at least call for me.'

'Well, yer can come up here any time yer like. What did yer mam and da say about yer gettin' engaged?'

Bernie smiled; she had been so relieved when the letter had come giving her father's consent. 'Da is only delighted, Mam was a bit more anxious but I think she's pleased too.' In fact her mam had gone on and on about her not rushing into things, giving herself time to think, time to enjoy the grand life she now had with money of her own and every luxury. Tessie had written that marriage was for ever and there was plenty of time for husbands and children when she was a bit older and wiser. Was she absolutely certain that Jimmy was the *right* one? After all, she hadn't been walking out with *anyone* up to now. And what sort of a family did he come from? Were they respectable and more importantly were they Catholic? Bernie had become very impatient with it all in the end.

'Will they come over fer the weddin'?' Mrs McCauley asked, interrupting Bernie's train of thought.

'I don't know. Money is very tight and there's so many of them. Even if Ma would leave the young ones, sure she's no one to mind them.' And then there was the question of them having the right clothes for a wedding, even a simple one, she thought. It would all cost so much and they had so little.

'I'd pay fer them if yer really wanted them ter come over, Bernie,' Jimmy offered.

His mother cast her eyes to the ceiling but Bernie smiled.

'That's good of you, Jimmy, but we'll need all our money.'

'Yer will indeed! Now, will yer go an' see if there's any sign of yer da? I told him ter be back here by four o'clock at the latest. He goes ter the pub fer a couple of hours on a Saturday afternoon, it's his only treat. And yer can tell Frank and Tilly they can come in now too. I sent them out ter play otherwise they'd have the place a midden and be hoggin' the conversation.'

Jimmy did as he was bid and Bernie sipped her tea until a few minutes later Jimmy came back accompanied by a boy of twelve and a girl of ten, both of whom eyed her with open curiosity.

'So, you're Frank and you're Tilly? Isn't that a lovely name?' Bernie smiled at the child.

'It's Matilda Mary really but that's too much of a mouthful!'

Bernie laughed. 'When Jimmy and me get married would you like to be my bridesmaid?'

The child's face lit up. 'Oh, Mam, can I be? Can I?' she begged.

'Yer've started somethin' now, Bernie! She'll have me mithered ter death!' Mrs McCauley laughed but she was pleased. 'Of course yer can.'

Frank looked suspiciously at the girl who was going to be his sister-in-law. 'Yer won't want ter dress me up in a sissy suit, will yer?' He'd seen his mate Vinny Molloy subjected to what he considered the worst humiliation possible when Vinny's sister had got married: the wearing of a satin sailor suit complete with straw hat. In his opinion everyone went completely mad at weddings, what with dressing you up, making you stay clean and demanding you 'behave', which really meant you weren't even to think about enjoying yourself.

'I will not! Sure, whatever you wear for Mass will be grand,' Bernie laughed and Frank breathed a sigh of relief, deciding that Jimmy had made a good choice.

The kitchen door opened and Jimmy's father beamed at them all. 'I see the wee girl has arrived! You're very welcome in this house, Bernie!' Charlie McCauley held out his hand to his future daughter-in-law.

Bernie smiled and shook it, instantly liking the big man with the lilting Belfast accent who was an older version of Jimmy. She felt a part of the family already.

'Youse two wash yer hands an' then we'll all have tea. Bernie, there's no rush fer yer ter get back, is there?' Jimmy's mam began to lay the table.

'No, Molly doesn't finish until eight on a Saturday. I'm very lucky, I get Saturday afternoon and Sunday off. Mrs M. is very good to me.'

'Have yer told her yet that yer're gettin' married?'

Bernie shook her head. 'I'll tell her on Monday. I'll show her my ring but I won't be after wearing it for work, it might get ruined.'

Mrs McCauley nodded but wondered how Bernie's employer would take the news and if indeed she would consider letting the girl carry on working after she was married. It wasn't usual but it would certainly help them to get a good start and put a bit of money away for the hard times which would inevitably come. She might suggest it to Bernie later on.

Friends Forever

* * *

After they'd all eaten and the kids had once more been shooed out to play, Bernie helped Jimmy's mam to wash up while Jimmy and his father chatted companionably. All too soon Bernie realised that she would have to be getting back and Jimmy said he'd accompany her to Arnot Street.

'Don't take no nonsense from *that* one an' remember ter come an' see me soon. This door will always be open fer yer,' Mrs McCauley instructed as they left.

'I like her, I like them all,' Bernie said when they closed the door behind them.

'I knew yer would. Well, I wasn't absolutely certain about me brother an' sister but Mam an' Da were the important ones. Still, askin' our Tilly ter be bridesmaid was a good idea an' our Frank was made up yer don't want him ter get dressed up. Yer'll like our Lizzie an' Emily too, but I don't know about their husbands.'

'Sure, they don't matter. I won't be seeing much of them. I'll go up and see your mam next Thursday night. Molly doesn't get in until late. Do you think that's too soon?'

'No, she'll be made up ter see yer. Now, are yer goin' ter show the owld tartar the ring? Do yer want me ter come in with yer?'

Bernie looked a little doubtful but then she nodded. She had to try to make some kind of a stand.

Molly was already in and she grinned as they both came into the front room. 'Well? Did you get it? Let me look at it!' she demanded excitedly.

'Oh, Moll, isn't it just gorgeous? I'm so lucky! And I've been to meet all the family!'

'Isn't that the most *beautiful* ring *ever*,' Molly breathed and then she hugged them both. 'I'm so happy for you both, I really am!'

Jimmy looked a little embarrassed but put his arm around Bernie. 'We're goin' in ter show it ter the dragon.'

'Do you want me to come too? Shall I go in first and sort of announce you?' Molly offered.

'Would you, Moll?' Bernie was a little relieved.

Molly instantly left the room, beckoning them to follow.

Mrs Hayes had just made a pot of tea and she looked at Molly with mild irritation at being disturbed.

'Bernie would like to show you something and she'd also like you to . . . er . . . meet someone,' Molly blurted out. Before the old lady could reply she grabbed Bernie and Jimmy and hustled them into the kitchen.

'Mrs Hayes, I'd like you to meet Jimmy McCauley, my fiancé, and this is the engagement ring he bought me this afternoon from T. Brown's in London Road and we're hoping to get married in nine months or so and my da's given his consent.' Bernie hadn't paused for breath but held out her left hand and now stood waiting for the reaction. Any reaction.

The old lady looked down at the ring and then up at Jimmy and gave a very brief nod. 'Well, at least it's a nice piece of jewellery he's bought you and he looks decent enough, but I've not changed my mind. I think you are too young and you hardly know him, but it's your life.'

'It is her life, ma'am, but I love her, I respect her an' I'll look after her,' Jimmy said quietly but firmly.

'See that you do! She's a nice girl and she deserves a good life,' came the sharp reply.

'I . . . I was wondering if, now that it's official, can Jimmy call for me and see me home?' Bernie asked hesitantly.

'He can but there's to be no courting going on under this roof!'

Jimmy opened his mouth to speak but Molly shot him a warning look and he shrugged. Bernie would be out of this place in nine months and there was always his mam's front room.

'That wasn't bad, was it?' Molly said when Jimmy had gone and Bernie sat down on the sofa beside her. 'She didn't order him out and now you won't have to meet him on the corner. And it is a gorgeous ring.'

Bernie smiled. 'All I've to do now is tell Mrs M. on Monday.'

'She'll be delighted for you, I know she will.'

'I hope so and I hope she'll let me go on working for her after I'm married. I want to get a really nice home around me, it's something I never had. Something Mam never had. I always envied you that, Molly.'

'You'll have a lovely home, Bernie, and a lovely wedding. Wasn't it the best thing we ever did, coming to Liverpool?'

'It was, Moll, it really was,' Bernie replied happily.

Chapter Seventeen

———————

To Bernie's intense relief Ellen Montrose took the news very
well. She, like Tessie, did express some concern that Bernie
was so young and that she hadn't known Jimmy for very long, but
seeing the happiness that shone from the girl's face and believing
Bernie's earnest protestations that she was fully aware that she was
making a commitment for life, she wished them every happiness.

'I will be sorry to lose you, Bernadette, I've become fond of you
and you are a good worker.'

'You've been kindness itself to me, ma'am, and I was wondering
if I couldn't stay on for a time after I'm married? Jimmy is often
away overnight and it would help me to save, have some money put
by for times when I might need it. When I can't work.'

Ellen Montrose looked thoughtful. She had assumed that the
girl wouldn't want to work after she was married and had a husband
and a home of her own to look after, but she was showing
remarkable maturity in wanting to save. She smiled a little sadly.
'You mean when you have your first baby? You will have to give up
work then.'

Bernie smiled back a little shyly. 'I will so, ma'am.'

'It would suit me fine if you stayed on but I will have to speak to
my husband about it.'

Bernie nodded and returned her engagement ring to its box.

'It is a beautiful ring, Bernadette. Take good care of it.'

'I will so, ma'am. Now, I'd better get on with the washing. It's a
grand drying day, there's a nice bit of a breeze. I might even get
some of it ironed before I leave this afternoon.'

'Leave the ironing until tomorrow, I'll teach you how to make a nice light Victoria sponge cake. We'll make two and you can take one home to share with your friend as a sort of celebration,' Ellen offered, smiling.

They had a piece of the cake each later that evening and Bernie even took a slice through to their landlady as a sort of peace offering and also to show the woman that she was fast becoming a good cook.

'It's really lovely, Bernie, better than Mam makes, though don't ever repeat that to her or I'll be killed! ' Molly laughed.

'Sure, my poor mam wouldn't know how to start. We never had a cake or buns, just soda bread. It helps that Mrs M. has a decent oven to bake them in and not an open fire which is all Mam has anyway.'

'Will you have an electric cooker in your own kitchen, do you think – when you have one?'

'I hadn't thought. Would I be able to afford one? They must be shockingly expensive. I could have gas though, maybe they're cheaper but of course a range would be cheapest of all.'

'How much do you hope to save in nine months?' Molly asked, licking the last crumbs from her fingers.

'I don't know, Molly, I suppose it's up to you.'

'Me?'

'You earn much more than I do and we pool everything.'

'We have eight shillings left over after we've paid everything and we share that. You can save four shillings a week.'

'But, Moll, that's not fair on you! You earn more and when I've gone you'll have to pay everything yourself.'

'I'll manage, sure I'm not in the least bit extravagant and I'll have savings too, don't forget.'

'But you wanted to brighten this place up, get new things – and don't forget we're both supposed to be sending money home.'

'Your mam won't expect you to send anything home now, will she? She knows you'll need every penny to get a home together.'

Molly knew that Bernie diligently sent what she could afford to Tess on a regular basis and that Tess was grateful for the money. It had helped to improve the standard of living of the O'Sullivans in more ways than one for Bernie had also written to her brothers informing them that seeing as she could send money home out of her meagre earnings, then they could do more to fulfil their obligations to their parents. Tess had been delighted to receive the brief letters containing dollar bills that had begun to arrive.

'I know that but *your* mam will.'

'She knows I'll send what I can. Sure, the lads don't send a fortune and they earn big money compared to me. I'll get her some nice remnants and other things for the house.'

'Well, I won't be after taking money from you to put into my Post Office Savings,' Bernie said firmly.

'Ah, stop giving out about it! We're friends, aren't we, and friends help each other. Put your four shillings a week away, don't forget you'll have to have a dress and a veil and shoes and flowers. Do you think they'll come over at all?'

Bernie shook her head. 'Jimmy said he'd pay their fares but where would they all stay, Moll? Then they'd have to be rigged out and it would all cost a fortune! I can't afford clothes for them all and Mam won't leave the kids as she's no one to mind them. Sure, I'd love my da to give me away and to have my mam at my wedding all dressed up in a nice outfit and with a decent hat on her head but I've got to resign myself to the fact that it's just not going to be possible.'

Molly looked thoughtful. 'You could go back and get married in the church at Killina.'

'I couldn't ask Jimmy and his entire family to go to the expense of that.'

'They've got more money than your mam and da have. His da is in regular work and his two elder sisters are married and have husbands in work too. I'm sure Mam wouldn't mind putting Jimmy and his parents up for a few days and we could ask a couple of my aunties to take Frank and Tilly. The others could find cheap lodgings in Tullamore.'

Bernie bit her lip. It was an idea but she'd still have to dip into her savings to provide wedding clothes at least for her mam. 'And what about you? You'll be my chief bridesmaid, you'll have to come too and that will eat into your bit of savings. Oh, I don't know!'

'Think about it. See what Jimmy thinks; sure he won't want to see you upset on your wedding day by having no family at all around you.'

Bernie nodded. She would mention it to Jimmy but if he didn't think it was a good idea then that would be the end of it. She would just have to get married here and be *happy* about it. After all, she'd have Matty, Nellie and the kids – and Molly, and she was such a good friend that she was almost family. In fact she and Molly were closer than a lot of sisters were.

In her lunch hour the following day Molly went to Blackler's and looked at patterns for wedding dresses and priced white satin, taffeta, organdie and crêpe de Chine. Providing Bernie chose something relatively simple, she was determined to make Bernie's dress and her own and Tilly's. It would be quite a challenge but it would save her friend a fortune and ensure that Bernie had a gorgeous dress for the biggest day of her life, whether it was to be in Liverpool or Ireland.

She'd spent so much time in the dress material department that she only had five minutes to get back to Lord Street and hopefully grab a quick cup of tea. Dashing out of the door and into Great Charlotte Street she collided with a young man.

'Hang on a minute, watch where you're going!' he cried, then he caught her by her shoulders. 'God, it's Molly Keegan!'

Molly stopped apologising and a smile lit up her face. 'Billy Marshall!' Molly realised at once it was the young man who had taken so much interest in her at the dance.

'I never got the chance to apologise for that fiasco at the Charleton. By the time it was sorted out and that feller was carted off you'd disappeared. I've been to Blair Hall a few times, hoping I'd see you there. Have you moved from Hopwood Street?'

People were pushing past them and Molly felt embarrassed. Billy guided her to the doorway of a shop.

'Bernie's fiancé Jimmy got us out and took us home straight away. We . . . we've moved to rooms in Arnot Street but we haven't been dancing since.' She'd forgotten how handsome he was.

'I can't say I blame you. He was a right head case, that feller.'

'I didn't like him one bit! He ruined the night.'

'Where are you off to now?'

Molly suddenly remembered that she was due back at work. 'Oh, holy Mother! I'm going to be late back! I'll be killed!'

'Back where? I'm not going to let you disappear from my life again, Molly Keegan.'

'Work. I work at Frisby Dyke's in the soft furnishings department. I'm on my lunch hour. I have to go, *really* I do!'

'Will you come dancing with me on Friday or Saturday or even Sunday night? Will I call for you? What number Arnot Street?'

Even though she was delighted Molly remembered their landlady's rule and she knew there would be hell to pay if she were to have a gentleman calling for her so soon after Bernie's bombshell. 'I'd love to go dancing on Saturday night. I'll meet you somewhere.'

'Outside the Co-op on County Road, say eight o'clock?' he pressed.

'Nine, I have to work until eight.'

'God! Is Sunday better for you?'

'Yes! Yes, it is.'

'Eight o'clock on Sunday night then. It's a date.'

'Great. Now I really have to go. I'll have to run all the way to Lord Street!'

She was out of breath and perspiring when she finally got back almost ten minutes late. Mrs Stanley was not impressed.

'Miss Keegan, I expected to see you back here on the shop floor ten minutes ago and not looking as though you've been dragged backwards through a hedge.'

'Oh, I'm desperately sorry, Mrs Stanley! I didn't realise it was so late! I went to Blackler's to look at paper patterns and material and spent longer than I intended there and then I met someone who . . . delayed me.'

The manageress shook her head. 'That is not much of an excuse. You should watch the time more carefully and not allow yourself to be "delayed".'

'I won't in future. I mean I will watch the time.'

'Such behaviour does your chances of promotion no good at all, Miss Keegan, and you have been showing such promise that I was considering sending you on a course for curtain-measuring and -making.'

Molly bit her lip, cursing herself for lingering so long over materials. 'I really am very sorry, it will never happen again and I do so want to get on, Mrs Stanley, I *do*!'

'We'll see how you progress over the next two weeks and then I'll decide. Now, tidy yourself up and get on with your work,' the woman answered a little less curtly.

Molly wiped her face with her handkerchief and smoothed her hair down with her hands. She'd splash her face with cold water and run a comb through her hair at break time. She wasn't sorry she had literally bumped into Billy Marshall but she'd almost ruined her chance of getting on in her job and that meant a lot to her.

During the afternoon when she had a few minutes between customers she thought about seeing him again and going dancing. She hadn't been out for ages and while she was excited about Bernie's engagement it wasn't the same as actually going out with someone like Billy Marshall and enjoying yourself. Of one thing she was certain though: it wouldn't end up like her night out at the Charleton.

'Where's he taking you? What will you wear?' Bernie asked that evening after Molly had imparted her news, her eyes shining.

'I don't really know, except that we're going dancing, and I suppose I'll wear the blue and cream frock I wore last time. Nothing else is really suitable.'

'Sure, why don't you treat yourself to something new? Mrs M. says you can get some nice things in C and A in Church Street and they're very reasonable. I was asking her if there is anywhere that's "cheap and cheerful" as Nellie always used to say. Not that Nellie could ever afford to shop there. Mrs M. doesn't either, she likes Owen Owen and Lewis's, but she's heard about C and A. You don't have time to make anything.'

'I dare not go out looking at frocks in my lunchtime!'

'You can as long as you watch the time. Ah, go on, Molly! Treat yourself. He's bound to take you somewhere decent.'

Molly made up her mind. 'I will so, if I can find something at a good price. I do want to look nice. Not that there's anything serious going on. I mean that I want to get promoted, I want to make more of a career out of my work.'

'You always were far more ambitious than meself, and good luck to you if it's what you want, Moll, but you might find that your feelings change later on.'

'I might and I might not.' Molly laughed, but determined to go and have a look in C & A – but not until at least Thursday.

Chapter Eighteen

———◆·❈·◆———

MOLLY BOUGHT A PALE apple-green rayon dress trimmed with white in the basement of C & A where things were considerably cheaper than she had imagined. She had confided to Bernie that it hadn't made a huge hole in her savings and Bernie had said that later on she might go and have a look there herself for something to wear as a 'going-away outfit', not that they would actually be going anywhere for a honeymoon.

'What did Jimmy say about where you'll be after getting married?' Molly enquired.

'He said he didn't mind where we got married but if I really would be happier with my family around me then he'd talk to his mam about it.'

'You see, didn't I say he'd understand?' Molly was now practising tying the length of white satin ribbon she'd also bought around her head.

Bernie giggled. 'You'd better not let herself back there catch you with Billy Marshall.'

'I'm not that much of an eejit! Didn't I say I'd meet him outside the Co-op?'

Bernie said she looked stunning when on Sunday evening she came down wearing the new dress, new headband and Bernie's white beads and bangle. Her auburn hair had been washed and it shone, a fact Bernie had insisted was due to the new shampoo that contained real 'henna', which was especially for redheads, although neither of them knew just what henna was. Molly sincerely hoped it wasn't some sort of hair dye. Only extremely bold girls dyed their hair; they were considered very fast.

'Yer look really great, Molly! Yer can walk up the road with us so the owld dragon won't think yer're meetin' a feller, not that it's any business of hers in the first place!' Jimmy offered. He had come to call for Bernie to take her to see his mam to discuss what he called 'this weddin' palaver'.

'Thanks, I will. I don't want to be causing trouble.'

'We won't walk the whole way with you, Moll; the tram stop is just on the corner. Sure, you don't want him to think you're not fit to be out on your own. That you've to take us along wherever you go,' Bernie said, grimacing.

They were as good as their word and Molly continued along the main road on her own. She smiled when she saw the familiar figure waiting for her. He looked extremely smart in a pair of the very wide cream flannel trousers known as Oxford Bags that were the height of fashion, and a sports jacket, a clean shirt and natty tie.

'Don't you look the height of style!' Molly said admiringly.

'I could say the same about you. That colour really suits you, especially with your gorgeous red hair. Have you the temper that goes with it?' he joked.

She laughed. 'I have not!'

'I bought you this, shall I pin it to your dress?' He held out a single white rosebud.

Molly blushed. No one had ever bought her anything like this before. 'Do you have a pin? Oh, it's so pretty!'

Billy duly produced a pin and fastened it to the neckline of her dress. 'There, a rosebud for my "wild Irish rose"!'

'Ah, give over with all that flattery!'

Billy tucked her arm through his. 'Right, we're going for the tram. We'll go to Swainson's, you don't get any drunks or rough-necks there.'

Molly thought fleetingly of their landlady's quarter to ten deadline. She'd discussed it with Bernie and had decided to ignore it. Bernie would be back by ten and had said she would make sure that Mrs Hayes thought they were both in by calling up the stairs to Molly a few times. Molly was to tap quietly on the window of the front room when she arrived back and Bernie would let her in so Mrs Hayes wouldn't hear the sound of the key in the lock.

Molly had enjoyed herself enormously and she decided as the evening wore on that she really did like Billy; perhaps he was a bit of a flatterer but she had to admit that she *liked* being told she was the best-looking and most stylish girl in the room, and that she danced very well for someone who swore she could hardly dance at all. She had refused all the offers of dances with other young men. In the interval he had bought her orange squash and chocolate biscuits and as they got off the tram and walked towards the top of Arnot Street she didn't care in the least that it was nearly eleven o'clock and she was very, very late indeed.

'Do I really have to leave you at the top of the street? Can't I see you into the house? What's wrong with that? It's what any decent feller would do,' Billy protested.

'I know but I've already explained what Herself is like and, believe me, I don't want to be told to pack my bags!'

He sighed. 'Then I'll just have to kiss you goodnight here. I will see you again, Molly?'

'You will indeed. I've enjoyed myself so much, Billy, thanks.'

'Can I see you one night in the week?'

Even though she really wanted to Molly shook her head. She had to be cautious at least for a while. 'I'd like to see you again next Sunday.'

'Shall we go to Swainson's again or would you like to do something else?'

'Swainson's would be just grand.'

'Same time, same place?'

She nodded.

He took her in his arms and kissed her and when he released her she swayed a little. She felt excited, dizzy, happy. Was this how Bernie felt about Jimmy? Was she falling in love with Billy Marshall or was she just deluding herself?

'Goodnight, lovely Molly!'

'Goodnight, Billy,' she replied before turning away and walking quickly down the street. What had Bernie said about her feelings changing? Oh, will you pull yourself together, Molly Keegan! she told herself sternly. It's the first time you've ever been kissed properly; don't go losing the run of yourself over it. How many girls has he kissed before? You certainly aren't the first! And you might not be the last either, a little voice inside her head warned her. He was a real charmer.

'Holy Mother of God! I thought you were never going to get home!' Bernie hissed as she eased open the front door. 'Take off your shoes or she'll hear you! Aren't I worn out holding imaginary conversations with you!'

'Sorry! I was having such a grand time that I forgot about the time.'

Bernie grinned. 'Come on upstairs. We're both supposed to be in bed. I've been sitting in the dark for ages.'

They crept upstairs, avoiding the creaking board on the landing and after Bernie had shut the bedroom door tightly Molly switched on the light and then sat on the bed.

'So, you had a great time? Are you seeing him again?'

'I am so, next Sunday night. We're going dancing again.'

'Will you try and get back a bit earlier, Moll?'

Molly nodded. She hadn't really been fair to her friend; after all, Bernie had abided by their landlady's rules.

'I don't mind, really I don't, but at least if I get thrown out I can go to Jimmy's mam, you'd have to go back to Nellie.'

That was a very sobering thought and Molly grimaced. She really would have to be in earlier next week, whether Billy liked it or not.

'How did you get on? Was anything decided?' Molly asked.

'It was. I had to explain just how hard up Mam and Da are and Ma, as she said I must call her now, said they would all go over. I'm to be married in Killina on the Saturday and there's no need for you to be writing to your mam, they'll all stay in lodgings in Tullamore for the weekend and get the ferry back on the Sunday night. Ma said that she's been saving too as Jimmy's da has been working a bit of overtime. I didn't think we'd be going back so soon, Moll, will you mind?'

'No. Won't we all be coming back on the Sunday night and Mam will be able to see for herself that I'm doing just grand.'

'All I've got to do now is find the money to rig Mam out.'

'I've already decided that I'm going to make your dress and mine and young Tilly's.'

'Oh, Moll, will you? I had a look at some in town yesterday and they cost a fortune!'

'You'll have a dress just as gorgeous as any of those at a fraction of the cost. You'll take the sight from the eyes of every girl in the parish, I promise!'

Bernie sighed happily. 'You're so good to me, Moll! What would I do without you?'

As summer passed into autumn Molly's romance with Billy Marshall blossomed although she only saw him once or twice a week. He pressed her to meet him more often but she wouldn't jeopardise the roof over their heads. She was fully aware that their landlady knew she was seeing someone but as long as she kept to the rules and paid the rent on time there was little the old lady could do or say. Molly had written to her mother, telling her that she was walking out with Billy, who was a respectable young man with a good job as a clerk in a shipping office, whose parents lived in a nice house in Everton with their daughter. She hadn't met them all yet but it would only be a short time before she did. And of course he was the same religion as herself.

Ita had written back warning her not to get too involved, to take care and to make sure he respected her. She wanted to be kept informed and she did of course hope that if Molly was still seeing him when Bernie got married that he would come over with the wedding party and she could meet him and see for herself if he was suitable. More to the point her father could meet him and have a serious talk to him.

'Oh, God! Can you imagine what Da will say to him?' Molly had wailed after reading that bit.

'Take no notice, Moll. I'm sure Billy won't.' Bernie wasn't sure that Billy Marshall was indeed the right one for her friend. Jimmy had made some enquiries about him and the results hadn't been very reassuring. He was what Jimmy called 'a fly by night' and 'a bit of a ladies' man'.

'Up to now he's never been out with the same girl for more than a few weeks, so I've heard. Gets what he wants and then dumps them – or dumps them if he can't get what he wants.'

Bernie had been upset. 'Molly's no fast piece! So, do you think he'll dump her?'

'Maybe she's different. Maybe she's the one who'll finally make that feller settle down. They have been courting for a couple of *months* now.' Jimmy tried to sound convincing.

'Oh, I hope so, Jimmy, I really do! I don't want her to get hurt,' she'd replied, but she'd said nothing to her friend.

Bernie was saving very hard, as was Jimmy. He worked overtime if there was any going and Bernie walked to and from work to save the fares. Twice a week she went to see Ma (as she now called Jimmy's mam) and she was growing even fonder of her future mother-in-law. Mrs Montrose often gave her a few groceries to take home, to help out with the finances and to ease Bernie's acute disappointment that Mr Montrose wouldn't hear of Bernie continuing to work after her marriage. It wasn't in the least bit respectable for a married woman to go out to work, he'd stated emphatically. Her place was at home looking after her hard-working husband. And just how would that husband feel if she continued to work? He would be pointed out as a man who couldn't afford to keep his wife and a man had his pride. Ellen Montrose had reluctantly agreed but had privately decided to give Bernie a wedding gift of money. She had some of her own that she'd saved over the years.

Bernie was delighted when by the end of October she had enough money saved up for the material for her wedding dress, veil and head-dress and had also managed to buy some smaller items from the list she had compiled of all the household goods and furniture she hoped to have by the time April 13 next year arrived. That was the date she and Jimmy had decided upon for the wedding, by which time Jimmy had said that he would have enough saved to buy all the furniture they would need and pay two months' rent in advance. She wasn't to worry about rigging out her family: he would give her the money to send to them.

'Aren't I the luckiest girl in the world, Moll?' she'd said a little tearfully.

'Aren't I? Billy's finally taking me to meet his family on Sunday,' Molly had replied, her eyes shining.

Chapter Nineteen

MOLLY WALKED SLOWLY DOWN the street towards home. It had been a lovely late October Sunday afternoon when she'd left and she had been so looking forward to the outing. Now the sun had gone, the air was damp and chilly and she was bitterly disappointed. So disappointed that she'd insisted she come home alone and Billy hadn't really put up much of an argument to dissuade her.

'I didn't expect you back so soon. What's the matter?' Bernie asked, catching sight of her friend's expression.

'Wasn't it a complete disaster? They hated me!' Molly was near to tears.

'Holy Mother! Why would they hate you? Isn't it the first time they've set eyes on you?'

'I wasn't what they were expecting at all, I could tell that.' She thought of the raised eyebrows of Billy's mother and the hostile expression that clouded Mr Marshall's face as soon as she'd spoken. She had remembered how Bernie had been welcomed into the McCauley family with open arms and how well Bernie got on with Jimmy's mam, so she hadn't been at all prepared for the undisguised disapproval she'd been faced with.

'What were they expecting? What had he told them about you?' Bernie demanded.

'He hadn't told them I was only seventeen, nor that I was Irish. They . . . they made it quite clear that they don't like Irish people. In fact a bit later on when we got a few minutes on our own Billy tried to apologise, if that's what you can call it. What he actually said was his da had told him never to bring an Irish "slummy" into the house and that's why he'd put off me meeting them.'

Bernie was outraged. 'Fine sort of "apology"! And we're not slummies! We're from the country! Did you tell him that?'

'I did so. I told him my da was a farmer and he *owned* his land and that we don't even live in Hopwood Street any more, we live in a nice area. Sure, it's a better area than they live in; there are a few houses in that street that look as if they belong in a slum and *they* certainly don't own their house.'

'And what has he against the Irish? They're not *Protestants*, are they?'

'No, but Billy says his da says the Irish are lazy, feckless drunkards.'

'The brass-necked *cheek* of the man! Sure, you get lazy, feckless drunks of all nationalities!'

'I know.' Molly was smarting with humiliation and Bernie was fuming. It was the first time either of them had come up against such prejudice, although they were aware it was rife and not only in Liverpool.

Molly managed a bitter smile. 'So, it was a bit of a cold atmosphere, *and* she managed to imply that I wasn't old enough to be courting. She said that I was barely older than his sister and that she wouldn't allow *her* to be going to dances or walking out. She said it as though I was a real bold piece and certainly not good enough for her precious son.'

Bernie tutted. 'And the "precious son" didn't have much to say for himself?'

'He did not and that really upset me.'

'Ah, take no notice, Molly, maybe . . . maybe he's not for you.'

Molly shrugged. Billy had disappointed and hurt her but she still loved him. She couldn't change the way she felt.

'What was the sister like? Was she there at all?' Bernie probed; she didn't want to pursue the subject of Billy Marshall's suitability. Further information on his character – provided by Jimmy – didn't improve his image, in her estimation.

'She was. She was very quiet and a bit plain-looking too, like her mam. Billy gets his looks from his da.'

'What about the house?'

'Clean and tidy. Decent enough furniture and they had a wireless and she had nice china cups.'

'So you got a cup of tea? At least she has some manners on her. Didn't Billy try to lighten things up at all?'

'Sort of but I think he's a bit afraid of his da. I was that upset that I insisted on coming home by myself.'

'Are you seeing him again?' Bernie enquired.

Molly nodded. She had wanted so much to get on well with his parents, to become friends with his sister, to be able to visit regularly the way Bernie visited Blenheim Street ... Maybe eventually an engagement ring might have been mentioned. They could have had a long engagement while she worked hard and tried for promotion – after all, she'd done so well on the curtain-making course that Mrs Stanley had hinted at it. She didn't want to live here on her own for ever. With Bernie gone it would be lonely in the evenings and she was beginning to realise that it would be something of a struggle financially. She too wanted a nice home of her own and a loving husband but Billy's family had made those dreams seem totally unattainable.

Bernie said nothing but resolved to talk it over with Nellie later that evening for she could see nothing but unhappiness ahead for her friend.

When Molly remembered that Nellie was to pay them a visit she decided to have an early night. She felt she couldn't endure Nellie's questions and comments about Billy or his family.

After Bernie had told Nellie of the ill-fated visit Nellie looked concerned. 'From what I've heard that Billy's no great shakes. If yer ask me *she's* too good fer *him*.'

Bernie sighed and looked worried. 'That's what I think too. Jimmy says he's a fly by night, that he only wants a girl for one thing and that he always dumps them eventually, although they've been courting now for a few months. I don't want her to get hurt, Nellie.'

'Neither do I, Bernie. Do yer want me ter try ter talk ter her?'

'Sure, I don't know what to do for the best. Maybe she'd listen to you and maybe she won't. Maybe it's best if I try first.'

'Well, do what yer think best, luv, but surely she's got some sense? She won't let him take advantage of her, will she?'

'Molly would never do anything like that, Nellie.'

'I hope not, luv, but yer never know. Now, don't let's waste any more time on that feller, tell me all yer latest news.'

'I'll put the kettle on first and there's a couple of slices of Dundee cake that Mrs M. gave me to bring home. I made it for their tea yesterday.'

'That'll be a real treat. It's years since I've had a slice of decent cake. Yer gettin' ter be a dab hand at bakin', Bernie,' Nellie said admiringly.

After their meal the following evening Bernie decided to talk to Molly about Billy Marshall. Molly was trying to remove a dirty mark from the pale pink lampshade she'd bought as shop-soiled goods last week, using a great deal of French chalk.

'So, you're after seeing him again next Sunday?'

Molly nodded, concentrating on the edge of the stain, her forehead creased in a frown.

'Will you say anything to him about how upset you were?'

'Of course I will.'

'And what do you think he'll say?'

Molly put the shade down on top of the pouffe and clasped her hands together. 'I hope he'll apologise and say it doesn't matter to him what nationality I am and that he really loves me and he'll make amends for their nastiness.'

'Does he love you, Moll? Has he told you?'

'I *think* he does. He says I'm the most gorgeous girl he's ever met and that he's never felt the way he does about any other girl before, nor has he ever been walking out with a girl for as long, so that must mean he loves me.'

Bernie didn't think so. 'But he hasn't *actually* said it?'

Molly shook her head.

'Oh, Moll, I don't want you to get upset but . . . well, I've heard things about him and not just from Jimmy, from Nellie as well.'

'What kind of things?' Molly demanded.

'That he's known as a ladies' man and a fly by night. That he always dumps his girlfriends. I don't want you to get hurt, Molly, really I don't! He shouldn't have let them treat you the way they did. He should have stood up for you. And if he really loved you he *would* have done. Jimmy would have gone mad if I'd been insulted like that! Nellie says you're too good for the likes of him and that she doesn't trust him.'

Molly's cheeks burned and her eyes filled with tears. She jumped to her feet, knocking the lampshade to the floor where it remained, forgotten.

'Well, he hasn't "dumped" me and he won't! He's not like that, he's *not*! How can you listen to such gossip, Bernie? Maybe he should have stood up for me but I told you he's a bit afraid of his da. That doesn't mean he doesn't love me.'

Bernie caught her hand. 'Oh, Moll, don't be angry with me, please? Don't let us fall out over him! I just want you to be happy, I don't want to see you hurt.'

'I will be happy, Bernie! I love him and I know he loves me and that eventually we'll get married.' It was very clear in her country-bred mind. They had been walking out for months and that meant he was serious about her. They would get engaged soon, she was sure of it. He *did* love her.

Bernie tried to steer the conversation into calmer waters. 'I thought you wanted to get on in your job?'

'I do but I want to get married too – at some time in the future.'

Bernie nodded. Well, she'd tried but she wasn't going to lose Molly's friendship, it meant too much to her. 'You will, Molly. One day you'll get married too.'

The following Sunday it was raining heavily which made Molly feel depressed. It meant they would have to go to the cinema or to a dance and there would be little chance of much privacy. Bernie was going to Jimmy's house as he had the night off; they were going to sit in Mrs McCauley's front room and look at a book of wallpaper samples – 'amongst other things,' Bernie had laughed.

It would be just great to sit in a nice cosy room, in front of a warm fire, and talk undisturbed, Molly thought enviously. Well, why shouldn't she? she thought rebelliously. The rent was always paid on time and she *had* a cosy room and a warm fire. Why did she have to go out in the rain and either hang around in doorways or sit in silence in a cinema or be jostled in a crowded dance hall?

The idea took hold and the desire to be able to sit with Billy in private added to it. She'd meet him and then bring him here. If they were very quiet Mrs Hayes wouldn't know. She'd go out at the same time as Bernie (it would be dark) and then come straight back with Billy – but the old lady would assume she was just coming in alone. Of course she'd have to make Mrs Hayes think she'd been out for some time by then. She'd have to go out somewhere a bit earlier and make sure that Bernie let her in very quietly so the landlady didn't know she had returned. Oh, it was all so complicated but thankfully Mrs Hayes never came into their rooms. She'd just have to be very, very careful and Billy would have to be very, very quiet. Lately she had begun to wonder if they should look for other lodgings where there was more freedom. Maybe she would once Bernie was married.

'Holy Mother of God, are you mad?' Bernie cried when she heard Molly's plan.

'I want to talk to him and I want some privacy. The only alternative is a shop doorway and sure, that's not very private, is it?'

'It won't be bad in this weather. Anyone with half an ounce of sense will be indoors.'

'And why shouldn't we?'

'You'll be killed if she catches you. She'll throw the pair of us out.'

'Then I won't let her catch me. It will be just this once.' Molly was determined. 'I *have* to talk to him. You know how important it is.'

'Winter is coming fast; there will be a lot of weather like this and maybe even worse to come.'

'I know. Oh, all these eejit rules and regulations are so . . . childish!'

'That's because she thinks we *are* little more than children. You will be careful, Molly?'

'Of course I will.'

'And it is just this once?'

Molly nodded firmly.

'All right so,' Bernie agreed reluctantly.

The subterfuge seemed to have worked so far, Molly thought as she let herself and Billy in, putting a finger to her lips to impress upon him not to make a sound. They went into the front room and then Molly took her wet umbrella through to the scullery off the kitchen.

'I see it's still raining then. Are you in for the night, Molly?' Mrs Hayes asked, glancing up from her knitting.

'It is and I am. Bernie has gone to Jimmy's mother's house, but she'll be back about ten. We've work in the morning.'

The old lady put down her needles. 'I can't knit for long these days, I've rheumatism in my fingers and it's always worse in damp weather. I think I'll be off to my bed before long. It's a miserable night.'

Molly agreed and it was with some relief that she closed the kitchen door behind her.

Billy was sitting on the sofa and she sat down beside him. 'You'll have to whisper, at least until she goes to bed. Her bedroom is at the back of the house so she won't hear us then.'

'It's bloody stupid, all this cloak and dagger stuff!' he hissed.

'I know and when Bernie is married I think I'll be after looking for somewhere else.'

He put his arm around her and drew her to him. 'We don't have to do any talking at all, Molly,' he whispered.

'Yes, we do! I . . . I want to know how you really feel about me, Billy. I was desperately upset last week and you didn't say much to help things.'

'I'm really sorry, Molly, I am. They've always been like that and they won't change. Me rowing and fighting with them won't make things any better. But let's forget about them, what they think isn't all that important. It's you who really matters to me.'

'Do you love me, Billy?'

'I've told you I've never felt like this about any other girl, Molly.'

'That's not saying "Yes I do". And you know I love you, I've told you so,' she said with hurt in her voice.

Billy was on the defensive. He did care about her but he didn't really want to be tied down just yet. He had no intention of getting married for years yet. He wanted to enjoy himself first for as far as he could see there wasn't much enjoyment to be had in marriage: not judging by those he saw around him. Well, as the old saying went: 'The best form of defence is attack.'

'You *say* you love me, Molly, but you don't *show* me that you do.'

'I do!'

'You'll never let me do more than kiss you.'

She drew away from him. 'Billy, you know I can't do anything . . . more.'

'You mean you *won't*, there's a difference. If you really loved me then you'd let me *love* you.'

'Billy, I do want you to love me but that . . . that's for marriage, you know it is.'

'But that might be years and years away. You can't expect me to wait that long, Molly, it's just not fair.'

Her heart had leaped at his first words – so he did want to marry her some day. Then it dropped like a stone. He wasn't going to wait. He'd find someone else. What had Bernie said she'd heard? That he always dumped his girlfriends. Was she too going to be 'dumped'? She couldn't even bear to think about that; life would be so miserable without him, there would be little or no point to it. But dare she even contemplate the alternative?

He sensed her weakening and pulled her close again, kissing her neck. 'I want you so much, darling, darling Molly. You'd really belong to me. You'd be all mine and I'd be all yours.'

Molly took a deep breath and pushed all the teachings of her religion, the strictures of society, the exhortations of her mother and Nellie and the warnings of her friend Bernie to the back of her mind. 'For ever, Billy?'

'For ever, Molly,' he said with a note of triumph in his voice.

Chapter Twenty

———◆❈◆———

MOLLY SAID NOTHING TO Bernie about what had happened between herself and Billy. Billy had gone by the time Bernie had come home, after promising that he'd be waiting for her at the top of the street next Sunday evening.

It hadn't seemed so awful, she'd thought as she'd lain in bed. The sky hadn't fallen on her. It had been a little painful but Billy had been very gentle and afterwards she'd realised that she loved him even more now for, as he'd said, they belonged to each other.

It was to be a thought she would keep firmly in her mind during the months ahead for she soon found that for them both it simply couldn't be 'just the once'. There were times when she fought long, hard battles with her conscience. She made excuses to Bernie as to why she didn't go to Confession and Communion and she was very thankful that Bernie was so engrossed in the plans for the forthcoming wedding, and the search for a decent house to rent and then furniture with which to fill it, that she didn't question her friend as closely as she once would have done. But Molly wondered just how long she could keep this up.

Bernie thought she had been very, very fortunate in getting the house in Ladysmith Road. It was a brand-new council house on what was being called a 'model estate' on the very outskirts of the city in Fazakerley. There were new shops, a cinema, a library and a community hall on the estate. The house had a garden both at the back and the front. It had two bedrooms, a lovely 'living room', a kitchen and even a small bathroom downstairs. The privy wasn't exactly inside, but it wasn't in the yard either. You went out of the back door and it was just on the left, she explained to Nellie.

'If I had a house like that I'd think I'd died an' gone to heaven! How much do they charge?' Nellie asked.

'Nine shillings a week but Jimmy says we can afford it as long as he gets a bit of overtime. They're quite strict; you have to prove that you have a steady job. He had to have a letter from the ferry company. Oh, Nellie, it's gorgeous! Ma said it's the best possible start we could have, she never had anything like it at all.'

'Not many in this city have, luv. There's not that many with steady jobs.' She frowned. 'Isn't it a bit far out, though?'

'The trams run there quite frequently. The numbers twenty and twenty-one. They go from the Pier Head to Fazakerley Terminus so Jimmy won't have much trouble getting to and from work. There are still fields and hedgerows and trees out there, it will be like living in the country again.'

'I keep fergettin' yer're a country girl. Are yer lookin' forward ter going back ter Ireland fer the weddin'? I wish we could afford ter go but we can't.'

'I am. Oh, I've so much to tell Mam.'

Nellie smiled at her. 'She'll be dead proud of yer, Bernie. Yer've done so well fer yerself and I bet yer'll look dead gorgeous.'

'I'm going with Molly next week for the pattern and the material. Now that Christmas is over they should be getting new stock in soon, so Molly says.'

'She's dead clever ter be able ter sew like that an' she's doin' so well at work. Is the romance still on?'

Bernie nodded. 'She's head over heels.'

'I'm surprised it's lasted this long. Maybe she's the one who has finally sorted him out.'

'It's been six months now so you never know. He's not taken her home again but I don't think she cares, not after the last time.'

Nellie sighed. 'Married life is hard enough without bein' at war with the in-laws. Yer need all the help yer can get.'

'At least I've no complaints there. We've all got on so well since the day I met them and I'm sure Mam and Da will like them too.'

'Put the kettle on, luv, and yer can tell me all the plans, in every detail. I'll have ter make do with livin' it second-hand, like.'

Molly had been just as impressed as everyone else when Bernie proudly took her to show her her new home.

'It's lovely out here, Bernie. Just think what these trees will look like in spring. Won't it be a joy to walk home?' she'd said enviously as they walked down the tree-lined road called Lower Lane. There was even a small thatched cottage halfway down, called 'Rose Cottage', and you could imagine it in summer with all the climbing roses in bright profusion around the door. 'You wouldn't think you were in a city at all.'

'Aren't I just the fortunate one? I wish I had a photograph of it to take to show Mam.'

'She could pass it around the parish so everyone could see how well you've done for yourself. I wouldn't mind living out here at all,' Molly said wistfully.

'Does he never mention getting married? You've been courting steady now for six months,' Bernie had probed.

'Not exactly. Sometimes he does say "in the future" but that's only when I really press him. I'll just have to be patient, I suppose.'

'Well, look how long some couples back home wait. Years and years.' But Bernie devoutly hoped that Billy Marshall wasn't going to turn out like the traditional Irish bachelor who never had the remotest intention of ever getting married. Molly had nodded; after all they were still very young.

The next two months were very busy ones for both girls. Bernie spent all her spare time furnishing the house in Ladysmith Road and writing to Tess to make sure all the proper arrangements were being made and clothes bought. She'd sent her mother the money to cover everything and Tess had already booked Jimmy's family into suitable accommodation in Tullamore, sorted out transport for them, seen the parish priest not only about the wedding itself but also a room for the small reception, and had started to look for outfits. She told Ita that her head ached and she was worn out with all the letters she had to write to Bernie and that Con O'Brien, the postman, had a track worn to the door with all the letters Bernie sent in reply.

Molly was busy at work for it seemed that half the city wanted to redecorate their parlours for spring and all her spare time was spent making Bernie's wedding dress and her own and Tilly's bridesmaids' dresses. Bernie had chosen white crêpe de Chine over white taffeta. The crêpe de Chine would drape nicely, Molly thought, for Bernie had chosen a fairly straight, mid-calf style with the fashionable dropped waist. The skirt also had the stylish 'handkerchief' hemline, which was complicated and would take longer to make. For modesty's sake it had long sleeves and a plain round neckline but Molly intended to 'dress it up' with a few rows of ruffles. Her own dress and Tilly's were of lilac crêpe de Chine over a deeper mauve taffeta and she was to have a wide brimmed picture hat. Tilly was to have a small Dutch-style bonnet, something the child was delighted with, never having had a hat of any kind in her life before.

'Oh, Moll, will we ever be ready in time? There's so much to do,' Bernie had cried in some panic when with just a week to go Molly hadn't been able to find the right colour ribbon to finish off Tilly's bonnet.

'We will so. Don't be losing the run of yourself, Bernie. I've a few more shops to try. I think I might go mad and go to George Henry Lee: I know they're expensive but I've heard they have the best haberdashery department in the city. It's only a bit of ribbon, it shouldn't break the bank,' Molly said firmly.

Bernie was very surprised when on the Sunday afternoon the weekend before she was due to go back to Ireland, Mrs Montrose arrived at the house in Ladysmith Road. Bernie had been giving her new table and chairs a final polish.

'Oh, ma'am, do come in and sit down.' She proudly plumped up the cushions on the sofa.

'I do hope you don't mind me coming unannounced, Bernadette, but I wanted to see you in private before you leave on Wednesday. And, if I'm really truthful, I wanted to come and see your new home.'

'Sure, I don't mind at all. Isn't it great to see you and you'll always be welcome, ma'am.'

Ellen Montrose looked around with admiration. 'I have to say it really is very nice, Bernadette. You have some lovely things too.'

'I'm very lucky, ma'am.'

'It's not all down to luck. You've both worked and saved very hard. I'm so sorry you can't continue working for me but, as Mr Montrose says, we have to think of Jimmy's pride. Will you be lonely out here? It's quite isolated and you did tell me that Jimmy is often away overnight.'

'I'll be just grand, ma'am. I've lived most of my life in an isolated place and there are trams and shops and everything.'

Ellen Montrose smiled. 'I was forgetting that.'

'And Molly will visit me and Nellie and I can go and see them and Ma – Jimmy's mam.'

'And you can visit me too.' Ellen Montrose knew she would miss Bernie and her chat.

Bernie looked a little flustered. 'Ma'am, I'm so sorry that I can't even offer you a cup of tea. Oh, I have the cups and the kettle but there's no food in the house yet.'

'Of course there isn't. You've not moved in yet and I haven't come to have tea.' She delved into her handbag and took out an envelope. 'I want you to have this as a wedding present.'

Bernie took the envelope and opened it. Inside was a nice card and a white five-pound note. 'Oh, ma'am! Oh, you really shouldn't have! It's too much!' She was quite overcome.

'Of course I should. I can afford it and it will help for a rainy day.'

'It's very generous of you, thank you and God bless you.' Bernie returned both the card and money to the envelope.

'You know I've been thinking about "rainy days". You're such a good cook now, Bernadette, that if ever you needed to work you could work from home. You could bake and sell cakes and scones and pies and that lovely barmbrack and soda bread. I'm sure there would be a market for it, especially the traditional Irish confectionery. Liverpool has a large Irish community, but I don't have to tell you that.'

Bernie nodded slowly. It was a good idea but she sincerely hoped she would never be in a position where she would need money so desperately.

'It is a good idea, ma'am, and that way I wouldn't be after upsetting Jimmy's pride either, but I hope there won't be any rainy days.'

'So do I and I'm sure there won't. Now, I'd better be getting back. Mr Montrose likes his tea at five sharp on Sundays. He goes to visit his maiden aunt at six. She's getting quite old now and looks forward to his visits.'

Bernie saw her out, thanking her yet again and reiterating that Mrs Montrose would be very welcome to call any time.

Molly was finishing a letter to her mother when Bernie got home and imparted the news of Mrs Montrose's visit.

'You have to admit that it's very good of her and it's quite a good idea,' Molly said. There was a note of weariness in her voice that Bernie noticed at once.

'I hope I never to need to work from home. What's the matter, Moll? You seem a bit down.'

'Oh, it's not easy to find the right words to tell Mam that Billy isn't coming over with us. She desperately wanted to meet him.'

Molly was very disappointed that Billy had refused to accompany them. She'd been excited at the prospect of showing him off to her family and friends. She was so much in love with him now.

'It will be great, Billy! You'll have a grand time and everyone will be only delighted to meet you!' she'd enthused.

Billy had turned his head away so she wouldn't see the expression in his eyes. His parents would go absolutely mad if he were even to hint that he was going to a wedding in Ireland with her. He'd sworn to his da that he'd given her up. His da would kill him if he discovered it wasn't all finished between them. Nor did he want to meet Molly's parents, particularly her da who was bound to demand to know what his intentions were toward Molly. Was he going to marry her or was he just stringing her along? And what could he say to that? If he agreed to marry her he'd be making a noose for his own neck and if he didn't he'd probably get a hiding from her da and all her relations too. From what she had told him about her da he'd realised it would be no use trying to soft soap him.

He'd turned back and taken her in his arms. 'Molly, I'm sorry but my grandad isn't at all well. He's over eighty and Mam doesn't think he'll last much longer. You know I'd come if I could but, well, I'm very fond of the old man and if he passed away when I was out of the country, enjoying myself, I'd never forgive myself. You do understand, don't you?'

She'd nodded miserably. She had been so looking forward to the trip but what could she say? She could see his point and she wouldn't want him to blame her for dragging him off to Ireland.

'I don't suppose it is easy for him,' Bernie said now. 'His grandad is very old and he has been sick. Sure, your mam can't find too much fault with that. And I'm sure one day you'll be taking him over to meet them, when you've a ring on your finger, and won't they only be delighted?'

Molly smiled at her. Bernie always did her best to cheer her up. 'He'll be missing a grand occasion.'

'He will so. It'll be a great day altogether.' Bernie grinned. 'Jimmy is taking two crates of ale with him, so he says, so he's bound to get on well with Da.'

'Just make sure he doesn't drink too much himself or the wedding night will be ruined,' Molly advised, returning to her letter.

Bernie smiled, rather embarrassed. In fact she was relieved that Billy Marshall wasn't going with them. His excuse sounded a bit thin to her and both she and Nellie agreed that he probably had other, more sinister reasons for his refusal. She was also certain that a shrewd man like Paddy Keegan wouldn't be taken in by Billy's flashy way of going on and that was bound to cause trouble between Molly and her da. However, with her usual tact she hadn't mentioned any of this to her friend.

Chapter Twenty-One

———◆◆◆◆———

DESPITE THE FACT THAT it was spring and therefore blustery the ferry crossing wasn't too bad. Jimmy had managed to wangle a cabin for Bernie, Molly, Tilly and his mam by slipping the steward a few shillings.

' 'Tis better than the way we had to try to sleep last time,' Bernie said after her future mother-in-law had remarked that it was a bit cramped.

'And it will be much quieter,' Molly added.

'I just hope those fellers don't go drinking that ale they brought with them tonight,' Mrs McCauley said caustically. 'Our Jimmy's not used to drink.'

'They'll have the train journey to sober up if they do,' Molly replied, grimacing.

'Bernie, let's try and stack these boxes up in some kind of order then, Tilly, you can get into this bottom bunk with me, and Molly and Bernie can share the top one. I'm too old to be trying to climb up and down this bit of a ladder.'

The boxes in which the wedding finery was packed and their cases were all somehow fitted in too and Molly and Bernie climbed up to the top bunk and settled themselves. Molly was glad that she had very generously been given the Friday off work. The others had all either taken time or altered their working hours.

It was a rather tired and travel-stained party who arrived at Tullamore Station the following afternoon. Molly's father had come with Dessie to meet them. Dessie was to take those who were staying in town to their lodgings.

'I never expected to see you two girls again this soon, that I didn't.' Paddy Keegan beamed as he hugged first his daughter then the bride-to-be. 'The two of you are to come on home with me. Sure, your mam and Tess are up to their eyes with the cooking. The kitchen is like a bakery and has been this whole week.'

'Then there'll be no shortage of food then,' Molly laughed, climbing up into the trap and wrapping the rug around her knees. It was still quite chilly and she hoped that tomorrow would be warmer or they'd all be frozen in their light frocks.

'Dessie is going to bring Jimmy and his parents out this evening to meet Tess and then you're all to go and see Father O'Brien at the Parochial House,' he informed them as they drove out of the station yard.

Ita and Tess were delighted to see them and exclaimed how well they looked and how stylishly they were dressed.

'And I have to admit, Molly, that your hair looks just grand short,' Ita said, stroking her daughter's shining auburn waves after Molly had taken off her hat.

'I still can't take it in that my Bernie is going to be a wife. Sure, I still think of her as a bairn,' Tess said, wiping away a tear.

'Mam, don't start weeping already!' Bernie cried.

'Save that for tomorrow, Mrs O'Sullivan, when you see how gorgeous she looks,' Molly added.

'Molly, put on the kettle. Tess and meself haven't stopped all morning and we're in the want of a cup of tea and you must be too. After that you'd best be after getting those dresses out of the boxes and hung up or they'll be destroyed altogether.' Ita wiped her hands on her apron and began to get out cups and plates.

'They'll need to be pressed anyway. I'll do them later on,' Molly offered.

There was so much to do and people seemed to be constantly coming and going and it was very late when Molly finally was left alone in the kitchen with her mother. Bernie had gone off with Tess to spend her last night as an unmarried girl in her parents' humble home. Dessie had taken Jimmy and his parents back into town and Paddy had gone to bed.

Friends Forever

'Are you happy over there, Molly?' Ita asked, peering intently at her daughter. Molly looked tired and a little dejected, she thought.

'I am, Mam. I like my work and I'm doing great. I brought you a few nice things for the parlour.'

'You've great taste, I have to say. And what about Herself? I think it's very good of her to keep her eye on you and make sure you're not out half the night and getting up to the Lord alone knows what.'

Molly's cheeks flushed a little at that. 'I just wish she wasn't quite as strict,' she said hastily, hoping that she didn't look guilty and wondering if she should mention the fact that she might be thinking of leaving the house in Arnot Street before long. She was hoping to get a couple of nice rooms in a house somewhere closer to the city centre, nearer to work, which would cut down on travelling time and fares. She'd heard there were some lovely big old houses up near where the Anglican Cathedral was being built; a few of them sometimes had rooms to rent.

'Has she not met this young man of yours?'

Molly shook her head. 'She doesn't allow gentlemen callers and she won't change her mind.'

'Your da and me are disappointed that he hasn't come with you. We were wanting to see what class of a lad he is.'

'I'm disappointed too, Mam, but he's really nice. You'd like him and so would Da. I did write and tell you why he couldn't come.'

'Is the grandfather at death's door?'

'I don't think he's *that* bad – but he has been very sick,' she added quickly, seeing the frown crease her mother's forehead.

'And has he mentioned getting married at all? Oh, I know Tess is delighted about Bernie but I don't want you rushing into things, Molly. You're still very young, just eighteen. I want you to enjoy your life, make something of yourself before you're tied down.'

'There's nothing definite, Mam, and I *am* enjoying myself. Haven't I already told you how well I'm getting on at work?'

'You've a good head on your shoulders and a clever way with colour and you're very handy with a needle. Would you not think

173

of starting your own business one day? With the soft furnishings, I mean.'

This had never occurred to Molly. 'Me? Start my own business making curtains and cushions and things? Sure, don't most people go to the likes of Frisby Dyke's?'

'If they have a big shop like that to go to. Not everyone does, and not everyone can afford to. It's just an idea.'

'The lady Bernie used to work for had an idea like that for Bernie.'

'And since when has Bernie O'Sullivan been good with a needle?'

'She can manage to turn up a hem and sew on a button now, but she's a grand cook, Mam. Her cakes are just gorgeous. Mrs M. taught her. She said if Bernie was ever really desperate she could make cakes and barmbrack and the like and sell them.'

Ita wasn't so sure that this was practical. 'Doesn't everyone do their own baking? Would they want to buy things like that? I make fresh bread every day.'

'Not in big cities they don't, Mam. You buy it in shops or you can even have it delivered to your front door. You can have everything delivered.'

Ita was sceptical. 'I don't know if I'd like that at all. I like to see what I'm after buying.'

'They just have *different* ways of going on in cities, Mam.'

Ita sighed. 'I suppose they do. And tell me, what is it like having the electricity and gas?'

'It's grand but I suppose after a while you just take it for granted. Like being able to catch a tram at the end of the street and not having to either walk or ride in the trap. But not everyone has electric or gas. Poor Nellie and her neighbours don't.'

'And was it very bad, living there?'

'It was so. I wrote and told you how desperate it was as soon as we'd moved.'

'If we'd known that before you'd gone over sure you'd have never gone at all. Bugs in the walls! 'Tis shocking!'

'She can't help it. It's the houses. Even the poorest cabin here isn't as bad, but we're out of it now and Bernie has a house the like of which her mam would give her eyes for.'

'I hope she's not making a mistake but I have to say I liked the lad and his mam and da, and sure anyone with eyes in their head can see he idolises her.'

Molly smiled. 'Bernie will be just fine, Mam, and so will I. Now, we'd better get to bed. We've to be up early.'

Bernie O'Sullivan's wedding was talked about for weeks in the Parish. Everyone said it did your heart good to see how a girl from such a poor home could do so well for herself.

Molly thought with pride how lovely Bernie looked as she walked down the aisle of the church on her father's arm. She was barely recognisable as the girl who had left here ten months ago. Dessie looked so proud and so smart in the new navy serge suit, white shirt and navy tie and his shiny black boots creaked a little with the newness. She had hardly recognised Tess who was resplendent in a plum-coloured costume with a long jacket and a box-pleated skirt. Her hat was dusky pink felt with a plum-coloured ribbon around the crown and she had black shoes with a small heel and cream stockings. She'd never seen Tess wearing stockings – ever. All the young O'Sullivans were neat and clean and well turned out too, although there had been some complaints and disappointment from Claire and Eileen that they hadn't been asked to be bridesmaids too. Tess had quickly put a stop to that by saying it was a wedding not a flaming May procession and there wasn't money for dresses that could never be worn again.

The Nuptial Mass was lovely and the wedding breakfast in the small hall was a veritable feast, so Mrs McCauley senior had said. Even Jimmy's two elder sisters couldn't find fault with anything. If Billy had been there to share the day with her, it would have been perfect, Molly thought sadly as – tired out and with aching feet after so much dancing – she accompanied her parents and brothers and sisters back to the farmhouse for a few minutes before she left for Dublin. Still, she had caught Bernie's bouquet and that meant that she would be the next bride. The thought cheered her up no end.

Chapter Twenty-Two

———❖———

Bernie was happier than she'd ever been in her life before. The years stretched ahead of her full of joy and contentment. She spent her days keeping her little house clean and tidy, baking, shopping, writing to Tess, visiting and entertaining her own visitors. But the time she enjoyed the most was when Jimmy had a day or an evening off and they would either go to the Rio, the local cinema, or would spend time in the garden.

Jimmy knew nothing about gardens but Bernie knew how to grow vegetables if not flowers. 'Sure, there was never the time nor the money nor the inclination to be growing flowers at home but it can't be all that hard. I've seen packets of seeds in Appleton's, the ironmonger's. Will I try some, do you think?' she'd asked him.

'Can yer plant them at this time of year? It's nearly summer,' he asked, leaning on the spade with which he was turning over what was to be Bernie's vegetable patch.

'Won't we be planting the vegetables? I know it's a bit late for some of them but that can't be helped; maybe it's the same with flowers.'

'Why don't yer get a book from the library?'

Bernie had looked apprehensive. She wasn't very good at reading and a huge place like the library was daunting. 'Maybe I will but if it's full of terrible long words I won't bother. It will have to be a case of trial and error.'

'Ma says they have books in the libraries on just about everythin' an' me da says I should learn somethin' about engineerin' and try ter get a better job.'

Bernie had looked at him with pride. There was nothing her Jimmy couldn't do if he put his mind to it. 'Will you?'

'I dunno, Bernie. I don't get much time off for studyin', like. There's the Mechanics Institute, a sort of school yer can go ter at night but my workin' hours aren't exactly what yer'd call regular, an' besides, I'd hardly ever see yer, luv.'

'I wouldn't mind that, not if it's really what you want.'

'I'd only be doin' it so we'd have more money an' I could give yer a better life, an' the kids – when we have any, that is – but if I was spendin' all my time at the books an' the Institute we might never have any.'

'Ah, they'll come along, you wait and see. Look at my mam. She had twelve.'

'Aye, but yer da wasn't always away from home, was he?'

Bernie had laughed. 'But he was always in the pub! I'll be happy with whatever you decide to do, Jimmy. I'm so proud of you, that I am.'

'An' I'll be proud of *you* when yer serve up our own spuds an' carrots an' cabbage with the Sunday joint,' he'd laughed.

'Sure, that day will be a long time coming if you don't get the ground ready.'

'I could murder a pint. It's thirsty work.'

'Get it finished and we'll get changed and walk up to the Railway pub by the station. You can have your pint and I'll sit on that little bench outside the station and enjoy the sun. I might be a married woman but I'm still not old enough to drink alcohol in a pub!' she'd reminded him.

Since returning from Ireland Molly had begun to think more and more about moving. It would help if she could find somewhere a bit cheaper too, she thought, for she missed Bernie's contribution to the budget. With Bernie gone it was more difficult for Billy to sneak in and out of the house and the long light summer evenings didn't help either. And he was becoming moody and offhand with her.

'Just tell the old bat you pay the rent, you're eighteen and you'll entertain who you like or just find somewhere else!' he'd snapped the last time she'd refused to allow him to come to the house.

'You know it's not as easy as that. Decent rooms are hard to find,' she'd pleaded, although these rooms had been found with little difficulty, she reflected.

'Well, I just don't see why we can't go to Bernie's house.'

'Billy, you know I can't be doing things like . . . that at Bernie's! We've had all this out time and again.'

He'd looked at her very coolly. 'I thought you loved me? I thought you wanted to belong to me?'

It had sent a knife through her heart. 'You *know* I do! But . . . but will you just be a bit patient? I promise I'll start to look for somewhere else.'

'Will you make it quick, Molly? You can't expect me to be hanging around on street corners waiting for you and then never being alone with you for more than a few minutes.'

'We could always go and just visit Bernie,' she'd said in desperation.

'What would be the point in that? All you two would do is gossip and I'd be bored stiff. And even if Jimmy was at home he doesn't like me and I don't like him.'

It had been the first time he had openly admitted that there was animosity between himself and Bernie's husband and it had made Molly feel even more unhappy. She had hoped that they could sometimes go out as a foursome but obviously that was now out of the question.

She'd buy a newspaper and scan the 'For Rent' column. She just might be lucky enough to see something around Myrtle Street or Faulkner Square. She wondered if she should bring up the subject of getting engaged, and then she could perhaps look for something in which they could start married life, but she decided against it. The tone of the conversation hadn't exactly been conducive to that subject. She'd wait until he was in a better mood.

Bernie was aware that Molly's romance wasn't all sweetness and light but she didn't criticise, she just listened to Molly when she poured out her heart, tried to reassure her and prayed that one day Molly would tire of Billy and meet someone nicer.

She had been thinking of Molly that afternoon when she'd been working in the garden. It was a very warm day and she suddenly realised that it was exactly a year since they'd first set foot in Liverpool. She sat back on her heels and admired the neat rows of vegetables that were just beginning to sprout leaves and the little rose bush she'd planted. The rest of her flower seeds weren't doing quite so well but they were just an experiment. She smiled wryly to herself as she remembered the dawning horror and panic they'd felt when they'd first seen Nellie's house in Hopwood Street. So much had happened in one short year and it had all been good. She'd never dreamed that when she'd first met Jimmy on the ferry boat that morning that a year later she would be married to him, deliriously happy and living in what for her was pure luxury. And what would this next year bring? A baby? A new job for Jimmy? And what about Molly? Her friend had also done well for herself – at work at least. Molly had shown such flair and expertise that she was being considered for promotion to deputy manageress, with the appropriate pay rise. That would certainly help with her expenses for she knew that, egged on by Billy Marshall, Molly was looking for somewhere else to live. She wished she could ask Molly to come and live with them but, much as he liked Molly, Jimmy would never stand for having Billy Marshall over the doorstep. She desperately wanted Molly to meet someone else because she shared Jimmy's opinion that Billy was only stringing her friend along; he surely never had any intention of marrying her. She also prayed that Jimmy was wrong when he said Molly must be giving in to him otherwise he'd have dumped her long ago. Sometimes she felt sure that Molly wouldn't be so foolish but at others she wondered if Jimmy was indeed right. She dared not even discuss that with Nellie for Nellie would be horrified and would take it on herself to put a stop to it one way or another.

Wearily she got to her feet and wiped the soil from her hands on her apron. She'd better get washed and changed and get a meal started. Jimmy was due home early tonight: he was going to go to the Mechanics Institute to find out how he could learn more about engineering. He'd be hot and tired and hungry and thirsty.

By half past eight she was seriously worried. He should have been home hours ago. The dinner was ruined but she was past caring. At first she thought maybe he'd changed his mind and decided to work on. Then she'd thought maybe he'd gone to see his da; next she'd wondered had the ferry been held up? But the weather was fine and calm. She'd gone to the front gate and looked up the road ten times but there had been no sign of him. Should she get the tram to his mam's house? Or to the Pier Head? She could leave a note in case he came home while she was out. Or maybe it would be best to go to the police station, but what could she tell them? That he hadn't come home on time? They'd make a mock and a jeer of her. Tell her he was probably in a pub propping up the bar or involved in a game of pitch and toss somewhere. It would be no use telling them he didn't gamble and he only ever had two pints at the most.

By nine o'clock, after half a dozen more fruitless trips to the gate, she'd decided to get a tram to the Pier Head and try to see someone on the ferry. It wouldn't be leaving until half past eleven. She'd leave a note, just in case. She'd put on her hat and a light cardigan and was halfway through writing the brief message when there was a knock on the front door.

Relief surged through her. Thank God! Thank God, he was home! She rushed to the door but even before she had wrenched it open the knowledge that he had a key and anyway he always came in the back way hurtled into her mind. Her heart dropped like a stone, her eyes widened with terror and her hand went to her mouth as she saw the burly figure in blue standing on the doorstep.

'Oh, sweet Jesus, no! No!' she cried.

'Mrs Bernie McCauley?' The constable's voice was low and full of sympathy. They hadn't told him she was so young. They probably hadn't known. 'Can I come in, luv?' Gently he put an arm around her shoulder and propelled her into the living room.

Bernie couldn't speak. Icy cold fingers were gripping her throat and she was having trouble breathing.

'There's been a terrible accident on the ferry. A freak accident. The ferry was late getting in.' He knew he was doing this very badly but it was the first time he'd ever had to do it. 'Sit down, luv, please.'

'What?' she managed to croak, sinking on to the sofa.

He sat down beside her. 'He . . . your husband was doing some maintenance work on deck and he slipped and fell.'

She grabbed his arm tightly. 'Jimmy can swim! He can swim!'

'He hit his head before he went over the rail. They got him out as quick as they could but . . . I'm sorry, luv. I'm so very, very sorry. He'd drowned.'

She crumpled up against his shoulder and he held her. She was little more than a kid and he wondered how long they'd been married.

Bernie couldn't cry. Tears wouldn't come but she was being torn apart inside. Her heart felt as though it was going to burst with pain and there were red hot knives behind her eyes. She was shaking uncontrollably.

'They're informing his parents, can I take you to them? You can't stay here on your own like this, luv. Or is there anyone else? Your mam? A sister?'

She didn't care where he took her. It didn't matter. Nothing mattered now. Nothing would ever matter again. His mam would be in shock too and Molly . . . Molly *couldn't* understand. Molly had never been married. 'Nellie. I . . . I want to go to Nellie's in Hopwood Street,' she stammered through chattering teeth.

He pulled her to her feet. He'd have to get some help. He'd need a car to take her into town or maybe even the hospital. Did she have no parents? he wondered. Then he remembered her accent. They were obviously too far away to help her.

Somehow he managed to get her to the police station. There they summoned a car after they'd managed to get a cup of hot sweet tea down her. Bernie hadn't wanted to drink it but they'd insisted; they'd also brought blankets and wrapped them around her. Dimly she'd heard them discussing whether or not they should take her to Walton Hospital and she'd managed to cry out that she didn't want to go there, she wanted to go to Nellie.

'What number Hopwood Street, luv?' the constable asked.

'Ten. Mrs O'Sullivan,' she answered in a choked whisper.

Nellie and the neighbours she was gossiping with on her doorstep all crossed themselves when they saw the police car drive up the narrow street.

'Jesus, Mary an' Joseph! That's bad news fer someone,' Maggie Hardcastle said ominously.

'Holy Mother of God, it looks like me!' Nellie cried, clutching the doorpost as the car drew to a halt.

'Is Matty 'ome, luv?' Maggie asked fearfully.

Nellie was confused. 'He is an' as far as I know all the kids are in.'

'It's Bernie! They've got Bernie in the back! Oh, sweet Jesus, Nellie! Somethin' must 'ave 'appened ter young Jimmy McCauley,' Agnes gasped, clutching Maggie's arm as Nellie flew down the steps to help Bernie from the car.

'What's happened? What's wrong? Nellie begged.

'Are you Nellie O'Sullivan?'

'Yes! What's the matter? Bernie, yer look terrible!'

'There's been a bad accident on the ferry and I'm afraid her husband was drowned. She's terribly shocked; she asked to be brought to you.'

There was a collective groan of anguish from the assembled women as Nellie took Bernie in her arms.

'Bernie, luv! Oh, God, I'm so sorry! Poor young Jimmy. Poor young lad.'

Bernie sagged against her and then the tears started.

Chapter Twenty-Three

MOLLY WAS ASTONISHED TO see Maggie Hardcastle standing on the doorstep.

'Mrs Hardcastle? What's wrong? It's half past ten, I was going to bed. Is it Nellie?'

'No, Molly, it's poor Bernie. Yer'd better get yer jacket, luv, an' come ter Nellie's with me. Bernie's there an' she's in a shockin' state.'

Molly didn't argue. She dashed to get her jacket and call a few words of explanation to her landlady. If Maggie had come all this way at this time of night it must be something bad, but why had Bernie gone to Nellie?

As they walked quickly up the street Maggie broke the news to Molly as tactfully as she could.

Molly couldn't believe it. 'He can't be dead! He *can't*! He's so young and so fit!' She clutched Maggie's arm tightly.

'He was both, luv, but it 'appens. God 'ave mercy on 'is soul. It was a terrible accident an' it shouldn't 'ave 'appened at all.'

'Poor Bernie! Oh, poor, poor Bernie!' The tears were streaming down Molly's cheeks. How would her friend cope with this? They had been married for such a short time and they'd been so happy. 'It's not fair. It's just not *fair*, Maggie,' she sobbed.

'I know, girl. Life's bloody *unfair*! Yer just manage ter get on yer feet and then the bloody rug is pulled out from under yer an' yer world comes crashin' down.'

Molly stumbled on, clinging to the older woman's arm as they made for the tram stop.

By the time they reached Hopwood Street Molly was calmer. The awful initial shock was passing and she knew she had to pull herself together before she faced Bernie. She had to try to give some comfort to Bernie; it would help no one if she just broke down too.

Nellie and Matty were sitting in the kitchen; there was no sign of any of their kids.

'Nellie, where is she? *How* is she?' Molly asked in almost a whisper. The house was very quiet.

Nellie dabbed at her eyes. 'I got her ter bed. His mam is with her. She . . . she came lookin' fer Bernie. Someone must have told her the police had brought her here. She's in a state herself but she's holdin' up well. His da has gone ter identify him; she said there was no way he would let Bernie face that. It would kill her. Agnes went ter the Dispensary and got somethin' off the doctor ter calm her down.'

Molly sank down on the wooden bench beside Nellie and took her hand. 'I don't know what I can do to help her, Nellie. What will I say to her?'

'What can anyone say ter her? What can anyone do ter help her, luv? An' the worst is yet ter come. Matty says there'll have to be an inquest and then she'll have ter bury him.'

'Oh, holy Mother of God!' Molly groaned. It didn't bear even thinking about.

'Maybe *she'll* be the only one who can help poor Bernie now. Maybe *she'll* be the one who can help us all ter get through it,' Nellie said, squeezing Molly's hand.

In later years Molly was to wonder how they both got through those dark and depressing days without losing either faith or hope. She watched her friend going through the motions of living, like someone in a daze or a dream; except for Bernie it was a nightmare from which there was no awakening.

They sat through the inquest together, hands tightly clasped. Molly valiantly fought back the tears but they slipped silently down Bernie's pale thin cheeks. She didn't bother to try to wipe them away as the circumstances that had robbed her of her very reason for living unfolded. The verdict was the one they had all anticipated: accidental death.

Bernie was staying with Jimmy's mam, something Nellie had urged her to do when Mrs McCauley had begged Bernie to go home with her.

'Yer'll be a comfort ter each other, luv,' Nellie had pleaded.

Molly had said nothing. She had wanted Bernie to go back to Arnot Street with her, where there would be few memories of Jimmy to torment her, but Bernie had gone to Blenheim Street with her mother-in-law.

The weather seemed to be an outright mockery of the day that was in it, Molly thought bitterly as on the morning of the funeral she walked with old Mrs Hayes to the tram stop. The sky should be grey and dull, not such a beautiful clear blue. It should be cold and damp and miserable, not warm and sunny. There should be a howling gale, not a gentle balmy breeze. But it was the first week of July, high summer. He was to be buried in St Anthony's, his old parish, where his friends and family would be near to him, not in the outskirts of the city. Bernie and his mother had insisted on it.

'God help his poor mother today. It's one of the worst things that can happen to a mother, to have to bury a child. And God help that poor young lass. Some part of me went to the grave with my Albert, God rest him,' Mrs Hayes said in a tone Molly had never heard her use before. 'But she's young and the young are resilient and she has her life ahead of her. She'll get over it in time.'

'It will take a long, long time. I've never seen her like this.'

'Have you spoken to her about coming back to live with you?'

'No, but I know she says she'll never, never set foot in the house in Ladysmith Road again. She says she couldn't bear it. Everything in it would remind her of him and all the happy times. She says she'd go out of her mind and I think she's right.'

'And there's too much of him at his mother's home and Nellie

O'Sullivan's house is out of the question, so she'll be better off with us. I can keep my eye on her when you're at work.'

Molly nodded. 'I'll try and get her to come home with us after . . . after it's all over.'

'And is that young man of yours putting in an appearance today?' The tone was sharp again.

'He said he'd try his best although it might be difficult.' Molly had only seen Billy twice since Jimmy's death. She knew he hadn't liked Jimmy but she hoped that he would come today, out of consideration to Bernie and herself. She also knew that he would be far from happy about Bernie moving back in with her.

Molly was touched by the crowds of people who followed the funeral procession along Scotland Road to the church. The traffic was at a standstill and even the ordinary passers-by stopped, took off their caps or crossed themselves. Throughout the Mass she glanced at Bernie, just eighteen years old and so small, so pale in her black dress, veil, shoes and stockings. So very young to be a widow. Almost like a child dressed in widow's weeds, she thought. But she was holding up well, so far.

When they filed out into the churchyard she caught sight of Billy and smiled wanly at him. He nodded back, but was then lost in the press of people and she turned her thoughts back to Bernie. This was going to be the hardest part of the day.

Bernie had felt totally numb up to now. Even though the sun was warm she'd felt cold. In the church she had shivered a few times and Ma had put her arm around her. But now as she saw for the first time the heavy brown earth that had been piled to one side of the grave a tide of misery engulfed her. He had gone; he had really gone. He was never coming back to her. He would never hold her, kiss her or love her again. She would never hear his voice, his laughter or his occasional curses. Her Jimmy was dead and now they were going to place him in the earth. It was no use trying to believe that his soul had gone to heaven, that he was looking down on her and would always protect her, as Father Ryan had said. She couldn't believe it, not now. There was only darkness, weariness and utter despair ahead of her. She could feel it pressing down on her, enveloping her and she was falling, falling into the darkness where they had lowered her Jimmy.

'Molly, quick, help me catch her!' Despite her own grief Flo McCauley had been watching Bernie and saw her begin to sway.

Molly caught her friend around the waist and the older woman also supported her.

Mrs Hayes delved into her battered black leather handbag and brought out a small bottle of smelling salts, which she passed over to Molly.

'Hold it under her nose, Molly,' she instructed.

'Sit her down, Flo. Put her head between her knees,' Nellie advised. 'An' move back a bit, give her some air.'

The mourners drew back a little and Molly dropped to her knees beside Bernie. 'It's all right, Bernie. You fainted. Sit up slowly now.'

The darkness was beginning to recede and Bernie just felt dizzy.

'Hold on to my hand now, Bernadette. Give yourself time, child.' Father Ryan too was beside her.

'What'll we do now, Flo? She's in no state fer the funeral tea.' Nellie was gravely concerned.

'She needs to rest. She needs some time to recover, somewhere quiet,' Father Ryan advised.

Bernie felt as though she was being stifled. She clutched Molly's hand. 'Moll, I have to get away from everyone! I can't stand all this. I can't breathe.'

Mrs Hayes stepped in. 'Father, can I ask you to arrange for some transport to take her back to my house?'

Nellie glared at her. 'What's the point of draggin' her all the way ter Arnot Street? Won't she be better goin' ter Flo's?'

'She'll have no peace and quiet there with everyone in and out,' the old lady snapped determinedly. The poor girl was in no state to cope with the customs that followed a traditional Irish Catholic funeral. She had been through enough already today. The poor child – and she was little more than that – needed looking after.

'Ladies, please don't let this degenerate into an argument,' the priest pleaded. Everyone's grief was raw and at such times tempers were short. 'What do you think, Florence? Would you be upset if Bernadette went back with Mary?'

Flo McCauley looked anxiously up at her husband who put his arm around her and nodded.

'No, I wouldn't be upset, Father. She *does* need rest.'

Thankfully Molly helped Bernie to her feet. At least she hadn't had to suggest it and for once she was very glad of Mrs Hayes's interference. Sometimes she wasn't an old dragon at all. She had a kind heart.

'Then I'll have a word with Tom Coyne. I'm sure he'll be only too glad to take the three of you there in one of his cars.' Father Ryan looked around for the undertaker and, catching his eye, made his way towards him.

With the help of the parish priest, Nellie and the undertaker, the little group was shepherded towards a funeral car. Bernie and the old lady were helped inside and Molly was thanking Nellie and promising to keep her informed of Bernie's progress when Billy tapped her on the shoulder.

'Can I have a private word with you, Molly?'

Nellie looked far from pleased but she said nothing and walked back to Mr and Mrs McCauley.

Billy guided Molly away from the car. 'What's going on? Is she all right?'

'She's far from all right, Billy! She collapsed with the grief of it all. She needs rest and peace and quiet, away from all the memories.'

'Is she going back to Fazakerley then?'

Molly just stared at him. Hadn't he heard her? Hadn't he understood at all? 'No. Didn't I just say she can't face anything that reminds her of him? She can't go back there. She'll never go back there.'

'But it's her home! She's got all that stuff. Where's she going to live?'

'With me.'

'For how long?' Billy was becoming annoyed.

'For as long as she wants to.'

'But what about us, Molly?' he demanded.

'We'll manage, Billy, we did before.'

'Molly, are you ready? We can't expect Mr Coyne to hang around all day. He has other engagements, I'm sure,' Mrs Hayes called impatiently from the car.

Molly turned away. 'I'll see you next Sunday, Billy,' she called over her shoulder.

Billy thrust his hands into the pockets of his trousers and stepped back, annoyed. Did she really think that they could carry on as before with Bernie in the house? He wasn't happy about this at all.

Chapter Twenty-Four

———•➤•◆•◄•———

MOLLY WAS SERIOUSLY WORRIED about Bernie. She was very depressed and alternated between bouts of abject miserable silence and terrible sobbing. Except for the fact that Mrs Hayes bullied her into eating she would have starved and Molly knew that she hardly tasted what she dutifully swallowed. Each night when she got home from work she would go first to see the old lady and ask how Bernie had been that day. She hated to leave her but there was no help for it.

Both Nellie and Flo McCauley had called to see Bernie. Nellie was still not entirely happy that Bernie was alone for most of the day with the landlady, a woman she considered to be not particularly sympathetic. Flo tried her best to comfort Bernie and rally her spirits but she was battling with her own grief and loss.

'I think she'd be better off with people around her an' people what care about her,' Nellie said to Flo after their last visit.

'Molly does care about her an' so does the old lady, in her way. At least she's makin' her eat,' Flo had answered dispiritedly.

On Friday night when Molly got home Mrs Hayes informed her that Bernie had gone to bed. She'd cried for nearly the whole afternoon and was totally exhausted.

'I gave her some hot milk and two aspirins and when I looked in she was fast asleep. Don't go disturbing her. She gets little enough sleep.'

Molly sat down at the kitchen table and eased off her shoes. It had been a long, hot, weary day.

'There's fresh tea in the pot and a slice of ginger cake. I want to talk to you.'

Molly helped herself to both and hoped she wasn't in for a lecture of some kind. She was in no mood for that.

'I know it's very early days but have you any idea what she is going to do with that house?'

'She won't go back.'

'That's not what I'm saying. It's full of furniture which can't stay there for ever, and no doubt the council will want the house to rent to someone else. I know it's not been long, but she is paying rent on it and I doubt she can afford it.'

Molly sighed. The old lady was right. She didn't know if Bernie could afford it, but how could she possibly broach the subject to her friend?

'I thought I'd write to the council and explain the position and see what they have to say. They could at least give her a few weeks' grace.'

Molly nodded. 'She has some really nice things there.'

'Which may well come to the attention of thieves.'

'I suppose I could pack some things up and bring them here. Is there anywhere we can store them? I don't want her to get upset.'

'We could put them up in the attic until she decides what she wants to do. I did mention it to her but she said she just couldn't think about it now. It will cost money to put the heavy furniture into storage but at least it will be well looked after and out of sight. Heller's on County Road would take it. It's a reputable place.'

Molly thought about their financial position. Now that Jimmy was dead Bernie had no money except what they had managed to save and the funeral expenses would have to come out of that. She herself had very little in the way of savings and now she would have to work to keep them both until such time as Bernie could think about getting a job, or maybe even going back to Mrs Montrose, if her former employer hadn't found someone else. She had wondered if it would help Bernie to go home to Tess for a visit but that now seemed out of the question with the expense of storing the furniture. 'How much would Heller's charge?' she asked.

'I'll go along tomorrow and ask them and perhaps on Sunday we can go out to Fazakerley and pack some things up and bring them back. Maybe that cousin of hers would come and sit with her? Her husband could come and give us a hand?'

Molly nodded. 'As long as I'm back by teatime; I'm going out in the evening.'

'With that young feller who insisted on talking to you?'

'Yes. I'll call and see Nellie on my way to work in the morning.'

The old lady didn't comment but she hadn't liked the look of him at all. Far too flash in her opinion and he certainly had no manners, haranguing Molly like that at such a time.

Nellie thought it was a good idea and agreed to come and visit Bernie on Sunday after lunch. She said Matty would be delighted to help them.

The house had such a desolate look, Molly thought as she let herself in with Bernie's key. It was as though somehow the tragedy of losing Jimmy had seeped into the walls. Everything was a little dusty for nothing had been moved since that terrible night when Bernie had left for ever. It had been Molly herself who had come to collect a few clothes and things for Bernie. That morning she had scraped the cold, congealed mess that had been Jimmy's supper into the bin in the yard.

'Where shall we start?' she asked the old lady.

'Mr O'Sullivan, will you bring those boxes in here, please?' Mrs Hayes asked sharply for Matty was standing in the hall looking sheepishly around at the rugs and fine furniture. 'Molly, you start on the crockery and the vases and I'll get the things from the kitchen.'

Matty placed a pile of boxes on the table. 'What will ye be doing with the poor young feller's clothes?'

Molly bit her lip and looked at the old lady. 'Will she want to keep them?'

Mrs Hayes shook her head. 'I doubt it but let's not be too hasty.

Mr O'Sullivan, would you be so kind as to pack them up? Maybe we should ask his mother and father what they think we should do with them? His mother might like them.'

Tears started in Molly's eyes. Oh, this was so awful. All this sorting out and packing up had a pitiful finality to it; she was glad that Bernie didn't have to do it. Of course she would have to make some decisions in the future but at least she wouldn't have to make them here.

Matty had to make two journeys back to Arnot Street and it was almost six o'clock when all three of them made the final trip. Nellie had made sure that everything had been put into Mrs Hayes's bedroom, from where it would be transferred to the attic by Matty and Molly on Monday night.

'How has she been?' Molly asked of Nellie.

'Still very down, luv. Won't speak, just stares at the wall. Oh, it's hard work tryin' ter find the words that might give her a bit of hope.'

'I know,' Molly replied sadly.

'Molly, put the kettle on. I'm sure we could all do with a cup of tea.' Mrs Hayes glanced at Matty and the corners of her mouth lifted in a wry smile. 'I'm sure you'd appreciate something stronger but I'm afraid there's only tea.'

'Ah, I would so, ma'am, and if you don't object I'll be after having a quick pint in that pub we passed on the top road.'

'Well, I object, Matty O'Sullivan, so tea will be just fine,' Nellie stated firmly. Trust him to show her up by wanting to leg it off to the pub.

By the time they'd had the tea and some scones and Nellie and Matty had departed Molly realised that she was going to be late meeting Billy.

'I'm just going out for a few hours, Bernie,' she said, squeezing her friend's clammy hand, not even wanting to mention that she was seeing Billy in case it upset her.

Bernie just bowed her head and Molly dashed upstairs. She had a quick wash, changed her clothes, brushed her hair and jammed on her best hat. If she ran all the way and caught a tram for the few stops to Spellow Lane she wouldn't have kept him waiting too long.

Despite the fact that she only had to wait a few minutes for a tram, she was almost a quarter of an hour late. He hated to be kept waiting. 'Hanging around like a corner boy' was how he put it.

As she alighted she looked swiftly around. The road wasn't busy at this time on a Sunday evening and people who were going to the dance at Blair Hall hadn't really started to arrive yet. There was no sign of him and she bit her lip. Had he become impatient and walked off? She stood outside the entrance to the Co-op, her usual place, and looked around. It was still very warm and she wondered if he had gone into the pub opposite for a shandy. He wasn't a heavy drinker. Should she go and see? She shrugged: no, she wasn't going to go into a pub looking for him and risk being asked to leave. She did look a bit older than her eighteen years but she certainly didn't look over twenty-one and some publicans were very fussy.

She walked up and down for a few minutes, looking eagerly at every young man who came into sight, and then suddenly she felt cold, remembering how Bernie had waited in vain for Jimmy. Oh, had Billy had an accident? Had he been hit by a lorry or a tram?

Stop it! she told herself firmly. He was just late, that's all. He must have been delayed. Maybe he'd had to wait for ages for a tram; sometimes you did on a Sunday. They weren't as frequent on Sundays.

She examined her appearance in the shop window and then glanced up at the ornate clock set into the small squat tower on the roof of the building. He was really late. He'd never been this late before. She began to wonder just how long she should wait for him. Was he going to come at all or was she being stood up? No, he wouldn't do that to her. But where was he?

After an hour and fifteen minutes she finally admitted to herself that he wasn't coming. People were now pushing past her and crowding the entrance to the dance hall and their happy, excited faces and laughter made her feel even more miserable. Her head was aching and her eyes stung with incipient tears. Why? Why had he done this to her? He knew how terribly distressed she'd been over Jimmy and Bernie. How could he upset her even more by leaving her standing here? She needed him to hold her and comfort her and he'd just deserted her. Abandoned her when she needed him most.

She caught a tram home and walked slowly down the street. She couldn't say anything to Bernie and wouldn't to Mrs Hayes either. Oh, it was so hurtful and humiliating. She'd been fully aware of some of the pitying glances she'd attracted from young women on the arms of their young men. Glances that said: 'Poor thing, she's been stood up.' She kept asking herself why and then she remembered their last conversation. Was he angry that Bernie was back living with her? Was that the reason? Had he realised that now Bernie would have no money and that she would have to keep them both and wouldn't be looking for somewhere else to live? Oh, surely, surely not? He couldn't be *that* insensitive, *that* selfish. He loved her, he must know how she felt and how loyal she was to Bernie. But did he? Never once had he actually said, 'I love you, Molly.' As she tried to put the key in the front door she realised she couldn't see the lock. Her tears were blinding her.

'You're back early,' Bernie said quietly as Molly took off her hat and threw it on the sideboard.

She swallowed hard. 'I just didn't feel in the humour for an outing,' she managed to get out. 'It's so sultry out there and I've got a headache. I think I'll see if Herself has some aspirins and then I'll have an early night. Is there anything you want, Bernie?'

Bernie shook her head. Even in her grief she could see that Molly was seriously upset. It must be something to do with Billy Marshall, she thought tiredly, but she was too heartsore to press Molly on it.

Molly gave the same excuse to the old lady, who just nodded and handed her two small white tablets. 'Wring a cloth out in some cold water and place it on your forehead. It might help a little. It is very humid tonight. We could do with a good storm to clear the air.'

It was something her mam often said in hot weather and suddenly Molly wanted Ita's shoulder to cry on. She wanted her mam to hug her and soothe her the way she had when she'd been a child and had hurt herself.

'I think I'll go on up,' she choked.

'Molly, it's nothing to the way poor Bernie feels and you'll get over him,' the old lady said quietly.

Molly could bear it no longer. She rushed from the room and up the stairs to fling herself face down on the bed, sobbing as though her heart would break.

Chapter Twenty-Five

———•◦✦◦•———

MOLLY HEARD NOTHING AT all from him during the next two weeks. She had hoped that he might send her a note or even call at the house. She had never felt so utterly miserable in her life and there was no one at all she could turn to. Her pride wouldn't let her show her dejection and humiliation in front of either Mrs Hayes or Nellie. She just got through each day as best she could, always hoping against hope that there just might be some word from him.

At the beginning of the following month when the blistering August heat seemed to be stifling the city and Nellie was despairing of the dirt and the flies and the stench, Bernie announced that she wanted to go home to see Tess. The house in Ladysmith Road had been let to new tenants and all her furniture was in storage, paid for in advance out of the five pounds Ellen Montrose had given her as a wedding gift.

'I wish I could come with you,' Molly said after she'd heard Bernie's decision.

'You can't, Molly. You've your work and besides, I won't be much company.'

'That wouldn't matter, you know that.' Molly wished with all her heart that she could have gone but they were very busy at work with a big order for a house in Newsham Park. She felt that these days it was only because she worked so hard that she stayed in any way sane.

'I have to try to get on with life, Molly. You've all been telling me that and I know you're right but it's so hard. I thought maybe Mam could help me.'

'Won't it upset you when you go to Mass in Killina?'

Bernie nodded. 'But I have to face things and people and learn to live with the memories. Ma says in time they'll become less and less painful and one day I might even treasure them. I don't know if it's something she believes herself or if it's just something someone's told her, but I have to have something to cling to. I have to believe there is some hope for the future even when I feel I just want to die myself. I'll never, never stop loving him and missing him.'

Molly squeezed her hand, tears in her own eyes. 'Of course you won't. And if you're really sure about going back then we'll find the money from somewhere.'

'I am so and don't worry about the money, I've got enough left for my return fare and to pay Mam for my keep. When I come back, I'll have to think about work.'

'You know your home here will be waiting for you and I might have been able to have saved a bit so there's no rush about finding a job.'

'I don't want to be a burden to you, Molly, and I have been.'

'You *haven't*! You've never been a burden. You're my friend, you always have been and you always will be.'

'I'll tell Ma and Nellie next time they come.'

'They'll both be glad that you're feeling a bit better.'

'I wish I was, Molly, I really do but the truth is I'm not. And when I think about the ferry and crossing the waters of Liverpool Bay where he . . . died, I . . . I . . . think I might lose the run of myself entirely.'

Molly was alarmed. 'Bernie, you won't do anything stupid, will you? Oh, maybe Ma should go with you or even Nellie.' The ferry crossing might prove too much of an ordeal for Bernie. She might just snap.

'No. I . . . I'm too much of a coward. Oh, I've thought about it but I know I couldn't do it – and nor would Jimmy want me to. And if I did I'd never see him again in the next world.'

'Are you sure you want to go alone?' Molly pressed.

'It's something I have to face, Molly. I'll be all right, but what about you?' Bernie answered a little shakily.

'Me? Sure, I'm fine. We're just so busy at work that I'm worn out when I get home and the heat doesn't help.'

'You don't go out much.'

'Haven't I just told you I'm too tired? Now, you just rest while I go and tell Herself back there that you've decided to go to see your mam for a few weeks.'

Everyone was very relieved that Bernie seemed to be trying to come to terms with her loss although Molly impressed upon them that it was still very early days. She reminded them that Bernie faced more heartbreak when she returned for the first time to the church where she had been married and had to listen to the condolences of the Parish, sincere though they would be. She wondered too how much help Tess could be.

They'd all gone to see her off and Molly thought again how young, pale and child-like Bernie looked in her black mourning dress and hat.

'I just hope ter God it's goin' ter do her good,' Nellie said as they watched Bernie climb the gangway.

'I've done what I can but it's her mam she really needs,' Flo McCauley added.

'Yer couldn't have done more, Flo. At least she won't have ter put up with the heat an' stink of this city.'

'No, it's a lovely little place. Fresh air, green fields, peace an' quiet.'

'We could all do with some of that, Flo. Come on, let's go an' get the tram.'

Molly walked with them to the tram terminus; already she felt lonely without her friend, even though Bernie hadn't been much company lately – through no fault of her own.

'Look, Flo, it says there that the *Berengaria* will be open ter the public fer two days next week. Wouldn't it be great ter go an' see over her, see how the posh people travel?' Nellie drew their attention to a poster on the wall by the station for the overhead railway. It depicted the Cunard liner, reputed to be the biggest and most luxurious in the world, having once been the private property of the German Kaiser. 'Molly, luv, go an' ask that feller in the ticket office how much it'll cost.'

Flo looked at her in some confusion, knowing that neither of them had the time or money to spare for such things.

'I had ter get her out of the way,' Nellie hissed, jerking her head meaningfully. 'Look who's walkin' past the door of the Liver Building.'

Flo's gaze alighted on Billy Marshall and the laughing dark-haired girl he had his arm around. 'Poor Molly! Does she know?'

'I don't think so but she's better off without him, the swine! He's no bloody good an' your Jimmy, God rest him, knew it.'

'He did an' he always said she could do better. Well, now I hope she finds someone decent.'

'Thank God they've turned the corner. She's comin' back,' Nellie said with relief.

'He said it's one and sixpence for an adult and ninepence for a child,' Molly informed them. 'And to get there early because there's bound to be big queues.'

'Not with prices like that. It's extortion. Come on, let's be gettin' home.' Nellie took Molly's arm and propelled her towards the waiting tram, sincerely hoping that Billy Marshall and his new lady love were halfway up George's Dock Gate by now.

The hot sultry days dragged for Molly. She missed Bernie as each night she sat alone in the living room, dispirited and often restless. Occasionally Mrs Hayes would knock and ask her did she want a cup of tea and Molly would try to make conversation but it wasn't easy, particularly as the old lady often seemed to be living in the past.

This evening she had written to Bernie and had walked up the road to the red pillarbox on the corner to post it; at least the short walk killed a few minutes. She'd wash the detachable collar of her work dress and the stockings she'd worn today and then go to bed, she thought wearily.

'Molly, I've the kettle on and I'd be very obliged if you could hold some skeins of wool for me while I wind it into a couple of balls,' the old lady greeted her.

Molly managed a smile. It was tiring sitting with the loose skeins held over outstretched arms but she couldn't refuse.

'What are you knitting now?' she asked, fingering the fine two-ply pale blue wool.

'A matinée coat for Mrs Halliday's grandson. Her Ida had a baby boy on Monday,' Mrs Hayes replied, pouring the boiling water into the teapot.

Molly nodded. Mrs Halliday lived two doors up.

'We'll let that brew while we do the first skein.'

Molly dutifully draped the wool over her forearms. At least it was only a matinée coat so there wouldn't be too much to wind.

'You know sometimes I think Bernie might have been able to bear her loss more easily if there had been a child. She would always have had a part of him with her. But then I think it might have been worse. She's so young to have to bring up a child alone. I know what it's like. My Albert was only fifty-two when he died and my youngest was still at school.'

'I know she was hoping for one but . . .'

Mrs Hayes sighed heavily. 'No time. They had so little time together, but I'm sure when she comes back she'll feel much better, more able to cope and pick up the threads of her life.'

'I hope so. I hate to see her so miserable.'

'She *will* get over it, Molly, although it might take her years. She might even meet someone else.'

'Oh, I don't think she will ever love anyone else.'

'You are both very young and when you're young you think broken hearts never mend but they do. The pair of you have lifetimes ahead, who knows what the future holds for you both?'

Molly didn't want to go down this path. Her heart too was broken.

'Maybe when Bernie's much better Mrs Montrose might take her back. It was Mr Montrose who said that Bernie working after she was married was an affront to Jimmy's pride.'

'And who is to say he was wrong? But that woman was very good to Bernie.'

'I think she was very fond of her. She sent a lovely card and flowers and then a letter saying if Bernie ever needed anything she shouldn't hesitate to go to her. So, maybe she will take her back.'

Mrs Hayes finished the first ball, placed it in her knitting bag and then poured out the tea. 'Of course she might be better trying for something else. She will need to get out and meet people, mix more, not be alone with just Ellen Montrose all day. I expect you find plenty to chat about with the women and girls you work with?'

'I do so, although lately we've barely had time to talk, we've been so busy with that grand house in Newsham Park.'

'They must have plenty of money to be refurbishing a place like that. Those houses are enormous.'

'Mrs Stanley told me he's a judge.'

'He'd need to be. Now, let's get on with the winding.'

Half an hour later Molly finally made her way upstairs. The wool had been wound, the dishes cleared and her collar and stockings washed, rinsed and hung out on the line in the yard.

The bedroom was still warm and she pushed the window open wider. Why did the old lady think Bernie would be better mixing more? Why was she so sure Bernie would get over Jimmy and even find someone else? Was she trying to tell her that she was better off without Billy, that her heart would mend and she'd find someone else too? She sat down on the bed and began to take off her blouse. Would Bernie have been able to cope more easily if she had had a child? Would Jimmy's baby have been a great comfort to her or would it have been a terrible burden?

The word 'baby' stuck in her mind for some reason. And then she realised why. She clutched her stomach as a wave of sheer terror washed over her. Oh, God! She'd had no curse for almost two months. Over the past dreadful, chaotic weeks she had simply forgotten. She was pregnant! Oh, what was she going to do now? It was the worst thing that could possibly happen to her. She had been so stupid.

She crumpled up and lay on the bed, shaking. She hadn't seen or heard from Billy in weeks. He didn't know, how could he? He'd promised it would be all right, that this wouldn't, *couldn't* happen and she'd believed him. She'd trusted him implicitly. She'd loved him; she still loved him. The initial panic was wearing off. She wasn't the first girl to find herself in this predicament. He would have to marry her now; he would *want* to marry her. She was certain he would be delighted, once he got over the initial shock. His parents wouldn't be very happy but, well, he was over twenty-one, he didn't need their consent.

She sat up and wrapped her arms around her knees and breathed deeply. It would all turn out fine in the end. He was just angry with her for putting Bernie before him. She was certain he loved her and now ... now ... she *would* be getting married. She'd go to his house after work tomorrow night and tell him and then they could start to make plans.

Chapter Twenty-Six

MOLLY FELT A LITTLE sick next morning but after a drink of cold water she felt better. She hadn't slept much the previous night, she'd had too much on her mind; now she felt quite drained and there was a long day ahead of her. Before she left she informed the old lady that she would probably be a bit late in tonight as she had something rather important to attend to.

'Calling in to see Nellie?' Mrs Hayes asked.

'Yes, I might just do that too,' Molly answered as breezily as she could. She wasn't looking forward to having to tell her landlady that she would be getting married very soon.

As she walked up the road she thought that she wasn't really relishing telling anyone. There would be shock, upset and disappointment on the part of her parents, maybe even anger from her da. She knew people would talk about how foolish and sinful she'd been and she'd get a desperate lecture from the priest but the person she most dreaded telling was Bernie. How could she expect Bernie to be happy for her? Bernie didn't like Billy and had once tried to warn her how unsuitable he was. Even though it would have to be a very quiet wedding – there would be no white crêpe de Chine for her – it would bring heart-rending memories flooding back to her friend.

The day seemed to have no end, she thought at lunchtime when she gratefully sank down into a seat in the small canteen. All morning she had been trying to go over and over in her mind just exactly what she would say to Billy but she was often interrupted and found it hard to concentrate. Now she was feeling very tired;

she was also a little light-headed but she put this down to the fact
that she'd had no breakfast. Mrs Stanley had been quite sharp with
her when they had been checking the number of curtains and
cushion covers that were to be packed up for the big house in
Newsham Park and she'd felt tears stinging her eyes. She'd realised
that she'd have to leave her job soon and that Mrs Stanley would be
very disappointed in her, especially after giving her all that training
and the chance of promotion, which would now be totally wasted.
She enjoyed her work most of the time and would be sorry to leave.
Then she'd thought about her mam's suggestion. She could perhaps
set up a business herself when the baby was older, if Billy agreed.
She'd like that and it would be extra money for them, and as she'd
work from home there wouldn't be any question of Billy's pride
being harmed.

At last it was closing time and thankfully she tidied the cards of
braid and the tiebacks, and put away the rolls of furnishing fabric
that had been left out.

'You can sort out those sample books in the morning, Miss
Keegan,' the manageress said rather more kindly, thinking the girl
looked exhausted and washed out. They'd all been working hard
and she knew Molly was worried about her friend.

'I will so, Mrs Stanley, thank you.'

'Goodnight.'

'Goodnight. Let's hope this weather breaks soon. It's very tiring,'
Molly answered.

She had to wait almost half an hour for a tram to Everton Valley.
They were all full and even when she eventually managed to get on
one it was crowded. The waiting hadn't helped her mood: she had
butterflies in her stomach and the beginning of a headache. How
she wished it was all over and settled. Only then could she really in
any way feel relieved, relaxed and happy.

It was growing dark when she finally walked towards the
Marshalls' house and she began to panic. What if he was out? What
would she say? Would she have to wait on the street corner until he
came home? She hesitated for a few seconds and when she finally

reached up for the doorknocker her hand was shaking. Oh, please let him be in, she prayed.

Billy opened the door and she felt relief wash over her.

He was annoyed and suspicious. 'What do you want, Molly?' he asked in a loud whisper, glancing back over his shoulder down the lobby, hoping she hadn't come to cause a scene.

'Billy, I have to talk to you. It's desperately important.'

'I can't talk to you now. You know what they're like.' He jerked his head in the direction of the kitchen.

'You *have* to! Can't you ask me in?' Molly pleaded.

'No! And I'd have thought you'd have got the message by now.'

Molly misunderstood him. 'What message? I've had no letter or note from you. When did you send it?' Oh, she'd known he would have tried to get in touch with her, to say he was sorry.

'I mean we're finished, it's over between us. I'm courting someone else.'

She stared at him blankly. 'Billy, it can't be. You don't understand. You've . . . We've got to get married,' she blurted out.

Billy looked at her with even greater suspicion. 'What are you saying, Molly?'

'I'm . . . I'm expecting and you know it's yours.' Oh, she hadn't wanted to tell him like this. She'd wanted him to take her inside, sit her down and let her explain gradually.

Billy grabbed her arm and hustled her down the steps, closing the front door behind him.

'Where are we going?' Molly pleaded.

'Up to the top of the street. I don't want all the neighbours hanging out of their windows with their ears flapping.'

When they reached the corner Molly stopped under the street-light.

'Billy, did you hear what I said? Do you understand?'

'I heard you all right.' He was stunned.

Molly plunged on. 'So you see we have to get married – and soon – but everything will be just great, I know it will, when they all get used to the idea. I love you and I know you love me. Oh, I understand why you were angry with me about Bernie but it couldn't be helped. She's gone to visit her mam now. Billy, I love you so much, say everything is going to be fine?' She flung her arms around his neck.

Billy stared ahead of him, making no attempt to touch her. The stupid little bitch! The conniving little madam! She'd done this on purpose. He'd been sure she'd been doing something to make sure she didn't get pregnant; other girls did. She was just trying to trap him. Was she even telling the truth? Well, it wasn't going to work. He didn't love her and he wasn't going to marry her – he didn't want to marry anyone, not for years. But his da would kill him if he found out about this. He pulled her arms from around his neck.

'I'm not going to marry you, Molly. You're not going to trap me like this. You knew what you were doing. You should have made sure this didn't happen. I don't love you. We had our bit of fun but it's over. I just told you I'm seeing someone else. Go home. Go back to Ireland like your friend. Don't come knocking on my door again. I never want to set eyes on you again.'

Molly felt as though he had physically slapped her across the face. She reeled backwards and screamed, a cry of pure pain and shock. No! No! It couldn't be true. He couldn't just abandon her like this. She wasn't trying to trap him. She loved him, she'd given herself to him and she'd trusted him to take care of her and now . . .

'Billy! Billy, don't do this to me!' she begged, clutching his arm, tears streaming down her cheeks.

He flung off her grip. 'Tears won't wash with me, Molly! Go home. I'm going back now before they come looking for me.'

In total disbelief she watched him turn and walk quickly away. She slumped back against the wall. Oh, God! What was she going to do now?

A woman came around the corner and stared hard at her. 'Are yer all right, luv? Has someone upset yer, like?'

'I'm fine. I . . . I . . . really am,' Molly choked and turned and ran blindly across the road, narrowly missing being hit by a lorry, which swerved to avoid her. The driver yelled at her but she didn't even hear him. She ran on and on until she could go no further. Fighting for her breath she half fell into a shop doorway, her legs buckling beneath her. Oh, she could run for ever but she could never get away from the terrible predicament she was in. She was a single pregnant girl and he wouldn't marry her. She was ruined. Society would condemn and shun her. She couldn't even begin to think about what her mam and da would say and do. Her Church would have no pity or absolution. She would lose her job, her home, *everything*! Even Bernie would be ashamed of her. How cruelly she had been betrayed, used and cast aside. There was nothing left in life now – *nothing*. She couldn't, wouldn't think about the child she was carrying. She hated it. No, that wasn't true, she hated herself. She despised herself.

She crouched there sobbing and gasping for breath for what seemed like hours until at last she had made up her mind. There was only one thing she could do to end her torment. She would go down to the Pier Head, walk on to the Landing Stage, slip under the chain fence at the river's edge and step off. It wouldn't take long. The water was deep and murky and it would be over soon. All the terrible pain and guilt and shame would be finished. It was a sin but she wouldn't think about that. Bernie had said she was too much of a coward to take her own life but Bernie had never had to face what Molly had been forced to face this night. It would be another dreadful blow to her friend but she was sure that when Bernie found out what Billy Marshall had done, she wouldn't blame her.

Molly stared blankly ahead of her as the tram rattled through the city streets towards the Pier Head. The conductor spoke to her but she didn't answer him, she just held out her fare. There weren't many people around when she got off and walked slowly down the floating roadway. There were two ships tied up at the George's Landing Stage: the Isle of Man ferry *Mona's Isle* and the Birkenhead ferryboat *Mountwood*. A few people were standing watching the ships out in the river; it was a pleasant evening with a slight breeze. Molly didn't notice anything. She just felt cold as she walked on.

She skirted both ferries and walked to the furthest end of the Stage. She stood for a few seconds looking down at the inky black water, the wavelets that lapped the wooden posts iridescent with a film of grease and engine oil. The only barrier was a low, single-link chain hung between posts. She stepped over it. The water was cold and despite herself she cried out and began to thrash about, then she was sinking. The water closed over her head; it filled her mouth, her nose and her ears and she forced herself not to try to swim.

'Jesus Christ! She's gone in!' a man yelled from the Landing Stage, rushing forward.

A woman began to scream as she caught sight of Molly in the water.

Tearing off his tunic and thrusting both it and his helmet into the arms of the half-hysterical woman, the young dock policeman dived head first into the river. His boots were hampering him, as was the heavy serge of his trousers and his blue cotton shirt, but he struck out strongly and grabbed Molly by her shoulder.

Two other men had joined the man who had raised the alarm and one of them dragged the heavy cork ring from its hook and flung it in, hanging on to the rope to which it was attached.

'Grab it, lad! Grab it an' we'll pull yer in!' he yelled.

Constable Joe Jackson made a grab for it, caught it and hung on with his left hand, his right hand locked almost around Molly's neck.

They were both dragged out, Joe coughing and spluttering, Molly limp and pale, her hair plastered to her skull.

'Turn her over. Is she breathing?' Joe gasped.

'Just, lad.'

Joe began to try to pump the water from Molly's lungs while in the distance they all heard the clanging of an ambulance bell. The captain of the *Mona's Isle* had seen what had happened and had raised the alarm at the dock police station.

Molly began to cough.

'She'll live, thank God! They'll give yer a medal fer this, lad,' the man who had thrown the lifebelt said quietly.

'I don't want a bloody medal! It's my job. Direct that ambulance down here. Let's get her to hospital.'

'Yer'll 'ave ter go too, lad, yer must have swallowed a few gallons of that water and it's bloody filthy. God knows what yer could 'ave caught!'

'Don't worry about me, I've the constitution of an ox or so my mam says.' Joe managed a grin but inside he was shaking. He'd never had to do this before and at first he'd thought she was dead. He climbed into the ambulance after the stretcher and sat down, wrapping a blanket around himself. She was so young. What the hell had made her do it? More to the point, what was he going to do about her? Suicide was a crime but in his opinion she must have suffered enough already – only someone truly desperate would try to drown themselves. And she'd very nearly succeeded. Should he say she slipped and fell? Maybe when she recovered she would talk to him, tell him just what had driven her to it. He dropped his head in his hands, shock and exhaustion taking its toll.

Chapter Twenty-Seven

———◆►◀◆———

MOLLY OPENED HER EYES slowly and looked around. Where was she? What had happened?

'It's all right, you're safe. You're in the Royal Infirmary. You swallowed a lot of water so they're keeping you in overnight. They're keeping me here too.'

Molly closed her eyes as she remembered everything. She had failed and failed miserably. She had tried so hard but now it looked as if things had got worse. Why else would a policeman be sitting beside her?

'You slipped and fell in, didn't you?' Joe said quietly. Even though she was so pale and obviously distraught he thought she was a very pretty girl.

Molly shook her head, tears seeping from under her closed eyelids. She was just too drained to reply.

'You *did*!' Joe repeated emphatically.

Molly slowly opened her eyes and looked up at him. He was young, probably about twenty-two. He had short dark brown hair and the brown eyes that were looking down at her were full of concern.

'You . . . you pulled me out?'

'I did. You were lucky someone saw you *fall* and that I was just a few feet away and that the captain of the *Mona's Isle* was also very observant. A few more minutes and you'd have gone.'

Molly turned her head away. A few more minutes and everything would have been over if he hadn't intervened. 'I can swim,' she said tiredly.

'You see, you must have slipped. What's your name and where do you live?'

'Molly Keegan and I live in Arnot Street.'

'On your own?' Joe pressed.

'No. I lodge with an elderly lady.'

'Haven't you got any family?'

At the thought of her parents Molly covered her face with her hands and began to sob. She desperately wanted to throw herself into her mam's arms but, oh, her mam would be so ashamed of her and her da would be furious.

Joe reached down and took her hands. He felt so sorry for her. She appeared to be on her own. 'What happened to you, Molly? What's so bad that you could see no other way?'

'Sure, isn't there only one thing so . . . so terrible that can happen to someone like me?' she sobbed.

'Hush now, hush or you'll have Sister down on us like a ton of bricks and she'll chase me back to the men's ward. I'm only allowed in here in my "official capacity".' He smiled at her and wiped her face with his handkerchief. 'You're Irish, aren't you? Is your family over there?'

Molly nodded. He was being very kind.

'Don't you have any friends here?'

'My best friend has gone home for a visit but even Bernie will be so ashamed of me, she really will.'

Joe wasn't a fool. He knew exactly what she'd meant. Some lad had put her in the family way.

'No boyfriend? No fiancé?' he probed gently.

Molly groaned as she thought of Billy Marshall's callous betrayal. Oh, what was the point of trying to pretend? 'Not . . . not any more.'

Joe nodded slowly. 'What did he say? You *did* tell him?'

'I did but he . . . he said it was just a bit of *fun*! But I . . . I loved him. I believed him when he said he wouldn't let anything happen to me and now . . .' She couldn't go on.

It was such an old story, Joe thought. Why did they let themselves be duped like that? 'Sounds as though you're better off without him,' he mused without really thinking of the impact his words would have on her.

'Without a husband? Without a father for my . . . baby? Do you know what will happen to me? If I go home I'll be put away in an Industrial School and if I stay it will be a home for Fallen Girls and Women. I had a good job, a nice home, a future, now I have *nothing*. You should have left me to drown.' She began to cry again.

'I'm so sorry but I couldn't do that.' He felt so helpless. He was certain she was a decent girl who had just been naïve and trusting and some no-mark had taken advantage of that, but Authority in all its forms wouldn't be as tolerant as he was. 'It might not be all that bad, Molly. You could have the baby adopted and try to start again.'

Molly shook her head vehemently. 'No!'

'You won't try to do it again, will you?'

'I . . . I don't know.' Oh, she was so tired of it all. She just wished he would go away and leave her alone. Alone with her misery and despair.

'Don't tell me I'm going to have to handcuff you to me so I can keep my eye on you?' He was desperately trying to drag her out of the black depression she was in.

'You can do what you like, I don't *care*.'

'Right, Constable, I think its time you got some rest. Back to your ward, please,' the ward sister interrupted.

Reluctantly Joe got to his feet. 'Her name is Molly Keegan and she lives in Arnot Street, Walton, and she tripped and fell. She told me she can swim so there's no question of it being anything other than an accident.'

'I'm very relieved to hear it. I'll keep my eye on her.'

'Could you let me know when you're going to discharge her, please? I'd like to see that she gets home safely,' Joe asked in a low tone, glancing back worriedly at Molly who had turned her head away.

'I'm sure it can be arranged, providing you yourself don't suffer any ill effects from the river water.'

'I won't, I've been dumped in worse than that.'

'I wouldn't be too sure. I sometimes think you could catch bubonic plague from that water,' Sister said darkly.

Molly drifted in and out of a sleep filled with dark dreams and when she awoke it was as if a leaden dullness had seeped into her mind and body.

A doctor came and examined her and asked her a few questions, and then a nurse brought her clothes, which had been washed and dried in the laundry. She had just finished getting dressed when Joe Jackson appeared at the door of the ward.

'I see she's ready, Sister.'

'She is indeed. Now, young lady, take more care where you are walking in future. I don't want to see you in here again. You were very fortunate and you, young man, will probably get a medal from the Liverpool Humane and Shipwreck Society. It was very brave of you.'

'Everyone keeps telling me that but I don't want a medal, I was just doing my job,' Joe replied, ushering Molly towards the door.

'How are you feeling this morning?' Joe asked as they walked down Pembroke Place.

Molly shrugged. It was a beautiful morning but she didn't even notice.

'Did you get any sleep? Did you even try to think about what you're going to do now?'

'No. I can't. I just can't.'

'I thought about it.'

She looked up at him. 'Why do you care what happens to me?'

'Because I feel sort of responsible for you,' Joe answered, trying not to sound too intense.

'You don't need to.'

'Yes I do. Well, someone should care what happens to you. Are you absolutely certain you can't go home to your family? They must care about you.'

Molly felt the tears well in her eyes again. Oh, would he never leave her alone? 'They do care, but . . . but you don't understand what it's like there, it's even worse than here. My da is a farmer, he's respected, the shame would be desperate for him. He could never hold his head up again – ever! He'd disown me.'

Joe could see she was near to breaking point so he remained silent for a while.

'What about your friend, the one you mentioned last night?' he asked as they turned into London Road. 'Bernie, was it?'

'She's enough trouble in her life,' Molly answered and briefly told him of Bernie's terrible tragedy.

'I remember it. I was on duty when the ferry finally got in. I'm sorry, he was only a year younger than me. Is she the same age as you?'

Molly nodded.

'Why don't you write to her? If she's really your friend she'll understand. You stood by her when she needed you.'

'I can't! Hasn't she enough to cope with?'

'It was just a suggestion,' he said and for the rest of the way they remained silent.

Mrs Hayes opened the door to them. She'd been watching from the front-room window. She'd been up all night and she looked exhausted and very old.

'In the name of God, where have you been, Molly? I've been demented with worry. I went to the police station twice but they couldn't tell me anything.'

'I'm sorry you've been so worried, ma'am. They could at least have tried to make some enquiries,' Joe said. 'She had an accident. She slipped and fell into the river at the Landing Stage. We got her out but that water is so filthy they kept her in hospital overnight.' Joe made no mention of his part in Molly's rescue.

'What were you doing down *there* and at that time of night? You said you'd be a bit late but when it got to half past eleven I really began to worry—'

'Don't you think we should go inside, ma'am?' Joe interrupted, seeing the curtains of the house next door twitching.

'Oh, come in. I'm far too old for all this anxiety and upset.' The elderly lady walked down the lobby towards the kitchen and Joe gently propelled Molly after her.

Molly just wanted to go up the stairs to bed. She felt she couldn't face all the questions.

'What are you going to tell her?' Joe whispered.

Molly shook her head. What could she tell her?

'Will I put the kettle on, ma'am?' Joe asked as Mrs Hayes eased herself down into a chair.

'The constabulary are getting very high-handed these days even though they're not very efficient, but I suppose you might as well,' was the acerbic reply.

Molly sat at the table and covered her face with her hands.

'Didn't you go to see Nellie?' Mrs Hayes demanded. 'I asked that lot at Westminster Road Police Station to enquire there and they said they would but I'm sure they didn't.'

'I didn't.' Molly was forcing herself to think. 'I . . . I . . . thought I'd go down and ask about the ferry sailings . . . home.'

The old lady was suspicious at once. 'You know the times!'

'They're about to change them, ma'am. They do that at the end of the summer,' Joe put in quickly.

'You're thinking of going home?'

'I . . . I thought I'd go and see how Bernie is.'

Mrs Hayes looked at her hard. Oh, she knew Molly had been devastated by being dropped by that young blackguard but she also knew how much Molly enjoyed her job. Was there some other reason? She had genuinely been worried sick all night and had realised that she had become fond of the girl. In fact she was fond of both of them. In the long, dark hours she'd realised that if they left she would miss them both.

Joe poured them both a cup of tea. 'She misses her. It was a terrible tragedy. Maybe she should go home.'

'No! No, I'm fine here,' Molly protested.

'She has a very good job at Frisby Dyke's and she has a good home here and no doubt Bernie will be back soon. She's bound to feel a bit homesick from time to time. And talking about her job, they will be wondering why she hasn't put in an appearance this morning. You have telephones, don't you?'

Joe looked bemused but he nodded.

'Then you can make yourself useful and telephone them and tell them what has happened and that she'll be in tomorrow.'

'I can't do that, ma'am, they're for official calls only.'

'Do you want her to lose her job?' the old lady snapped.

Joe frowned. He supposed he could do it. 'No. I'll make sure they know.'

'And speaking of jobs, haven't you one to go to? We're both exhausted. Thank you for seeing her home.'

Joe realised he would have to go but he was worried about leaving Molly with such a bad-tempered old woman.

'You'll be at work tomorrow?' he asked Molly.

'Of course she will,' Mrs Hayes answered tartly.

He nodded. He finished early tomorrow, he'd call in and try to see her.

'I'd write to Bernie, if I were you,' he said before he turned and left.

'You do write to her. I sometimes wonder at the calibre of the members of the Liverpool City Police Force these days, I really do. Now, finish that tea and we'll both try and get some rest. I feel quite ill,' the old lady confided.

Molly got to her feet. There would be no rest for her; how could there be? Nothing was resolved; nothing could be resolved. Maybe he was right. Perhaps she should pour out her misery in a letter to Bernie?

Chapter Twenty-Eight

———◦•※•◦———

BERNIE HAD BEEN SITTING in the kitchen half-heartedly scraping carrots for a stew that Tess was preparing. In the last few days she had begun to feel a little better, to take a bit of notice of what was going on around her. It had been so hard when she had first come home. Neighbours had called to offer their sympathy and Mass cards until she had felt like screaming at everyone just to leave her alone. Somehow she had got through it, though, and she had survived her first visit to the little church at Killina where she had been married. She had gone to early Mass with just her mam. Tess had instructed Dessie to take the kids later. There hadn't been as many people there and they'd sat right at the back so her tears and those of her mam wouldn't be noticed. Father O'Brien had been very kind and his words had given her hope but now she realised that the person who had got her through it all had been her mam.

Apart from when she had arrived she hadn't been into town but Tess had said they would go tomorrow. It would do her good and she should buy herself some little thing.

'I don't need anything, mam,' Bernie had protested.

'Sure, 'tis not a matter of *needing*, Bernie. 'Tis a matter of taking some sort of *interest*. There must be something you're short on?' Tess urged. Each day she tried to get Bernie to do some small thing, some task, to try to edge her back to an interest in the future. She had been shocked to see how thin, pale and lost her daughter had looked when she'd arrived.

'Ah, I suppose the girls could do with some stockings with the autumn coming on.'

'Nothing for yourself?' Tess asked. Once Bernie would never have thought of stockings for her sisters.

'No, Mam. Is there anything you need?'

'There's plenty I'm after needing but I've done without for so long it's no hurt now,' Tess had replied. She was hoping that this Sunday afternoon she could get Bernie to agree to go and visit Ita with her. Of course Ita had been one of the first to come to see Bernie and she had called a few times since but it would be the first time Bernie had paid any kind of 'proper' visit to anyone.

'Are you nearly finished with those carrots, Bernie? I'm ready for them now,' Tess enquired, stirring the stew in the big iron cooking pot that hung over the fire.

'Just one more, Mam.'

'It should be ready for when your da gets in. Will we have a cup of tea?' Tess sat down at the table and wiped her hands on her apron, looking expectantly at her daughter.

Bernie at last rose and began to get out the cups.

Tess smiled to herself. She was sure it helped to keep busy. 'I was thinking that maybe on Sunday afternoon we could walk down to see Ita?'

Bernie looked up. 'Mam, I don't think I'll be much in the way of company.'

'Ah, now, child, you have to make a bit of an effort some time and I know Ita is worried about Molly. Sure, she hasn't heard a word from her for a while. I know you've had a letter so I thought you could put her mam's mind to rest a bit.'

'Molly's just grand, Mam. She's been working very hard and she doesn't get home until very late at the end of the week. They've had a big order to do for a judge's house.'

'Well, won't her mam want to know all about that?'

'Mam, I don't really know much about it. I haven't been in the mood to care much,' Bernie answered wearily.

'But you can tell her all kinds of little details about Molly's life.'

'Isn't it enough that we're going into town tomorrow? Isn't that enough outings for one week?'

Tess shook her head. Maybe she was pushing it a bit – going too fast for Bernie. 'Ah, well, we'll put it off until the week after, so,' she conceded.

The outing into Tullamore had been quite successful, Tess thought as they made their way home next afternoon. She'd managed to arrange for them to get a ride with John Fahey who had been going into town on some business. He was a pleasant enough man and had chatted to her all the way there. Bernie hadn't said much but then Tess hadn't expected her to. He'd arranged to meet them in the Market Square for the return journey.

They'd gone to Bracken's Drapery and Mrs Bracken had served Bernie with a good deal of consideration and she had been pleased to see how well Bernie had responded. Half a dozen pairs of woollen stockings in fawn and brown and black had been set out for their appraisal and Bernie had chosen black for Eileen and fawn for Claire so there would be no fighting over which pair belonged to whom. Tess herself had bought the few groceries she could afford.

'Looks like you've letters or maybe a parcel, Tess,' John Fahey said as they drew level with the grain store at the bend in the canal line and Con O'Brien could be seen coming towards them, pushing his bike.

'That'll be the day when I get a parcel. Sure, sometimes I think the lot beyond in America have forgotten about us entirely: there's hardly a letter sent these days,' Tess answered with some resignation.

'Maybe it's a letter then, Tess.'

'More likely a letter for Bernie from Molly.'

'Ah, well, I'll set you down here.'

'We're greatly obliged to you, John, that we are,' Tess thanked him as they both alighted from the trap.

' 'Tis a letter for Bernie, I've left it on the table, Tess,' Con informed them, then went on his way. It was the custom for him to leave the mail in the house if no one was in; the door was never locked.

Tess laid her few purchases down and handed the letter to Bernie. 'It's from Molly.'

Bernie managed a smile. 'Can you see through envelopes now?'

'Don't I know her writing? I'll put on the kettle, I'm parched.'

Bernie sat down and turned the envelope over in her hand. What would Molly have to say? Would she ask when she was coming back? Would she gently chide her for not replying to her last letter? She'd read it later; she felt so weary.

'Are you not going to open it then?' Tess asked.

'Later, Mam. I'll have a cup of tea and then I think I'll go for a bit of a walk. The kids will be in soon and I want a bit of time on my own. It seems to have been such a busy day – busy with people, I mean.'

'Suit yourself, child,' Tess replied. She'd learned when not to push Bernie too much. 'Have your tea and then take Molly's letter with you on your walk.'

Fifteen minutes later Bernie wandered slowly down the grassy bank of the canal where it widened after the Cappaloughlan Bridge. Autumn was already in the air. The leaves of the trees were beginning to turn gold and orange, the rushes and reeds at the water's edge were becoming dry and rustled in the breeze. The bog iris and water buttercup were dying and the cow parsley had long since withered. She'd always thought of autumn as a lovely season before, now it seemed full of sadness, reminding her that the long dark winter was ahead. Reminding her that a year that had started so full of hope and happiness was ending in such heartbreak.

She sat down on the stump of a tree that had been long since felled by a winter storm and thought about the months ahead. She would have to go back to Liverpool; there was no work here for her and her mam couldn't afford to keep her. Would Ellen Montrose take her back again? Did she want to go back? She sighed heavily and tore open the envelope. This time she would have to make an effort to write to Molly or her friend would start to get very worried.

She read the letter slowly three times and then folded it and pushed it into her pocket. She sat for a long time thinking about Molly and herself. She had been so utterly wrapped up in her grief that she had had no idea what had been going on, really going on, in Molly's life. Now she knew she had to make an enormous effort to put her sorrow aside and think of her friend. She could no longer indulge in the luxury of thinking only of herself. Molly was in terrible, terrible trouble and she was bearing it alone.

'Oh, Moll! Moll, you poor, poor thing!' she said aloud. Shock and pity and anger were all mixed up inside her. That swine! That utter *bastard*! She had to go back. Molly needed her desperately.

Tess noticed the change in Bernie instantly. There was a new purpose, a new determination about her. It was as though she had suddenly woken up from a sort of daze.

'Mam, I've decided that I've moped about for long enough. Everyone was right. I have to get on with my life.'

Tess nodded; she was wise enough not to question what had suddenly brought this about but she suspected that it was something to do with Molly. Bernie would tell her – in time. 'You don't know how relieved I am to hear that, Bernie.'

'I think I'll go back tomorrow, Mam.'

Tess was astonished. 'That soon? Are you sure?'

Bernie nodded. It wouldn't take her long to get her things together.

Tess recovered herself. 'Well, this evening will you come with me to see Ita? She might have something she wants you to take back for Molly.' Tess knew Ita would automatically think there was something wrong with her daughter if Bernie took off without even saying goodbye after receiving Molly's letter. She would worry herself sick. Tess herself was certain now that something was very wrong but she still didn't ask.

It would be hard, Bernie knew, not to arouse Ita's suspicions but she had to go. 'I will so.'

Tess was relieved. 'We'll go up after I've given your da and the kids their supper.'

Ita was delighted to see them and ushered them into the parlour. 'It's like a three-ringed circus in this kitchen tonight, all they can talk about is the hurling match on Saturday!' she said, casting her eyes to the ceiling.

She indicated that Tess and Bernie should sit down while she made up the fire with more turf.

'You're very welcome, Bernie. It's grand to see you getting out.'

'She's decided to go back and I think it will do her good,' Tess announced.

'You're certainly looking a lot better, Bernie.' Ita too was relieved and Bernie did indeed look far more alert. There was a spark of animation in her face now that hadn't been there for a long time.

'I feel better. I said to Mam that at last I realise everyone was right. Life has to go on. I have to make an effort. It won't be at all easy but I have to *try*.'

'It won't be easy, Bernie, but Molly will be a big help to you, I know.'

Bernie swallowed hard. She was going to have to be a big help to Molly, not the other way around. 'Molly has been the greatest friend anyone could wish for, so she has. I've decided that now I've made up my mind it's best not to trail around saying goodbye to half the Parish. It would only make it harder for me. I'm going tomorrow, that's why I came up tonight. Mam said there might be something you want me to take back for Molly?'

Ita looked at Tess in surprise. This was very sudden.

'I think she's right, Ita. It will only upset her again if she goes around to all the neighbours. Best to let her go quietly without any fuss.'

Ita nodded slowly. She supposed Tess was right; after all, she knew Bernie best of all.

It was Tess who made the tea while Ita went to scribble a few lines to Molly and gather up a few bits and pieces she wanted to send. When Tess and Bernie finally left, Ita kissed Bernie and told her to take care of herself and to tell Molly that she was to write a bit more often now and let her know how they were both getting on.

Bernie had agreed but she wondered just how soon Molly would write and what she would tell her mother. She had no idea at all of what they were going to do but they would sort something out. There was no way on earth that she was going to let Molly go through this on her own.

Chapter Twenty-Nine

MOLLY HAD BEEN LISTLESS and preoccupied. In the days following her ordeal Mrs Stanley hadn't failed to notice but refrained from commenting on it. The girl was obviously going through some kind of crisis which she hoped would resolve itself shortly. Molly had shown herself to be reliable and sensible in the past and Mrs Stanley hoped that she would soon recover her equilibrium.

Molly had felt a little relieved, slightly less panic-stricken after she'd written to Bernie, but only momentarily. What did she expect Bernie to do? She couldn't wave a magic wand and make everything all right again. She wasn't even sure if Bernie would come back or how soon she should expect a reply.

Mrs Hayes had been up each morning before she'd gone out to work, just to make sure she was none the worse for her ordeal – that there really were no ill effects from the notorious river water, was what she'd said. It had only made Molly feel worse.

She had been very surprised when she'd left the shop the following evening to find Joe Jackson waiting for her. He looked different out of uniform, she'd thought, younger.

'Have you come to check up on me?'

'I was worried about you. Did you write to your friend?'

'I did.'

'When do you expect a reply?' he'd asked.

She'd shrugged.

'Do you think she'll come back?' he'd pressed.

She'd shrugged again, wishing he would go away and leave her alone. She just wanted to go home and sleep, she was so tired.

'Have you thought at all about what you're going to do?' He wasn't going to give up on her.

'I don't *want* to think about it. Why are you pestering me? I'm not your responsibility.'

'I feel as though you are and, besides, I don't want to see you crushed, it's really not the end of the world.'

'It's the end of my world,' she'd answered.

'You could build a new one.'

They'd reached the tram stop and she'd rounded on him. 'You mean go somewhere else? Take the emigrant ship again?'

'I didn't mean it literally.'

'Will you just leave me alone, please?' she'd begged, thankful that her tram had arrived.

He hadn't replied but he'd stood aside while she'd boarded and watched the tram as it moved slowly down Lord Street, wondering if he had unwittingly planted an idea in her head – an idea that he wasn't at all happy about.

Unknown to Molly he had visited Mrs Hayes twice during the subsequent days, trying to sound the old lady out as to Molly's mood.

'You're taking a great interest in her but I have to say you're an improvement on the last one.'

'What was the last one like?' he probed.

'Flashy and with no manners.'

'Do you know his name?'

'I don't and I've no wish to. She's a good girl and I'm fond of her so if you've any intentions towards her I'm telling you now that I keep a strict eye on her. She's only eighteen,' had been the sharp reply.

Not sharp enough, he'd thought sadly, wondering how she would treat Molly when she found out. Was she fond enough of her to forgive her?

'I'm glad to hear it and my "intentions" are solely to make sure she is all right.'

'That's a pity. I like you,' the old lady had stated.

He'd been amused. She was very blunt.

On his second visit she'd informed him that a telegram had arrived from Ireland and he'd been relieved. Her friend at least had made some effort to contact her; maybe it would be to say she was coming back.

'What do you think they'll both do now?' he'd asked.

'They'll pick up the pieces and get on with their lives,' Mrs Hayes had said, giving him a long hard look.

Molly had to fight down the tears of pure relief when she got home and opened the telegram. Bernie was coming back! She would be here tomorrow!

'Well?' Mrs Hayes demanded.

'She's coming back. Tomorrow.'

The old lady nodded. 'You must have given her a shock. Maybe it was just what she needed.'

I gave her a shock all right, Molly thought sadly, but just what Bernie could do to help she still didn't know. At least they could talk and cry over it together and right now she knew that would be some comfort.

When she finally arrived back in Arnot Street Bernie was relieved to find Molly had gone to work. At least she was trying to keep up the appearance of normality. After a brief chat to the old lady during which she learned of Joe Jackson's visits she went to see Jimmy's mam. Flo was delighted to see her and equally delighted that she was starting on the long road to rebuilding her life. She didn't press Bernie too much on her future plans, however. She knew how hard it was to think ahead; she herself only took one day at a time.

Molly hurried home from work that night and as soon as she saw the familiar figure of her friend waiting for her in their living room she burst into tears of relief and flung herself into her arms.

'Oh, Molly! Why didn't you tell me sooner? When I think I could have lost you too I go cold all over! I couldn't have stood it. I just *couldn't* have!' Bernie cried.

'I'm sorry. I was so desperate I couldn't think straight!'

They collapsed on the sofa.

'Tell me every word that swine said,' Bernie demanded.

Molly shook her head. 'No. I don't even want to think about him, Bernie.'

'And you are sure?'

'More than sure. Oh, what am I going to do?'

'What are *we* going to do, you mean. I'm not leaving you to face this on your own.'

Molly had been thinking about the situation. 'Maybe we should go somewhere where no one knows us – America or Australia?'

'We can't run away from it, Molly, and sure, wherever we go there's bound to be someone who knows someone from home. Anyway, if your mam and mine knew we were out there – and they would have to, we can't just disappear – they'd have the brothers and sisters down on top of us.'

Molly realised this was indeed true. 'Then . . . then there's nothing for it but a home for fallen women.'

'I won't let you go into one of those desperate places! We'll move. Herself will throw us out anyway so we'll go before that happens. We'll move to another town. We could go to London and find somewhere to live! We could say we were both widows. Ma saved the bits out of the newspapers about Jimmy. I'll work to keep us all, Molly, if you want to keep the baby – if you don't want to have it adopted. I wouldn't mind what kind of work I did, I could even bake cakes and buns and sell them too.'

Molly was feeling much calmer. They could move; they might indeed be able to manage. 'Later on maybe I could work from home, set up my own soft furnishings business. But what would you tell Ma and Nellie? You'll have to tell them why we're moving.'

Bernie smiled at her, seeing the distracted, hunted look disappear from her eyes. 'We'll think of something, Molly. We'll cope. We'll build a new future and it will be grand.'

Molly smiled for the first time in weeks. 'You're the greatest friend anyone could ever have.'

'Friends always look after each other.'
Molly squeezed her hand. 'It's us two against the world, Bernie.'

Augusta Hayes closed her eyes and silently eased the door shut. She hadn't meant to eavesdrop, but she had been overcome by her curiosity and the desire to see the two girls reunited. Well, she *shouldn't* have, she told herself as she made her way rather unsteadily towards the kitchen. She felt old and ill and very shocked. How could Molly have demeaned herself so much? How could she have behaved like *that*? How could she have forgotten everything she had been taught? Oh, it was outrageous that the girl should have brought such shame to her family and to herself. She'd been determined to keep a watchful eye on them both, that's why she had laid down rules and regulations, to protect them. With Bernie she had succeeded. Even though she hadn't approved at first of her marrying so young, at least she had been married. At least Bernie hadn't disgraced herself – disgraced them all!

She took a glass from the cupboard and poured a small amount from the bottle of medicinal brandy she kept hidden away at the back of a cupboard. Molly had seemed such a sensible girl, such a steady girl, a good girl. She *was* a good girl, she told herself firmly, she had been very, very stupid to believe the lies that young blackguard had obviously told her. She shook her head in disbelief. Molly's behaviour was an affront to the moral code she believed in. What was she to do?

Both girls assumed that she would automatically throw them out, but could she? She was very fond of them. She had grieved with young Bernie and Molly's recent experience at the Pier Head had caused her real anguish and worry – and now it appeared that it had been no 'accident' at all. If she demanded they leave life would be so lonely without them. Her own two daughters seemed to have very little time to spare for their mother and her sons had moved to distant parts of the country.

Yet if she allowed the girls to stay would she be seen to be condoning Molly's behaviour? She could imagine what her family and her neighbours would think of her. But just what would happen to them if they went to London or any other city? How would they survive? Bernie's optimism might well be misplaced. If they stayed, she would have to face some degree of humiliation and not least from Bernie's dreadful cousin, Nellie, who was bound to upbraid her for her lack of supervision. Oh, what was she to do? She poured herself another medicinal drink. She would have to think very carefully. All their futures depended on what she decided tonight.

Chapter Thirty

———◦◦◦◦———

FOR THE FIRST TIME in weeks Molly slept well but Bernie lay awake for a long time trying to see what the future held for them both. It didn't look very rosy at all, despite all her optimistic protestations to Molly. How *would* they manage? There would be all the additional expenses of moving to a different town and finding decent lodgings, never mind jobs. Molly wouldn't be able to work for very much longer and she herself was still only fit to be a domestic servant. The more she thought about Molly's predicament the more her anger at Billy Marshall's behaviour grew. His treatment of poor Molly was nothing short of diabolical; he shouldn't be allowed to get off scot-free after ruining her friend's life. Molly had had a great career ahead of her, she'd been up for promotion and might possibly have met a really decent young man and had a happy marriage. Eventually she might have had children who would have been welcomed into the world without the terrible stigma of being illegitimate, something that would haunt this child all his or her life.

She knew that if her Jimmy had been alive he would have done something to ensure that Billy Marshall didn't escape some form of retribution. Well, now it was up to her and before she finally drifted off to sleep she had decided just how she would do it.

While Bernie had tossed and turned, sleep had eluded the old lady too. She wrestled with her conscience, with her affection for the two girls, with the vision of what her own days would be like if they left and, like Bernie, when her tired eyes finally closed she had made up her mind.

239

She had intended to be up early next morning but it was the front door slamming as Molly left for work that woke her.

She found Bernie in the kitchen making a fresh pot of tea when she finally arrived downstairs.

'She's gone to work then?'

'She has so. Will you have a cup of tea?'

'I will, thank you. I intended to get up earlier; I wanted to talk to you both.'

Bernie eyed her with surprise as she poured out the tea.

Mrs Hayes stirred in the sugar slowly. 'I . . . I overheard you talking last night. I know I shouldn't have listened but the fact remains I did.'

Bernie looked at her in horror. 'Then you . . . you know?'

Augusta Hayes nodded.

Determination filled Bernie's eyes. 'Well, I'm going to stand by her! Sure, she's not going into one of those desperate places! She's not a bad girl, she's *not!*'

'Am I saying she is? She's been a very, very foolish girl and now she'll have to pay, and pay dearly, for that foolishness, but I'm not having the pair of you running off to London or anywhere else. Aren't you in enough trouble already and God knows what will happen to you both in a place like London.'

Bernie stared at her, open-mouthed. 'You mean . . . you mean we can stay?' she finally stammered. She had never expected this.

'I do. Oh, don't think I'm condoning what she's done and I can tell you that there will be some very cutting comments from people in this street about my allowing you to stay here but I'm not going to lose any sleep over that! Did you decide whether her parents should be told, in time? At least her poor mother?'

Bernie shook her head. 'It would kill them. There was a girl in the Parish, Maggie O'Dwyer, her family were quite well off, and she . . . she got into trouble. Maggie's mam was friendly with Molly's mam at that time and, oh, it was terrible! They disowned her entirely. Mr O'Dwyer forbade them all to even mention her name again and even struck it out of the family Bible.'

'Good God!'

'That's what it's like. It's a desperate, desperate thing to have happen to you.'

'What happened to her?'

'She was sent off to the nuns. I'll always remember the day she was sent away and Molly's mam telling my mam how heart-broken Mrs O'Dwyer was and how destroyed altogether Mr O'Dwyer was with the shame of it all. As far as I know she's still working in the laundry. No one will sign for her to come out and she's nowhere to go even if it was allowed, and no man would marry her. So, you see, Molly couldn't tell her parents and I wasn't going to let poor Molly end up in one of those places. I wasn't going to let her be treated like that.'

Augusta nodded. Molly certainly didn't deserve such treatment; it bordered on the barbaric. 'Have you given any real thought to work? She won't be able to work for very much longer.'

'I was thinking last night that maybe I could find work in a shop and then of an evening I could try baking soda bread and barmbrack, traditional Irish confectionery, and then selling it to some of the bigger grocers. I could drop it off on my way to work the following morning. I'm going to have to earn enough to keep both of us.'

'It's an idea but there might be no call for it. I suppose you'll be wanting to turn my kitchen into a bakery?'

'I hadn't really thought that deeply about it. It's still all a bit of a shock.'

'Indeed it is and believe me I'm getting far too old for such shocks, but I still feel some responsibility. I thought I was making sure that neither of you got into trouble, but I suppose it just goes to show that where there's a will, there's a way. Maybe I was too strict. Maybe I should have allowed gentlemen callers, then at least I could have seen what kind of company she was keeping.'

'And what good would it have done, except cause rows and fights? I tried to warn her about him, I did, but she . . . she loved him. I never liked him and neither did Jimmy. Poor Molly, she trusted him. She believed him when he said he wouldn't . . . well, that nothing would happen to her. I hate him!'

'And no doubt she will too, given time. Now, if it was that young Constable Jackson she'd taken up with I'd have been quite pleased.'

'Has she seen much of him? She only mentioned about him dragging her out of the river and seeing her home from the hospital.'

'He's been to see me a couple of times, to see how she's getting on. He assures me there's nothing more to it and that's a pity, but you can't blame him. What man would want to take on that reprobate's child?'

Bernie nodded sadly. 'Poor Molly. Oh, I was in a desperate state when she told me what she'd done! She must have been out of her mind with it all to walk straight into the river. Thank God your man was there.'

'And thank God he had the sense to tell everyone that she slipped and fell in. I was out of my mind with worry when she didn't come home all night. I thought she was dead and but for him she might well have been and then what would I have told her parents?'

'I . . . I thought about doing something. I didn't want to live without Jimmy, but I'm just not brave enough and I knew I'd never see Jimmy again if I did. She's either very brave or she was not in her right mind and I prefer to think it was the latter.'

The old lady nodded her agreement. 'Will you tell that cousin of yours?' she asked, hoping the girl would say no.

Bernie nodded. 'Ah, she'll have ten fits but I . . . I need her help. At least I need Matty's help.'

'What for?'

Bernie looked secretive. 'Oh, just an idea I had last night. Nothing for you to worry about.'

'Just as long as I don't have her here on my doorstep ranting and raving about me not looking after you girls properly. I don't need her to rub it in.'

Bernie reached across the table and took the old lady's hand. 'You won't. Sure, you don't know how relieved I am that you're not throwing us out. I really didn't want to leave Liverpool. We'll cope with everything – even your neighbours. Thank you. God bless you for a good, kind-hearted woman.'

Augusta Hayes tutted. 'My neighbours I can ignore; my two stuck-up daughters will be a different matter.'

'But you never see them.' Bernie had never heard the old lady make any such comments about them before.

'That's because the pair of them moved out to Southport when they got married and they don't like to be reminded that they were brought up in a terraced house in Liverpool by a widow trying to make ends meet. Nor do they approve of me taking in lodgers. Oh, they've really got above themselves, have those two. Married a pair of brothers in the "Retail Business", as they put it. That means they're shopkeepers but I have to admit that the shops they own are big ones. Grocery shops, five or six of them.'

Bernie was curious. 'Do they never visit you?'

'They come two or three times a year. Always at Christmas, bringing me expensive and usually utterly useless gifts. Perfume it was last time! What would a woman of my age want perfume for?'

'What about your sons?'

'Harold lives and works in London; George is in Dover and Bertie seems to spend his time travelling the world. He goes away to sea; he's based in Southampton.'

Bernie thought how sad it was that the old lady had been left alone but then she thought of her own brothers and sisters who were thousands of miles away from home. At least her mam and da had each other and the younger kids – but who was to say that when they were old enough they too wouldn't take the emigrant ship, just as she had?

'Well, I suppose I'd better go and see Nellie and Ma,' she said, getting to her feet.

'How is poor Mrs McCauley?'

'She says she takes each day as it comes.'

The old lady nodded. 'It *will* get easier, Bernie. Time *does* heal.'

Bernie bit her lip. 'I miss him so much.'

'Of course you do, child. You'll always miss him.'

'Going home helped a lot. Mam was very good and I did begin to see that I have to get on with life.'

'Worrying about Molly will also take your mind off . . . things.'

'It will so. I might even tidy myself up and go and see if there are any jobs to be had.'

'That's a good idea. I might have a nap after I've done some housework. I feel quite exhausted.'

Bernie went first to see her mother-in-law who was delighted to see her looking more like her old self but not so delighted to hear of Molly's predicament. 'She isn't the first, Bernie, and she won't be the last,' she said sadly. She was very thankful that Mrs Hayes was showing the girls such kindness and consideration. Knowing of the woman's strong sense of morality, Flo knew it was no easy decision she'd made.

Nellie's views were predictable, so Bernie thought after she'd bluntly informed her cousin about Molly and listened to Nellie's tirade about that 'owld one' and her rules and regulations and look how she hadn't had a clue what was going on under her very nose.

'She's being very good about it all, Nellie, and it's hard for her so the last thing we need is you giving out to her.'

Nellie slammed the teapot down on the table. 'All right, Bernie, but iffen I could get me hands on that bloody Marshall feller I'd . . . I'd cut his balls off! God fergive me fer me language! I saw him the night yer went back ter see yer mam, bold as bloody brass with another girl hangin' on his arm. I sent Molly off on a bit of an errand so she wouldn't see the swine! Flo was with me.'

'It's not right that he gets away with it. He's ruined her life. He's ruined *her*! I was thinking, Nellie, isn't there *something* Matty can do about him?'

Nellie stared at her hard and a grim smile lifted the corners of her mouth. 'Oh, aye, there is! We don't take kindly around here ter the likes of him treatin' one of us the way he's treated Molly – an' she is one of us. The fellers around here will sort him out, you just leave it ter me, girl. Billy Marshall will rue the day he ever took advantage of Molly, they'll give him something permanent ter remind him! His days of playin' fast an' loose with the girls will be over. I won't tell them who the girl is, mind. We don't want it talked about in all the pubs an' alehouses around here. It's enough

244

fer them ter know that a decent young girl has been took advantage of. Matty might guess but I'll sort him out!'

Bernie nodded slowly. 'They . . . they won't kill him, will they? We don't want *that*.'

'No, he's not worth swingin' at the end of a rope fer, but he might well end up in hospital. Now, let's have a cup of tea. I'm feelin' a bit better about it all now.'

'So am I,' Bernie agreed. In her opinion rough justice was better than no justice at all.

Chapter Thirty-One

———————

THAT MORNING MRS STANLEY was relieved to see that Molly seemed a little better. She made a mental note to talk to the girl about her forthcoming promotion at the end of the week, when she had finalised it with management.

Molly herself was determined to try to economise and save every halfpenny she could. She would walk a couple of stops to save on the tram fare; she would make things like stockings last longer; she would only have a cup of tea and maybe a bun for her lunch and she wouldn't have her hair cut. She would let it grow again; it was cheaper. She was determined to be more positive when she and Bernie discussed the future in greater detail when she got home from work that evening.

Bernie was waiting for her and she was surprised to see that Bernie was looking far happier than she'd seemed last night.

'Have you had a good day then?'

'I have so. Come on in while I tell you the news.'

Molly was a little fearful. 'What now?'

'I had a long talk with Herself this morning, after you'd gone to work.'

Molly felt her heart plummet. 'Oh, God!'

'No, it's great news! The best! We can stay.'

Molly sat down on the sofa. 'You told her about . . . me?'

'Not exactly. She overheard us.'

Molly groaned. 'Oh, God, Bernie!'

'No, it's all fine, Moll.' Bernie told her about last night's conversation with Mrs Hayes and her discussions with Flo and

Nellie. 'They're both sworn to secrecy. Oh, Nellie did start giving out but in the end she agreed with me. You were just too trusting, you've been stupid, you made a mistake.' Bernie said nothing about the retribution that was to be wreaked on Billy Marshall.

'I suppose I'm thankful, in a way, that it's all out in the open now,' Molly said a little tentatively. She still had them all to face but at least they knew. She got to her feet. 'I'd better go on in and see Herself and thank her.'

Bernie nodded. Things were looking a little brighter now.

Molly took a deep breath and opened the kitchen door. Augusta Hayes was sitting in her chair, her knitting in her lap.

'Well, I suppose I'll have to start knitting for you now.'

Molly sat down at the kitchen table. 'I'm so, so sorry I let you down.'

'You let us all down, child, but more importantly you've let yourself down. You've foolishly ruined your life and for what? A few minutes of pleasure.'

'I know but I . . . I loved him.'

The old lady noticed that Molly had said 'loved', so she hoped the child didn't harbour any notions that she was still 'in love' with the blackguard. 'If he had truly loved you, Molly, he would never have taken advantage of you. He would have respected you.'

Molly nodded miserably. She would never get over the utter humiliation of it all.

Augusta Hayes decided to change the subject. 'How much longer can you work?'

'Another two months, I hope, if I . . . I don't get too big. And I'm going to save hard.' Molly gave a little shudder. She prayed she wouldn't get too tired in the coming months or begin to show too much; Mrs Stanley might notice and put two and two together. Then she would be dismissed out of hand and everyone in the entire shop would know of her shame. Oh, it was still so terribly hard to cope with everything that faced her. Apart from the financial strain there would be months of gossip from the neighbours, the ups and downs of her health, her fear of labour and the heart-breaking knowledge that her child would suffer terribly by being branded illegitimate.

'It's going to be hard for you, Molly, and I don't mean just the next months.'

'I know, but I can't change things.'

Augusta decided to be more practical. 'It's going to be very hard on Bernie too and she obviously doesn't want to go back to Ellen Montrose.'

'No, she doesn't. She feels as though she has to move on, do something different, be with more people other than just Mrs Montrose.'

'I can understand that. She mentioned something about shop work and of course her rather fanciful baking venture. Could you not get her something at Frisby Dyke's? You seem to be well thought of there.'

'I can try; sure, it's the least I can do. You are being very good about it all. I really don't deserve it.'

'I couldn't turn you out. I've grown very fond of you both and seeing as the pair of you are going to become more like family than lodgers, you can start to call me Aunt Augusta. Now, if you'll put the kettle on we'll have something to eat.'

Bernie thought that things were certainly taking a turn for the better when Molly told her about her talk with the old lady. 'Won't it be desperate odd to call her "Aunt Augusta"?'

'I suppose we'll get used to it, in time.'

'It should be Great-aunt Augusta, sure she's old enough to be our granny.'

'And she suggested that I try to get you a job and I will.'

Bernie looked hopeful. 'That would be grand but I couldn't manage anything too complicated, nothing like your job.'

'You've no confidence in yourself. You could do my job without too much trouble.'

'How could I? I haven't the way you have with matching colours.'

Molly was about to answer when there was a loud knock on the front door.

'I'll go,' Bernie offered, praying it wasn't Nellie who, despite her assurances, had changed her mind and come to upbraid the old lady. She was surprised to see a policeman standing on the doorstep but quickly recovered herself.

'You must be the one who dragged her out of the river.'

Joe Jackson grinned a little sheepishly. 'And you must be her friend, Bernie. You don't know how glad I am that you came back.'

'How could I leave her? And I can never thank you enough for what you did.' Bernie liked him instantly and not just because he had saved Molly's life. She felt instinctively he was the sort of lad you could trust and rely on. In some ways he reminded her of Jimmy.

'Is that that young man from the constabulary?' came the strident voice from the kitchen.

'She doesn't miss much, does she?' Joe whispered.

'It is so,' Bernie called back.

'I suppose he's come to see Molly so you come in here to me, Bernie, and send him in to her.'

Bernie managed a wry smile. 'She's changed the rules but it's a bit like bolting the stable door after the horse has fled,' she said *sotto voce*, then she called, 'I'll do that, Aunt Augusta.'

It was Joe's turn to smile. 'The rules have certainly changed!'

Bernie opened the parlour door. 'Go on in with you.'

'I thought it was you,' Molly said, indicating that he sit down.

Joe instantly noticed the change in her. She'd lost that look of utter despair and defeat. 'You look much better.'

'Things *are* much better, far better than I could ever have hoped for.'

'Because Bernie's here?'

'Yes and because she – Aunt Augusta, as we now have to call her – knows about me and she wants us to stay and Bernie's told her mother-in-law and her cousin Nellie and, well . . . they've all been so good about it.'

Joe smiled with relief. 'You see, I told you it wasn't the end of the world. Not everyone is totally heartless. Those who know you well know you're not a bad girl.'

'Just the biggest eejit who ever left County Offaly.'

Joe didn't want to upset her by agreeing so instead he looked around the room. 'It's very nice in here. These are pretty.' He indicated the cushion covers.

Molly smiled. 'It's a bit old-fashioned so I made those to try to brighten it up a bit. I had great plans for this place but now . . .'

'You'll just have to put them on hold for a while, that's all. Have you had time to make any plans with Bernie?'

'I'm going to try to get her a job where I work and I'm going to save as hard as I can until I have to leave. We'll manage somehow.'

Joe looked thoughtful. She was trying so hard to be brave about it all. 'I don't earn a fortune but if you're ever really desperate I'll always help out. Don't ever be tempted to go to a moneylender, they'll bleed you dry and if you can't pay up they often use some very rough ways of trying to make you.'

Molly was really touched. 'I won't, but . . . but you've been so good already, I can't ask you for money.'

Joe patted her hand. 'You can, I mean that. I don't want to see you driven to desperation again. I care what happens to you, Molly.'

Molly smiled. He obviously still felt responsible for her. 'I won't be. If we can just manage until after the baby's born, then I'm going to try to set up my own little business making soft furnishings. I can work from home.'

He grimaced. 'Have you told Aunt Augusta that?'

It was Molly's turn to pull a face. 'Not yet. Sure, I'm giving her time to get used to Bernie wanting to start a confectionery business in her kitchen in her spare time.'

'You're very industrious, the pair of you.'

'We'll have to be to make ends meet, although Bernie says she's going to sell all the furniture she's got in storage.'

Joe nodded. 'I suppose all this is taking her mind off her loss.'

'It is.'

'A bit of a blessing in disguise.'

Molly shook her head. 'How could it be a blessing?'

'You just never know, Molly. At least you're well rid of *him*.'

Molly didn't reply. She had the awful feeling that every time she looked at her child she would be reminded of Billy Marshall.

* * *

Billy was feeling quite pleased with himself. He'd managed to extricate himself from a very sticky situation without his parents finding out and the new love in his life, Evelyn Higson, was proving to be very amorous indeed: she was besotted with him, hung on his every word, bent over backwards to please him. And what's more there was even talk of him getting a rise in his wages at work. That's why he'd indulged in a few more pints than usual tonight. He felt a little light-headed but delighted with himself just the same.

He'd got off the tram at the bottom of St Domingo Road, crossed over and begun to walk up the back entry that ran behind the houses. He'd go in the back way, through the yard, into the scullery. It would save a lecture from his da about wasting money getting bevvied.

It was almost pitch dark in the 'jigger' (as the entries were known) and he was concentrating on avoiding the rubbish strewn on the cobbles, so it wasn't until he nearly collided with someone that he looked up and realised his way was blocked by what looked like a group of four men.

'Sorry, mate, I didn't see you for a minute,' Billy muttered.

'Oh, yer're goin' ter be bloody sorry in a minute, lad, an' I'm not yer "mate"!' Bert Hardcastle spat at him.

Billy tried to bluster but he was feeling decidedly uneasy. 'Who the hell are you?'

'We're a few friends of a young girl you know. A young girl you took advantage of, got pregnant and then dumped.' Matty's voice was dangerously quiet.

'What young girl? And who the hell are you?'

'You know bloody well who we're talking about, lad! We don't take kindly to wee innocent girls being taken advantage of and then being cast aside when they're carrying your bastard!' Big Charlie McCauley's hand shot out and he grabbed Billy by the throat.

Billy tried to yell but he was being throttled, then pain exploded in his gut and in his back. He tried to lash out but the blows rained down on him.

Five minutes later he lay on the ground, his battered and bleeding face pressed against the dirty cobbles, his body a mass of bruises. Two of his teeth had been knocked out and blood oozed from his swollen lips.

'Every time yer look in the mirror yer'll remember what yer did ter that poor little lass! Yer days of chasin' the girls are over, they'll all run the other way when they see yer comin', yer useless effin' no-mark!' Bert Hardcastle gave him a last contemptuous poke with the toe of his boot.

'Come on away now, lads, before someone calls the scuffers!' Matty urged and they walked quickly back down the entry, out on to the road and towards the nearest tram stop.

Chapter Thirty-Two

I N LATE SEPTEMBER MOLLY managed to get Bernie an interview for the position of sales assistant in the haberdashery department at Frisby Dyke's.

'Sure, you can manage haberdashery: it's buttons and ribbons and trimmings and needles, pins, reels of thread, things like that. It's only three days a week for now but it will be full time come November when things start to pick up for Christmas and they get all the decorations in,' Molly informed her, thinking that by November she would have left and feeling depressed at the thought.

Bernie was terribly nervous during the interview but was delighted when she was told that she could start the following Thursday. The recommendation by Miss Keegan, a rising star in the soft furnishings department, had certainly helped her application, she was informed when she acceded the job. Bernie replied that she would work as hard and as diligently as her friend but felt so sad that Molly's bright career was ending.

Mrs Stanley had had a long chat with Molly and told her that by the beginning of the following month she would almost certainly be able to offer her promotion to the position of Senior Assistant. Molly had listened with a heavy heart but had tried to put on a brave face and appear enthusiastic and grateful. She cursed herself time and time again for the fool she'd been. She felt nothing but anger and hatred now for Billy Marshall. How could she ever have thought she loved him?

She had made her peace with the parish priest, but not before she had received the most damning lecture of her life. His words had been so harsh that she'd been reduced to floods of tears and finally Augusta Hayes had lost her temper with the man. She snapped at him that even Christ himself had shown compassion and forgiveness to Mary Magdalene and she'd been a common prostitute. All Molly had been guilty of was loving and trusting one out-and-out blackguard. She wasn't the 'disgusting, lewd harlot' that he'd called her and nor was he even to think about writing to inform her parents. He'd left in high dudgeon but Molly did feel better about her immortal soul for, as Bernie had said to comfort her, 'Herself has a point. Didn't Jesus forgive her and didn't she become Saint Mary Magdalene?'

'I'm definitely no saint but I'm not a common whore either,' Molly had sniffed but she took comfort from Bernie's words.

They'd heard from Joe Jackson that Billy Marshall had been badly beaten up. He'd been found lying in pools of blood in the back jigger and had had to spend a week in hospital.

'Sure, it serves him right! I've no sympathy for that feller at all!' Bernie had remarked caustically.

Molly had said nothing but she'd noticed the look Joe had shot at her friend.

'Did you have anything to do with it?' she'd asked when Joe had gone.

'All I did was tell Nellie and Flo what an out-and-out *swine* he was, and they agreed,' Bernie had answered innocently.

'You didn't tell Matty?' Molly had probed.

'Nellie probably did and sure you know they sometimes take the law into their own hands.' Bernie had shrugged the incident off.

Molly felt so guilty on being promoted. She really *should* have told Mrs Stanley that she would soon have to leave but she just couldn't bring herself to do it. Oh, was there no end to the mortification, she thought? But she needed every penny she could get: the promotion meant a rise of four shillings in her wages.

Bernie was settling in very well; the girls she worked with were friendly and helpful and she enjoyed chatting to the customers, most of whom were pleasant enough.

'You wait until Christmas week; they won't be so flaming pleasant then! We have to put up with the height of abuse from some!' Maggie, who was in effect her supervisor, warned.

Bernie just shrugged. 'Ah, sure, isn't everyone in a desperate state come Christmas Eve with all the fuss?'

The nights were certainly drawing in and the weather was getting colder, Molly thought as, one Friday evening in late October they both walked to the tram stop. These days Molly got very tired and she had already let out the seams on her working dresses.

'I'm going to have to face it, Bernie. I can't stay at work much longer. Mrs Stanley said this afternoon that I must really be enjoying my work now, because she was sure I'd put on some weight and wasn't it a good thing when I'd looked so pale and ill after my unfortunate experience down at the Pier Head. I'm not going to be able to hide it for much longer.'

Bernie nodded slowly. 'When will you tell her?'

Molly sighed miserably. 'I think I can last another two weeks.'

'I'll be on full time then. We'll manage, Moll. Isn't it a good thing that ordinary dresses are so loose? And with it being so cold we're all bundled up in coats and scarves so you'll be able to hide it from most people.'

'It's not going to be much of a Christmas this year, Bernie.'

'It wouldn't be much of a Christmas for me anyway even if you weren't in this position,' Bernie answered. It would be her first Christmas as a widow. She and Jimmy had only had one Christmas together and last year she'd been so happy. Her heart ached for him as it did every single day.

Molly took her hand and squeezed it. She wished with all her heart that they could both turn back the clock to a year ago.

When they arrived home they were surprised to find that the old lady had visitors.

'It must be those two bold rossies of daughters. No one else comes here,' Bernie hissed, hearing female voices.

'Molly, Bernie, come on in here and meet my two daughters!' came the imperious command from the kitchen.

'Just let us take off our coats and hats and tidy ourselves up a bit, Aunt Augusta! Sure, we're not fit to meet company,' Bernie replied, then she pushed Molly in the direction of the stairs. 'Get up there and into that green frock,' she hissed.

When they both finally came down they had changed and tidied their hair. The old lady looked far from happy and the two well-dressed women in their late thirties had similarly grim expressions on their faces. They looked uncomfortable sitting on the hard wooden kitchen chairs.

'This is my eldest daughter Vera and this is Maud, the other one,' Augusta said flatly.

Bernie chose her words carefully. 'I'm Bernadette – Bernie – and this is Mary – Molly. It's pleased we are to meet you. Aunt Augusta has been very good to us; it's like a home from home here and we're both very happy.'

'So we hear, not that we approve of her taking in lodgers,' Vera replied curtly. She was a plump woman with pale skin, grey eyes and light brown hair, which had obviously been permanently waved. Her blue merino wool two-piece was expensive and the single row of pearls around her neck was real.

'We don't all have husbands with a fortune in the bank; indeed some of us don't even have husbands. Bernie is a widow too,' Augusta snapped.

'I'm sorry to hear of your tragic loss, you're so very young.' Maud's tone was gentler and her blue eyes were kind.

Bernie smiled at her. She was obviously the nicer of the two. 'Will I put on the kettle, Aunt?'

Vera raised her eyes to the ceiling and pursed her lips. Aunt indeed! It was ludicrous. Mother was becoming very odd in her old age, taking in these two little Irish chits and having them call her 'Aunt'. She would have to speak to Richard about it all. Who knew where it would end?

'Don't make a fresh pot for us, we have to get back. I'm expecting the decorators tomorrow morning. I've persuaded Richard to refurbish the sitting room.'

Bernie noted that she stressed the words 'sitting room'; obviously she objected to the word 'parlour'. 'Will you be after having new soft furnishings?' she asked innocently.

Augusta shot her a suspicious look but said nothing.

'Of course. I've already been in to Boothroyd's,' Vera answered rather smugly, gathering up her handbag and gloves and moving her coat from the back of the chair.

'Molly's the Senior Assistant in the soft furnishings department at Frisby Dyke's.'

Vera didn't look impressed. 'So Mother informed me.'

Bernie ignored her tone. 'She's fantastic at matching colours and she can sew and she can measure for curtains and pelmets.'

'Can you really, Molly?' Maud seemed interested and was lingering instead of putting on her coat and hat. Vera was concentrating on fixing her dark blue velvet cloche hat securely.

'I can and we're not nearly as expensive as some shops. We stock some really good materials and a fine range of colours.'

'I've nagged Edward into agreeing that we buy some new curtains and cushions and maybe a lampshade or two for our sitting room, but he won't hear of having it redecorated. He's not all that fussy about the house and says he can't put up with the disruption.'

'I doubt Richard Hesketh has much choice but to put up with it,' Augusta muttered and received a withering look from her eldest daughter.

'Maybe you'd like to come in and see us? I could help you choose materials,' Molly offered.

'Maud, do you really want to traipse into Liverpool when we have shops like Broadbent's and Boothroyd's and Highton's?' Vera was getting impatient. If they didn't get a move on the train to Seaforth would be crowded with dreadfully common dockers.

'Well, Edward doesn't really like me spending a fortune on the house,' Maud said thoughtfully,

'Tight-fisted,' her mother muttered.

'He prefers me to spend it on myself,' Maud continued, shooting her mother a meaningful look. 'If I bought all the material and trimmings, could you make the curtains and cushions for me, Molly?

I'm assuming it would be much cheaper than having them made in the shop? Do you have the time?'

Vera paused, her hatpin suspended in mid air. Had Maud gone completely mad? Who knew what kind of a mess the girl could make of things?

'Oh, she has the time but don't you think you can take advantage of her by expecting her to do it all for half of nothing!' Mrs Hayes interjected. 'There's a lot of skilled work involved.'

'Mother, I'll pay her a fair rate!' Maud snapped irritably.

'See that you do.'

'I'd love to make them for you but please don't go saying anything about it when you come in to buy the materials.' Molly was delighted. Whatever Maud Hesketh paid her would be very welcome indeed.

'Of course not. If anyone asks I'll tell them it's entirely my affair where I have them made, for all they know I could be running them up myself. I'll come in tomorrow, after lunch.'

'Do you think you could get someone to measure the window so we'll know how much you'll need? It would be a great help and would save any waste.'

'Indeed. I'll have Edward do it tonight. Now, Vera, are you ready? If we don't hurry we'll be caught up in the late rush.'

'I've been ready for the last five minutes! Well, goodbye, Mother. I hope those blankets will be useful, they're pure wool and you always say we usually bring you rubbish that's neither use nor ornament, so this time we thought we'd be practical. We'll call as usual at Christmas with Richard and Edward.'

'You don't have to drag those two out here. I know they'd both rather stay at home in front of their fires and have a few hours' peace and quiet with you two out of their way.'

'They feel it's their duty,' Vera answered acerbically.

'It's been nice to meet you both,' Bernie intervened, feeling an argument was brewing.

'And I'll see you tomorrow, Mrs Hesketh,' Molly added.

'It would suit me if they all stayed away! Bernie, put the kettle on,' Augusta Hayes said flatly when her daughters had departed.

'Why don't you get on with them? Was there a fight or some-thing?' Bernie was openly curious.

'There was indeed. As soon as the pair of them got the engage-ment rings on their fingers you would have thought they were marrying into royalty. Oh, we weren't good enough by half. No indeed. They didn't want their own brothers at the wedding – they had a double one – "showing them up" with their scouse accents and bad manners. *They* managed to lose their scouse accents overnight! I was only tolerated if I said nothing and wore the outfit they bought for me. Well, I told them a few home truths, I can tell you. Their poor father would be turning in his grave at the carry on of them and if he'd been here there'd have been none of that at all! He called a spade a spade did my Albert and he wouldn't have stood for such nonsense.'

'Did you go to the wedding?' Molly asked.

'I went under sufferance and I spoke to no one the whole long day. They all thought I was very odd but, believe you me, it's *that* lot who are odd. I didn't mind the old father, he was still alive at the time.'

'And have either of them children?' Bernie asked.

'No. Vera wouldn't have them messing up her grand house and Maud wouldn't have them ruining her figure! What a pair!'

'Well, at least we might make some money and if I do a really good job they might recommend me to their friends.'

'I wouldn't count on it, Molly, although not everyone with money is prepared to waste it paying over the odds for things. Even those with a fortune in the bank like to think they're getting a bargain from time to time.'

'I'd say it was more like "value for money",' Bernie said sagely.

'Call it whatever you like but just make sure she pays you something decent, Molly.'

'I will, Aunt,' Molly replied, sipping her tea thoughtfully. It would certainly be worthwhile asking Maud Hesketh if she knew of anyone else who could use her services.

Chapter Thirty-Three

———

TRUE TO HER WORD Maud Hesketh arrived the following
afternoon and Molly spent nearly an hour with her choosing
materials and braids and lampshades. It was all too heavy for Maud
to carry home so delivery was arranged for the Monday of the
following week.

'You'll have to come out to collect it, Molly. I couldn't have
asked them to deliver it to Mother's house or they would have been
suspicious, it being your address as well,' Maud said quietly as she
took her leave after paying for the goods. She was very pleased with
the quality, the selection and the price and had said so to Mrs
Stanley.

'Will I come out after work next Tuesday?' Molly asked.

'Yes indeed. Mother has the address. You can get the train; we
live very near to the station.'

Bernie had decided that as there was a great deal of sewing
involved and hopefully more in the future, Molly should have a
sewing machine.

'We can't afford one!' Molly had protested.

'We can if I do a swap with some of that furniture. Heller's stock
treadle sewing machines. When they're folded down they just look
like a table. We could keep it in the hall. Sure, you can't do all that
sewing by hand. You're tired enough when you get home from
work as it is.'

Augusta had agreed and so she and Bernie had gone along to the
large furniture shop on County Road. As Bernie had some nice
pieces in storage, it was agreed that a new Singer treadle would be

delivered the following week, in exchange for a sideboard and a chest of drawers.

'So, there you are, Molly, everything you need to start up your business. A machine and your first order,' Bernie had announced on their return. She was pleased to see Joe Jackson sitting in the kitchen with Molly.

'She'll need someone to help her carry all that stuff back home. It's heavy and I notice Her Ladyship had it delivered, no dragging it home on the train for *her*,' Augusta remarked, looking pointedly at Joe.

'I could go with you, Molly. I'm on an early shift next week, I finish at five,' Joe offered.

'Good, then that's settled. Meet Molly from work and you can get the train out there and be back before it gets too late. You can have some supper here when you get back,' Augusta instructed.

'When does she want them all finished for?' Bernie enquired, thinking she could buy all the necessary thread at cost.

'I don't know. I'll have to discuss that with her when I see her. It's the cutting out that takes the time. After that it's all straight seams.'

'You're sure you're not taking on too much, Molly?' Joe asked. She was looking a bit washed out, he thought.

'Not a bit of it and besides, we need the money.'

'Well, if you need any help carrying things, I'll do it,' he offered.

Molly smiled at him. He really was very thoughtful. A comparison with Billy Marshall flitted through her mind. Billy Marshall was totally thoughtless and hard and selfish. He had no morals, no ethics, no sense of responsibility. Joe was kind, generous, caring and had a huge sense of responsibility not only to herself but to Society. They were both handsome men, although Billy Marshall's looks were what most people would call 'flashy' while Joe was handsome in a quieter sort of way, but what did looks matter anyway? It was character that was really important. And she was trying to rid herself of all thoughts of Billy Marshall.

Joe was waiting for her on Tuesday evening and they walked to Moorfields to get the train out to Southport.

'Do you have the address?' Joe asked after he'd paid for their tickets.

'I do so. We have to get off at Birkdale Station; it's number twelve York Road but we'll have to ask the way. Aunt Augusta didn't know. The house has a name too, "Springbank".'

'Oh, very posh!' Joe laughed.

It was a very grand house, Molly thought when they finally found it. It stood in its own grounds and was reached by a gravel drive between well-tended lawns and flower beds, empty now except for a few neatly trimmed evergreen bushes.

'It's a very big house for just the two of them,' Joe said, somewhat in awe of the high-gabled Victorian-style building. 'He must have pots of money.'

'Apparently they own five or six big grocery shops.' Molly tentatively rang the doorbell and they stood on the step, listening to it jangle through the hall.

A young girl of about Molly's age dressed in the black and white uniform of a domestic servant opened the door.

'We've come to see Mrs Hesketh about the new soft furnishings,' Molly informed her.

'Madam is expecting you. Come in and wipe your feet, please,' was the prim reply.

Joe handed the girl his hat and then they both followed her down the hallway to a wide door on the left. The girl knocked and then announced them.

It was a beautiful room, Molly thought. She'd never seen anything so grand. It was huge with a very high ceiling and two large windows. The furniture was all expensive, if a little worn, but a fire burned in the ornate fireplace making it appear welcoming and homely.

'Good evening, Molly. You found us easily?' Maud Hesketh indicated that they both sit down.

'We did, thank you, Mrs Hesketh. This is Constable Jackson, a friend. He's come to help me carry everything. It was all delivered on time?'

'Oh, yes, indeed. I've only unpacked the lampshades. I thought it would be easier for you to manage if I left the rest as it was.'

'That was good of you. Can I ask when you'd like them to be ready?'

'I'd like everything to be finished by, say, the end of November, in plenty of time for Christmas. We entertain quite a lot at Christmas, as do Vera and Richard.'

Molly nodded. It would be hard going but she'd do it. 'I can manage that.'

'Good. Now, I've been having a word with Vera regarding the cost and I'm prepared to pay you five guineas. As you see there are two very large windows and then there are the pelmets and the cushions.' She considered it a very reasonable price compared to what Vera was being charged. Edward had said he thought it a bit excessive but when she'd told him what Boothroyd's were charging he'd changed his mind.

Molly was surprised; she hadn't expected quite so much even though there was indeed a lot of work involved as Maud Hesketh wanted everything edged with braid and the cushions piped.

'Thank you, that's very generous. Might I ask, Mrs Hesketh, that if you're happy with the results – and I'm certain you will be – you recommend me to your friends? I'm trying to start up my own business, you see.' Molly was acutely aware that by the time all the soft furnishings were completed she would be showing and that very probably Maud Hesketh would want nothing more to do with her, let alone recommend her to her friends, but she had to *try*. Any bit of work would help.

'That's very ambitious of you. Does Mother approve?'

'She does so.'

'Well, if I'm satisfied then I'll recommend you. I have to say I was quite impressed by your sense of colour and style. Myself, I would never have thought of putting those colours together but I think they'll look very well in here. Quite elegant, in fact.'

Molly smiled and stood up. 'If you don't mind, I'll just check on the measurements. I don't want to make a single mistake.'

'Please do,' Maud instructed and chatted quite pleasantly to Joe while Molly, with the aid of the tape measure she'd brought with her and a pair of steps the young maid had been instructed to bring in, measured the wide, large windows.

Joe was a little concerned as he watched her. There seemed to be a lot of stretching involved and the steps didn't look very safe to him.

'Will I give you a hand, Molly?' he asked.

'Not at all, I'm nearly finished and then we'll get off home and leave Mrs Hesketh in peace,' Molly replied brightly, although she was feeling rather weary.

'You would have thought she could have offered you a cup of tea, knowing you'd come so far and straight after work,' Joe remarked as they walked back to the station. He'd insisted on carrying all the heaviest parcels and he was surprised to find just how much all this material weighed. Molly carried the smaller parcels of braid and fringe and piping cord.

'Sure, I don't suppose it entered her head. Anyway I couldn't see your one in the uniform being very pleased at being asked to serve tea to a "tradesperson", which is what I am.'

'Well, it wouldn't have hurt her. It's what she gets paid for, after all. It's a job.'

'We'll get supper when we get back and it shouldn't take too long,' Molly said consolingly.

They had to wait twenty minutes for a train. Molly was cold now and her back had begun to ache badly.

'Are you sure you're all right? You don't look it.' Joe was concerned as he found them both a seat.

'I'm just tired and my back hurts.'

'You should have let me do the measuring. I'm sure all that reaching up isn't good for you. Especially not after a day on your feet and dragging all the way out here.'

Molly managed a smile. 'Stop fussing. Sure, I'm grand.'

But by the time the train reached Hall Road Molly was feeling dreadful. She was hot and sweaty and in a great deal of pain. 'Joe, I think we're going to have to get off at the next station. I . . . I think I need some fresh air.'

'Do you feel faint?' Joe was alarmed. She looked terrible. She had no colour at all in her face and there were beads of perspiration on her forehead.

'A bit. I've desperate pains in my back.'

Joe gathered up the parcels. 'Can you walk? I'm not a lot of help loaded down with this lot.'

Molly got to her feet as the train pulled into the station and managed to alight, watched anxiously by Joe, but as she made for the bench on the platform she stumbled. Then, with horror, she felt warm stickiness ooze from her and she knew it was blood.

'Oh, holy Mother of God!' she gasped as pain tore through her.

Joe dumped the parcels on the ground and put his arm around her. 'Molly, what's wrong?'

'I . . . I think I'm losing . . . it, Joe! I know there's . . . blood and . . .' Her words ended in a scream of pain.

'Just sit there! Don't move. I'm going for help.' Joe looked around and spotted the station master and, thankfully, another policeman. He dashed over to them and explained. The station master nodded and rushed into the booking office to telephone for an ambulance.

'Will you come with us, mate?' Joe asked his comrade. 'I can't manage her and all this stuff and it was expensive. I can't just leave it here.'

'Aye, give it here. You could have done with some transport to cart this lot around.'

Jo grimaced. 'On what they pay us? And she can't afford it, she's trying to start her own business. I hope that ambulance isn't long.'

'They're pretty good, they'll be here soon.'

Joe went back to Molly and took her hand. 'Hang on, Molly! There's an ambulance on its way. We'll have you to hospital in no time.'

'Oh, Joe, it hurts! I'm so frightened!'

'Hush, Molly! It's going to be all right. I'm here and I won't leave you! There's no need to be frightened.'

Molly clung to him tightly until at last they heard the clanging of the ambulance bell.

* * *

Bernie was getting worried. 'They should have been back by now. Do you think there's something wrong? Would the trains be off, do you think?'

'I doubt it but at least Joe is with her and he's got sense. If she'd been on her own I would be more worried. Maybe they stayed longer than they intended, although I can't see Maud offering them tea and biscuits.'

'Well, I'll give them another half an hour and then maybe we should go and ask at the police station if there has been some kind of accident that would delay the trains.'

'We'll get no sense out of that lot! The last time I had dealings with them they were no help at all,' was the caustic reply.

It was three-quarters of an hour later when Bernie ushered a police sergeant into the kitchen.

'Molly's in Stanley Hospital,' Bernie announced, her face pale. 'Joe got in touch with the sergeant here at Westminster Road Police Station. Joe and another policeman are with Molly. She was taken ill on the train and they got off; the other policeman is helping Joe with all Molly's things.'

'What happened?' Augusta demanded.

'No need to get upset, ma'am; she's going to be just fine now. She was taken ill on the train and thankfully young Jackson had the presence of mind to call an ambulance. It's appendicitis, so I'm informed. He got word to us and said he's staying with her for a while.'

Augusta shot a warning look at Bernie. So, she'd miscarried; at least Joe had had the sense to get her to hospital. 'Thank you, we were getting worried. Bernie, will you get our coats? We'll go up and see how she is.'

'Maybe it would be better if you waited here?' the sergeant said. 'By the time you get up to the hospital it will be late and, if you'll excuse me for saying so, ma'am, you're not a young slip of a thing like this lass here, you're better waiting by your fire with a cup of sweet tea. I know it's a bit of a shock.'

Bernie looked at the old lady with concern. 'Perhaps he's right.

It's no use us dragging all the way up there and then not being allowed to see her.'

Reluctantly Augusta nodded. 'Very well.' Oh, waiting for news was so hard, especially when you cared – and she had come to care a great deal for young Molly.

Chapter Thirty-Four

———•◦•———

JOE HAD DISCUSSED MOLLY'S plight with the ambulance man and the fact that he would have to ask the local police to inform Bernie. The man had been both compassionate and sensible.

'They'll know at the hospital right away what's wrong with her, son, but you don't have to let the whole world know. Mind you, they won't be all sweetness and light, not with her not being married, like,' he'd added.

'I have to get word to her friend and the old lady she lodges with; they'll be worried sick.'

'Then tell them it's appendicitis. That comes on sudden, like, and the pain is terrible,' the man had suggested and Joe had nodded, for Molly was obviously in agony.

For Molly the next hour was pure torture. She had never experienced anything like it and there was so much blood that she began to think she was going to die. She could think of nothing but the pain and she sobbed in terror until the sister told her sharply to pull herself together. She was young and healthy; it was a simple miscarriage; she would survive and in the circumstances it was something of a blessing. Molly bit back her cries. Couldn't the woman see the torment this was causing her – and not only the appalling cramps that were racking her body. She was losing her baby and that was tearing her heart in two. It didn't matter who its father had been, it was *her* baby, a part of her, she had carried it inside her all these weeks, she had begun to love it and now it had lost its chance of living. That was far from a blessing.

When Joe was finally allowed in to see her she was pale, worn out and tearful.

He took her hand and squeezed it. 'It's all over now, Molly. How do you feel?'

'Weak and tired and . . . Oh, Joe! The poor wee thing!'

Joe bent and wiped away the tears with his handkerchief. 'Hush. Maybe it's all for the best, Molly. A child should have two parents to love and care for it. It would have been so hard for you managing on your own.'

'I know and at first I didn't want it but I sort of got used to the idea and I wouldn't have minded, really I wouldn't.'

'You'll have another, one day. When you're married with a nice home of your own.'

Molly shrugged. She was exhausted.

'Look on the bright side. You won't have to give up your job now. They said you'd be able to go back to work after a few days' rest. We'll tell them you had appendicitis. Apparently that comes on suddenly.'

Molly managed a wry smile.

'Now, you'd better get some rest. I've still got all these blasted parcels to get to Arnot Street.' He was gathering them all up when the sister appeared.

'I'm glad to see you're leaving but before you go I hope you'll have a serious talk with her about her morals – or lack of them.'

Joe's expression changed and his eyes hardened for Molly had uttered a broken little cry. 'I beg your pardon, Sister?'

'I would have thought that it was obvious. What's happened is a blessing. She has been given another chance. You should impress upon her that from now on she should behave as a decent young girl and not a trollop!'

Molly looked stricken and tears welled up in her eyes.

'How dare you sit in judgement on her! You don't know anything about her! She's no trollop – far from it! She was innocent and someone took advantage of that. She *is* a decent young girl and it's certainly not your place to make any kind of comments about her!'

The woman's cheeks were red with anger and she compressed

her lips tightly. She hadn't expected such an outburst from him. What was the constabulary coming to these days, defending cheap little tramps!

Joe turned his back on the nurse. His anger redoubled when he saw the stricken expression on Molly's face.

'You rest now, Molly. Don't you take any notice of *her*. I'll come and take you home when you're ready.'

'My arms feel as though they've been dragged from their sockets with the weight of all this stuff! I've carted it on and off three trams,' Joe said when he reached Augusta's house.

Bernie ushered him in. 'How is Molly? Has she . . . ?'

'She's miscarried. She's tired but she's going to be fine.'

'Oh, thanks be to God!' Bernie was very relieved. 'I was so worried.'

'Is there any point at all in us going to the hospital?' Augusta asked.

'I wouldn't bother going all that way tonight. She'll be asleep by now and it's what she needs.'

Bernie nodded. 'You must be worn out and starving yourself.'

Joe sat thankfully at the kitchen table while Bernie put on the kettle and warmed up the supper.

'Sure, 'tis a bit dried up now,' she said ruefully looking at the meal that had been cooked hours ago.

'I don't mind.'

'I don't suppose Maud even gave you a cup of tea,' Augusta remarked.

Joe shook his head. 'We really weren't there long. I don't think it helped much that Molly was reaching up on a pair of steps remeasuring those huge windows, not after a day on her feet.'

'I thought Edward Hesketh had done that?'

'Oh, you know Molly, she wanted to make sure.'

'Well, she won't have to give up her job now,' Bernie said.

'I tried to tell her that maybe it was a good thing, but she's upset. She said she'd accepted it.'

'She's bound to feel like that but it *is* for the best. She can get on with her life now and she's learned a valuable lesson in human nature. We'll go in and see her tomorrow,' Augusta said, getting to her feet. 'Well, I'm worn out with it all, so I think I'll go to my bed.'

When she'd gone Bernie cleared away the dishes and then sat down facing Joe. 'I'm so glad you were with her. What would she have done if she'd been on her own?'

'She just couldn't have managed all that stuff on her own.'

Bernie twisted her wedding ring around on her finger. 'You're . . . fond of Molly, aren't you?'

'I am. What are you getting at, Bernie?'

'I want the best for Molly – she's the greatest friend anyone could have.'

'I want the best for her too. She's been through enough.'

Bernie took a deep breath. 'Do you love her?'

Joe smiled. 'I don't know and that's the truth. I like her, I admire her but despite everything, I don't know her very well – yet.'

'I knew almost right away that I loved Jimmy. I want Molly to have someone like my Jimmy to love her and look after her and I want her to be as happy as I was.'

Joe reached across the table and took Bernie's hand. She looked so sincere and yet so young and vulnerable. 'Bernie, she couldn't have a better friend than you and I'm so sorry that you and Jimmy had such a short time together. I *am* fond of Molly and maybe I will grow to love her but she might not grow to love me. She might not even want to try. All this might have put her off men for life.'

'I don't think so! She likes you and she trusts you and you always seem to be there when she needs you most. I just . . . I just wanted to ask, that's all.'

Joe smiled. 'I'll be around for as long as she wants me to be and who knows?' He shrugged.

Bernie managed a smile. 'So you don't hold what she did against her? A lot of people would.'

'She was too trusting, too besotted with him. Anyone can make a mistake.'

Bernie nodded. 'Sure, you're one of the nicest people I've ever met. Even Aunt Augusta likes you!'

'That's high praise indeed. Well, I'd better be getting home or Mam will think something terrible has happened to me. She always thinks the worst. She hates me being in the Force, she wanted me to join the Merchant Navy, like my da, but I get seasick on the Mersey ferry.' Joe laughed.

'I'll get this stuff put away, and then I'm off to my bed. I'll have to go in a bit earlier in the morning to let Mrs Stanley know about Molly.'

Molly came home three days later, accompanied by Joe and the old lady.

'You'll be fine now, child. A bit more rest and then you can look forward to living the rest of your life without any burdens,' Augusta said when she collected her, shooting a cutting glance at the ward sister whose attitude to Molly was still decidedly hostile and openly disapproving.

'I've cried a bit but I'm getting used to it,' Molly replied a little shakily.

'I sent word to that daughter of mine, telling her her new soft furnishings might well be a bit late and I wanted to hear no hysterics from her about it.'

Joe grinned; he could well imagine the tone of that letter.

'Oh, I'll have them done on time,' Molly said.

'We'll see. I'm not having you wearing yourself out. Things will be hectic enough with Christmas approaching. Do you think a visit to see your mother would help you at all?'

Molly shook her head. She was very thankful now that she hadn't told her mam. She had been thinking about it all and she had decided that if one day she was lucky enough to get married and have another child, she might then tell Ita about what had happened. Mam would be shocked and possibly upset but it would be something just the two of them could share. She knew her mother would never divulge the secret to her da. 'I really don't have the time to go to Ireland. You said yourself how hectic things get at Christmas.'

'You really don't want to go exhausting yourself, Molly,' Joe urged. She still looked wan and tired.

'I won't. A few more days' recuperation and I'll be as fit as I ever was.' She was beginning to feel that that was true. A sense of relief was slowly washing over her. She could start again. She could look forward, make new plans – or rather implement the old ones. She had a good job, the beginnings of what might one day be a thriving business, a comfortable home. And she was so lucky to have people like Bernie, Augusta and Joe who really cared about her.

Epilogue

Christmas, 1929

MOLLY SAT BACK ON her heels and admired her handiwork. The little fir tree they'd bought looked lovely, she thought. They'd decorated it with tinsel and baubles and little candles, all bought from the market stalls.

'Ah, doesn't it look just gorgeous! We never had a Christmas tree or decorations at home.' Bernie was making paper chains from strips of red and green crêpe paper twisted together. They'd put up bunches of holly and mistletoe too.

'Dust harbourers!' Augusta muttered, but she was secretly pleased. It was years and years since this house had been decorated like this for Christmas. It really felt like the happy home it had been when her Albert had been alive and the children had been young, and for the first time in three years her youngest son, Bertie, was coming home for Christmas. Of course she'd have to put up with the annual visit from Vera and Maud but even that wouldn't be the trial it usually was this year.

'We'll have a great time. I'm so glad I got Maud's things finished on time; the money has come in very useful.'

'I hope you're saving some of it. You worked your fingers to the bone for it.'

'I am, Aunt, and I really didn't mind. She was so pleased with everything and said she would willingly recommend me.'

'So she should. I bet Vera was seething that she paid through the nose for her stuff.' Augusta looked a little smug.

Bernie grinned at Molly. 'Ah, you should have seen it, Aunt! It looked gorgeous and everything matched so well.' Bernie had accompanied Molly and Joe to the house in Birkdale, ostensibly to give them a hand in putting up the curtains and pelmets but really because she'd been eaten up with curiosity.

'I wouldn't be giving up your job too quickly, Molly, even if you get more orders. They might dry up and then where would you be?'

'I've no intention of doing so. It might take me years and years to build up a business that will bring me a good living. When is Bertie arriving?' she asked to change the subject.

'Not until the day after tomorrow, Christmas Eve. His ship docks tomorrow and he's getting the train up from Southampton.'

'What's he like?' Molly asked.

'He's like his da, God rest him. The image of my Albert when he was young.' The old lady's gaze went to the photograph of a rather stern-looking man with dark hair and eyes, dressed in an old-fashioned suit, which stood on the sideboard.

'Quite good-looking then,' Bernie mused. 'It will be strange having a man staying here.'

'He's only here for a few days. They sail again on New Year's Eve but it will be good to see him. He's not a bad lad, he writes and sends me a few pounds every now and then, which is more than I can say for the rest of them.'

'Well, I'm looking forward to seeing your Maud again. There's something I want to ask her,' Bernie announced.

'What?' Augusta demanded suspiciously.

'Molly and I talked it over. You remember I said I wanted to start a bit of a confectionery business? Well, we thought after Christmas, when Bertie's gone, I could bake some soda bread and farls and barmbrack and Molly suggested I wrap them in green and white gingham with little labels marked 'Traditional Irish Confectionery' and see if the two Mr Heskeths would sell them in their shops.'

'I wouldn't be asking favours of those two!'

'She has to start somewhere and why not with them? She's good and we'll do it all up to look attractive and appealing,' Molly intervened, seeing Bernie's disappointed look. She wanted Bernie to succeed; Bernie needed something to strive for. She enjoyed her work at Frisby Dyke's but there was still a huge gap in her life. Bernie had not yet got over losing Jimmy and while starting a modest business venture was no substitute at all for him, Molly felt it would help a little.

'I suppose it will do no harm to ask, but don't hold out too much hope. A pair of hard-nosed businessmen, those two are.'

'Then they should be able to spot an opportunity when it presents itself,' Molly said firmly.

Augusta got to her feet. 'And I suppose you'll be turning my kitchen into a bakery?' She sighed resignedly. 'Well, I'll go up and sort out some bedding to air for the camp bed for Bertie.'

'Do you need any help?' Molly asked.

'I do not. But I'd be grateful if you could tidy up in here.'

Bernie began to gather up the scraps of coloured paper. 'I think this is going to be the best Christmas she's had in years, despite what she says.'

Molly reached for her hand. 'I know and it will be a . . . nice one for us too, despite everything.'

Bernie nodded a little sadly. 'Last year I was full of plans for my wedding. I thought this Christmas was going to be so desperate that I couldn't bear to even think about it but . . . but we've got a lot to be thankful for, Molly. We've got our health and strength, good jobs, good prospects, a nice home—'

'And each other,' Molly interrupted.

'And you've got Joe. Isn't he taking you out to the Empire and for a meal as a Christmas treat?'

Molly nodded. 'He's very good to me.'

'Do you think you could ever love him, Moll?' Bernie asked tentatively.

'Are you matchmaking, Bernie McCauley?'

'He's fond of you, he told me so,' Bernie said obstinately.

'Did he indeed? Oh, I don't know, Bernie. I like him a lot . . . but it's not the same. You of all people should know that.'

Bernie nodded. 'I don't think I'll ever love anyone the way I loved Jimmy.'

'Would you two girls just listen to yourselves!' Augusta Hayes had marched back in with an armful of bedding. 'You're like a pair of old women whose lives are best part over! You've your futures ahead of you and bright ones they seem to be too. You've got families who care about you, you've got myself to worry and fuss over you and you've got each other – you're the best of friends! Now, put the kettle on and let's have no more looking back. Look to the future – who knows what it will bring?' she instructed firmly, setting the bedding down on the table.

The two girls smiled at each other. She was right. No matter what the future brought they would always have their friendship.

'Friends for ever,' Molly said, and Bernie nodded her agreement.